OF DUBIOUS ORIGIN

OF DUBIOUS ORIGIN

DAVID I. SANTIAGO

Arte Público Press
Houston, Texas

Of Dubious Origin is funded in part by grants from the National Endowment for the Arts and the Texas Commission on the Arts. We are thankful for their support.

Recovering the past, creating the future

Arte Público Press
University of Houston
4902 Gulf Fwy, Bldg 19, Rm 100
Houston, Texas 77204-2004

Cover design by Ryan Hoston
Cover photo by Jordanna Santiago

Library of Congress Control Number: 2025028553

♾ The paper used in this publication meets the requirements of the American National Standard for Information Sciences—Permanence of Paper for Printed Library Materials, ANSI Z39.48-1984.

25 26 27   4 3 2 1

For the most beauteous of all

CONTENTS

PART II

PART III

PART IV

PART I

CHAPTER ONE

Israel Gets a Job, Loses a Job and Has an Idea

Six months after completing his associate's degree in geography from the College of Lake County, Israel Cruz was still at home, undecided about his future. This was evidently a family trait, as his brother, Judah, was also living at home, not having decided about his own academic options (which were admittedly limited) after graduating from high school, despite the coaxing from his parents to make up his mind.

Israel had found work as a remote temporary worker, manually digitizing objects from satellite images into a mapping database for the city of Waukegan. This was not the most thrilling of occupations, although it was related to his degree and involved converting geographic features into points, lines and polygons. The work reminded him of the tracing exercises he had done in kindergarten, such as "I can trace my name!" and "Let's trace shapes!" He knew there was more to the field of geography than this but wasn't able to find employment aligned to the more interesting courses he had taken at school, like Cultural Geography or the Great Mysteries of the Earth. Tracing and data entry seemed to be the in-demand field for his level of education and experience, and if he was being honest with himself, it wasn't particularly in demand.

He had only stumbled into the job because one of his college professors, Dr. Ritter, had taken pity on him after receiving several calls from Israel's mother pleading with him to intervene. After making a few inquiries to colleagues in and around the North Shore, he found Israel work as a contract GIS technician.

The job was good while it lasted, but his heart wasn't in it, and this showed up in the myriad of quality issues he introduced into the GIS database. He once corrupted multiple feature classes while distractedly watching TikTok videos, causing the city's GIS platform to go down for nearly a week and forcing the system administrator to work over the weekend.

"You need to double-check your work," his supervisor had said, but at that point, the damage had been done, and he was let go two weeks later.

The next three months were not his finest. He descended into his parent's unfinished basement, setting up a lair under the bare wooden stairs, cramming into it a small gaming desk, a gaming chair, a twenty-four-inch monitor, an Xbox console, assorted RGB lights and wires crisscrossing in various directions. Although he shared a room with his brother, he wanted more space to himself "to think about his next steps," he had told his parents. The family's nine-hundred-square-foot, two-bedroom cottage, a vintage Cape Cod (as described by his father), was the smallest and among the oldest houses in the neighborhood. Israel had always felt claustrophobic at home, which he believed contributed to his mediocre grades in high school, but it wasn't until this latest setback that he decided to take action and carve out his nook.

The basement afforded little more space than the bedroom he shared with his brother, as it was packed with storage bins stacked on top of each other, a washer, dryer, laundry bin and workbench covered with tools, screws and nails. It was a little more private than the bedroom. He secured a

Brazilian-style rainbow-colored cotton hammock to the wooden support posts under the stairs, which he slept in at night, along with a heavy wool blanket and wool socks, since the basement was not insulated. As the temperature dropped in the fall, he thought of placing sandwiches, fruits and other perishables next to the hammock, since the basement was effectively a cold cellar, but he decided against it after seeing mice scurrying under his feet.

Most of Israel's thinking about his future involved plotting weapons upgrades in Assassin's Creed, dodging hostile attacks and using Ikaros to scout enemy positions. When he needed a break from his combat exploits, he would scroll through social media on his cell phone, sometimes for hours, idly flicking through postings from various influencers about gaming, travel, music and sports.

Of particular interest to Israel was the celebrity influencer Maria Maia Coelho, also known as M&M, a Portuguese supermodel, reality star and supposed former love interest of none other than the soccer star Cristiano Ronaldo. Her social media postings consisted largely of video clips explaining her personal experiences with fashion and beauty brands. Although discussions about eyeliner and lip balm weren't generally top of mind to Israel, he couldn't take his eyes off M&M and developed what might be considered an obsession with her. The bikini-clad videos of her applying the newest sunscreens in the Algarve may have contributed to his fever.

The net effect of his extended periods of isolation in the dark, damp, subterranean, digitally enhanced setting was Israel's perpetual inebriated-like state when he emerged upstairs for food, bio breaks and the occasional package. He developed a gnarly, bushy black beard that blended into his curly, unkempt hair, and he could have readily been mistaken for a vagrant.

Israel was not an unattractive young man when he paid better attention to his hygiene and grooming, although he was not one to grace the covers of *GQ* or *People* magazines. He had a somewhat large Roman nose, dark olive skin (when exposed to sunlight) and large brown eyes. He was of above-average height and below-average weight and had a slightly bent gait, mainly because of bad posture and distracted thoughts. Most of all, he looked ordinary. His appearance was reminiscent of so many different peoples, it was nebulous. He had been mistaken for Italian, Assyrian, Arab, Cuban, Rajput, Persian, Bavarian, Brazilian, Albanian, Turkish, Spanish, French and Berber. People would come up to him on the street and speak to him in Hindi or Hungarian. People would stare at him and ask him where he was from. He would invariably reply that he was from Highland Park, even though he knew what they were really asking about, and he found the whole exercise taxing.

He once rode on the Metra next to an elderly Kazakh woman wearing a white *aq kiymeshek* who smiled at him knowingly but said nothing. He had become accustomed to that look, a look that suggested he was surely one of them, even though he was fuzzy at best about their culture and traditions.

These encounters had influenced his decision to study geography, which he insisted was a perfectly practical and employable discipline. Perhaps he was right about the career possibilities, but he had not advanced far enough in his studies or gained enough professional experience to corroborate his assumptions. Still, geography was inescapable, and for Israel, the question of his place in it was impossible to ignore. It slapped him in the face every time someone asked him about his origins, if he spoke Punjabi, if he followed the Argentine Primera División, if he knew where to find halal.

And then there was the matter of his name: Israel. A country. A place. The Holy Land. In the Levant. Part of the Fertile Crescent.

Ironically, it was his father who had lobbied for the name, even though he was Puerto Rican of the Evangelical persuasion. His mother, who had grown up in a conservative Jewish household, had preferred the name Richard, but she eventually agreed. His dad had his charms.

The more Israel thought about his origins, the more frustrated he became. *Everyone's always asking me where I'm from, but I never know what to say.* He wished he had the clarity of the Irish Catholics reveling during Saint Patrick's Day or the Indians celebrating Diwali.

His father insisted that Israel and Judah were a mixture of Jewish and Spanish origins. But when Israel pointed out that Abuelo and Abuela lived in Puerto Rico, his father agreed and said he was also Puerto Rican, but mostly Spanish.

"What are you saying?" Israel would ask. "Is your side Spanish or Puerto Rican?"

"Yes," his father would reply.

His mother would say that Israel and Judah were Jewish because she was Jewish. She was very proud of her heritage.

"But you converted to Christianity before I was born. How can I be Jewish?" he asked.

"It's part of Jewish law," she would reply.

Perhaps more confusing was his father's insistence that his mother was of Sephardic origins from Spain.

"I thought your grandparents spoke Yiddish," he said.

"That is true," his mother would say.

"I've never met a Spanish Jew," he would reply.

"We have a strong oral tradition on my side," she would add. "Knowledge of our origins has been passed down for generations."

What had *not* been passed down were any of the native tongues that someone of such distinct ethnic identities would be expected to know. He spoke no Spanish. His father refused to speak the language in the house and had encouraged him to study French in school, even though his last name was Cruz. So, Israel studied French and picked up a few swear words in Spanish over the years. His high school, being in a predominantly Jewish neighborhood, did offer Hebrew, but he never went to Hebrew school or temple and felt at a disadvantage to his more authentic Jewish classmates, so he decided against it.

When he was twelve, his parents had hired a rabbi of questionable credentials who attempted to teach him Hebrew prayers and how to read the Torah. The lessons took place in their living room and required an upfront payment of a not-so-insignificant sum, but when the rabbi failed to show up after the third lesson despite the down payment, his parents became disenchanted with the idea, and he never had a bar mitzvah. This was of little concern to Israel, but as he got older, he sometimes regretted not having that rite of passage under his belt.

One afternoon, after his mother and father had returned from work, Israel lumbered up to the kitchen for basic sustenance. He was bleary-eyed and gaunt, not having eaten all day, and had a slight tremor in his right hand from holding the Xbox controller for several hours. As he made his way unsteadily past the dining room table to where his father Estephan, his mother Ida and Judah were seated, he did not greet them. This snub was not intentional. He was not in the right state of mind. The dampness and cold had stunned his brain. The virtual and physical worlds had coalesced further than he had intended. All he knew was that he needed water and any leftovers that might be in the refrigerator. It was a matter of survival, like surfacing from an underwater cavern.

His failure to acknowledge his family did not go over well with Estephan, who slammed his fork down on the table and glared at his son. Still unaware of his father's growing irritation, Israel bent down and placed his head in the refrigerator, scanning the contents of the shelves.

"For God's sake!" shouted Estephan, causing Israel to jump and bang his head against one of the refrigerator shelves. "We work all day, even your brother, Judah, and you can't acknowledge our presence?"

Israel turned toward his family, blinking and rubbing his head. He noticed Chinese takeout on the table and heard his stomach rumble.

"I thought if we gave you some space, you might figure out what to do with your life," Estephan continued. "But this has got to stop."

"Estephan, please don't do this now," said Ida, with bags under her eyes.

"When do you suggest we have this conversation?" asked Estephan. "When we find him collapsed unconscious on the basement floor? Look at him? He's a mess!"

Israel scratched his armpit and smacked his lips. The smell of chicken lo mein was intoxicating.

"All I'm saying is this can't go on," said Estephan. "You need to get a job. Or better yet, finish your application to transfer to Northern or U of I. I don't understand what you're waiting for."

Israel stepped slowly toward the rectangular laminate dining room table. He was ravenous now, and there was an unopened takeout box at the edge of the table, near Judah, who was closest to him. Estephan narrowed his eyes as Israel approached the table, then snatched the takeout box and put it in his lap. Israel's eyes bulged, and he shook his head in confusion.

"You're not getting anything until we have a conversation," growled his father. "You don't work. You don't pay the bills. You don't study. You don't help around the house. I have no idea what you actually do all day, but it doesn't benefit the members of this household in any way. In fact, in all candor, you're useless, wasting away. I don't even know who you are anymore."

This comment hit Israel in the gut and seemed to wake him from his stupor.

"Maybe it would be best if you just packed your things and left," said his father.

"Estephan!" cried Ida in protest. "Enough!"

Ida glanced at Israel, who stood morosely in front of them, staring at his feet.

"I mean, you look awful, honey," said his mother. "Your father is running out of patience. It's been three months, and there's been no progress with figuring out your next steps. You've missed the transfer deadline for the spring semester, and you haven't even attempted to apply for a job."

Ida reached for the box of lo mein, its contents half eaten, and raised it in the air. "Come on, now," she said. "You need to eat something. And maybe when you're done, you can take a shower."

Later that evening, Israel was lying in the hammock in the basement, bundled in the wool blanket, staring at the amber colors projected onto the ceiling by his mood light. He was unsettled and, for once, was not on a device.

His father's words *I don't know who you are anymore* rang in his head. *Just who do you think you are?* Israel pursed his lips. *I never knew who I was,* he countered to himself. *It's never been clear. How can I commit to a college degree or choose a career if I don't know who I am and how I fit in? That's the problem.*

He had to admit that he wasn't happy. He was irritable. He couldn't focus. He had lost weight and felt rudderless, drifting in a foggy sea, unable or perhaps afraid to right the ship. *Where am I to go? What am I to do?*

He heard the door squeak open, and the overhead stairwell lights flicked on. Someone cleared their throat. He felt his hammock shake from the impact of each heavy, plodding step, until his brother stood before him, Milky Way bar in hand.

"Whatcha up to?" asked Judah.

"Nothing. Just hanging out," said Israel, his left arm hanging limply over the side of the hammock.

"Cool," said Judah, doing a quick scan for another seat. "Mind if I sit down?"

"Actually, yes," said Israel, but it was too late, and Judah plopped down next to his hip, causing the hammock to sag in the middle.

Judah bore some resemblance to Israel. He had coarse black hair, dark olive skin and a small aquiline nose. He was several inches shorter than Israel, stockier, with noticeable love handles when wearing a tight-fitting shirt. His appearance did not belie his mild manners. He was passive and never did well in competitive situations.

He enjoyed cosplay and comic books. He owned an Avengers Endgame Captain America costume, medieval Viking vests, Jedi-style robes with oversize hoods, a Doctor Strange high-collared cloak, a red haori with faux leather buckles on the sleeves and premium waxed Austin Brown perforated leather motorcycle gloves. He owned mob psycho wigs, Afro-style wigs, mohawk wigs and butterscotch-blonde-pigtail wigs. He had skull coin necklaces of varied plastic and cheap metal construction. He had always dreamed of attending Comic-Con and socialized with a tight circle of local cosplayers who shared his interest in embodying characters other than themselves.

Judah had a passing interest in cooking, and although he loved to eat, his job at the Pancake House had dampened his desire to attend culinary school. He knew he'd have to decide about his education. His mother wouldn't allow him to call it quits after high school, but he wasn't in a rush to figure things out.

"Been thinking about Comic-Con," said Judah. "It's taking place in July this year."

"Oh yeah?" replied Israel, uninterested.

"Might be able to save up enough money to go," he said. "It's in San Diego, you know."

Israel watched the amber hues change slightly on the ceiling.

"You should come with me. They have a gaming hall."

"I don't know," said Israel. "It's hard to plan that far in advance. So much going on."

Judah nodded his head in agreement. "Might be good to get out of the house. I mean, it's a bit ..." Judah paused to find the right words, "... isolated down here."

Israel said nothing.

"The first word that comes to mind is *forsaken*," Judah added.

"I find the accommodations suitable," said Israel.

"Right. Righto," said Judah, scratching his chin. "*God-forsaken* is probably the better descriptor."

The hammock groaned as Judah adjusted his position and looked at the ceiling.

"Anyway, Dad was a little animated at dinner," said Judah, changing the subject. "Hope you didn't take it the wrong way."

Israel crossed his arms and glanced at Judah. *Was there a correct way to react to his offensive remarks? Suggesting I leave? His firstborn son? The supposed apple of his eye? First in the line of succession?*

"I'm made of Teflon," said Israel. "Those types of comments just bounce off of me."

"It *is* ironic, though, that he questioned who you were," Judah continued. "I mean, it's pretty obvious you're his son."

"I've been aware of that for some time."

"I've also been wondering lately ..."

"Don't tell me you're unsure of our parental origins," said Israel.

"Not exactly. Just never seem to get a straight answer about our family tree. It's been on my mind lately."

This got Israel's full attention. He sat up in the hammock, leaned on his elbows and looked directly at Judah. "You've been thinking about that too, huh?"

"I came across a 1974 edition of *Captain America* at Comics Planet and Gaming. It caught my attention because I never knew there was a story about him becoming disillusioned with the US government. He actually abandons his Captain America identity, feeling that he can't serve the corrupted government when he learns it's linked to global terrorism, and takes on a new superhero identity known as Nomad. A man without a country, with no patriotic markings on him at all. As I was skimming through the comic, I got into a conversation with Micah. We talked about how awesome it would be to cosplay Nomad, how unique it would be, and then Micah started talking about his own identity crisis, being adopted from South Korea by an Italian-American family. He said that after going to Comic-Con this summer, he might book a flight to Seoul so he can track down his real mother and father. That got me thinking a bit about our family and how there are a lot of questions about Mom and Dad's ancestors."

Israel leaned back in the hammock and placed his hands behind his head. He tried to visualize what the Nomad superhero looked like, and his thoughts drifted to Assassin's

Creed. Images of ancient Greece. Being an outcast Spartan mercenary. Embarking on a journey of discovery to uncover truths about a mysterious past.

"I was thinking," continued Judah, "that maybe we should order DNA tests. We'd have to save up to buy them, but it might help reveal more about our family."

"I don't know … the technology seems sketchy," said Israel.

"You think so?"

"Look," said Israel, "I think I've just about had it with this quest to discover our true identity. I mean, it drives me nuts that Mom and Dad keep on telling us we are Spanish this, Jewish that, when none of it adds up. We have like zero connection to any of it, other than our names. So, I've come to a logical conclusion."

"You'd like to meet Geraldo Rivera?"

"What? Why?"

"Because he's the only other person I know who has a Puerto Rican father and Jewish mother."

"Uh, no. Definitely not."

"He's got a great mustache."

"His mustache *is* rather stylish."

"Then what's your logical conclusion?"

"My logical conclusion is that I'm giving up our heritage and becoming Portuguese."

"You mean," said Judah, furrowing his brow, "that you'd like to become a Portuguese national?"

"Yes, in fact, I'm planning on moving to Portugal," said Israel. From now on, I'm one hundred percent Portuguese. No more half this, half that. I am Portuguese. Plus, Cruz sounds like a Portuguese name."

"What you're saying is that you're giving up being Puerto Rican and Jewish or whatever exactly we are?"

"Yes, *exactamundo*. I'm tired of the ambiguity. I hereby relinquish my ethnicity and proclaim that I am Portuguese."

CHAPTER TWO

Israel Makes Plans and Gets into an Argument

The following morning, the basement was black and frigid in the dismal hours before the early January sunrise, but a small light shone through the darkness. It was just past six in the morning, and Israel was fully awake, flipping through articles about a special Lusitanian supermodel on his cell phone. Research on this subject was nothing new, but the timing and degree of focus was extraordinary. For months, Israel had barely risen before noon, but that was not the case this morning. He was not groggy but alert, his eyes darting back and forth across the tiny device screen.

Maria Maia Dulcinea Coelho

From the Open Encyclopedia

Maria Maia Dulcinea C., commonly referred to as M&M, is best known for being a Victoria's Secret Angel, Giorgio Armani beauty ambassador, Best Female Model at the Globos de Ouro (Portuguese Golden Globes), cover girl for *Vogue* and the *Sports Illustrated* swimsuit issue, winner of the Fashion Personality of the Year, social media influencer with over thirty million followers, beauty products reviewer and promoter and presumed former love interest of Cristiano Ronaldo, the famed soccer player.

Early Life

Born in Lisbon, M&M grew up in Setúbal and attended the University of Lisbon.

Career

M&M was discovered at the age of 17 and exploded onto the modeling scene after coming in as the runner-up for Top Model Portugal in 2015. She has been featured prominently in television ads for H&M, Zara and L'Oreal and has amassed a passionate following on social media.

Personal Life

M&M owns a home in Cascais, Portugal, and a villa in Bellagio, Italy, where she stays during trips to Milan to meet with various sponsors. In 2017, she was allegedly spotted with Cristiano Ronaldo exiting the Savoy Palace in Funchal, Madeira, although the reports could not be independently verified.

Now, Israel was not the stalker type. Despite his unkempt appearance, he'd had, at one point or another, girlfriends. Even though those had been fleeting relationships and involved only two young women, he did not exhibit any behaviors toward the opposite sex that would immediately cause them to run for cover.

What had recently transpired, however, was the blurring of lines between reality and fantasy, and he assumed he could win the heart of the rich and famous supermodel. There were examples of celebrities marrying people of the common ilk—

Matt Damon and Luciana Barroso, Adele and Simon Konecki, Paul Rudd and Julie Yaeger—and Israel figured he had just as good a chance as anyone to woo M&M. As far as he could tell, she was still single, probably overworked, and could use someone to lean on, despite his extremely modest means and lack of professional accomplishments.

The questions for Israel this morning were a) how to move to Portugal and b) where to settle once he arrived. He was confident about his destination; renting an apartment in Cascais or nearby Lisbon would do. There appeared to be a train that ran between the two cities, and he was confident that he could find work in the capital since there were likely more opportunities there than in Cascais. Although the latter was a more appealing destination, given its proximity to his subject of interest, he might fare better in his romantic endeavors if he had a white-collar job in Lisbon. There were plenty of companies in the area, and he was sure his firm command of English would make him a hot commodity in the Portuguese tech scene.

He thought of Google and Apple and the various improvements he could bring to their mapping software. His lack of a four-year degree was of no concern to him. In fact, lacking one was likely an asset. He was merely following in the footsteps of other great tech pioneers such as Bill Gates and Mark Zuckerberg. The one question that vexed him was how to handle the multiple job offers. Negotiation was important. He would need written offers from the two ... no, three or four companies attempting to recruit him.

Let me start by thanking you for this offer, thought Israel, rehearsing one negotiating scenario in his head. *I am excited about this opportunity with Google. I am especially looking forward to the initiative around leading a team of engineers for the company's next generation of holographic maps. Portugal has world-class technologists, who yes, happen to be less expensive than their American counterparts, and I just so happened to be in the Lisbon area when this wonderful opportunity presented itself. Now, before I commit, in the interest of full disclosure, I wanted to mention that I was also offered roles at Apple, Facebook and Microsoft and am considering my options as I decide the best fit. Can we discuss adjusting my compensation package? I would love to join Google, but the market is strong, and I also need to do what is best for my career.*

"That sounds about right," said Israel aloud, and he mentally checked off job prospecting from his list. "I will start applying for positions once I arrive."

Moving to Portugal was a little more complicated. There were short-stay visas, long-stay visas, golden visas, possibly silver and bronze visas, and various options in between. As he was a US national, no visa was required for stays of up to 90 days in a 180-day period, which meant that he could fly to Portugal, then figure out the long-term residency requirements later. His pending job offers would also surely include a sponsorship clause, enabling him to have a long-term work visa while applying for citizenship.

He thought about going over to the Portuguese consulate to discuss immigration options in more detail, but that would have involved taking the train to downtown Chicago, which was inconvenient and involved prolonged exposure to sunlight, which he needed to work up to. Plus, there was much to learn via Google keyword searches.

Around seven o'clock in the morning, he listened to his mother grinding coffee beans and realized that he might, for the first time in many months, be able to drink hot coffee. His mother always brewed enough for the entire family, and Israel usually finished off the cold and acidic contents of the pot after everyone left for work.

When he made his way upstairs about fifteen minutes later, he found his parents busy rushing between the kitchen and the living room.

"Your ties are in the closet," said Ida.

"I already looked there!" Estephan exclaimed, coffee mug in hand.

"Ugh," sighed Ida, marching into the living room. "Look right over there. The tie rack has fallen on the floor."

Israel poured himself a cup of coffee and leaned against the kitchen sink, savoring the smell of the fresh brew, its steam rising into his nostrils. His parents had begun carpooling to work to allow Judah to drive to his job at the Pancake House. Judah worked the afternoon shift and had not yet left.

"I'll start the car," said Ida from the living room.

"You didn't start it yet?" asked Estephan. "It's fifteen degrees outside."

"Will you stop complaining?" retorted Ida. "You were the one that got up late this morning."

"I have a bail hearing with one of my defendants in an hour," Estephan said, stepping into the kitchen with Ida in tow. "There's so much …."

Estephan stopped dead in his tracks and spilled some of his coffee on the floor.

"Oh my God! You scared the living daylights out of me! What are you doing up so early?"

Israel took a sip of his coffee, exuding an air of calm and composure. "I've decided on my next steps," he said.

"Is that so?" asked his father, narrowing his eyes.

"That's wonderful," said his mother, peering around Estephan's shoulders. "I can't wait to hear all about it. Tell us this evening. We're running late."

"Right. Please do tell us about your plans this evening," added his father, who patted his pants pocket. "Ida, have you seen my wallet?"

Later that afternoon, Israel was sitting in the barber's chair at Giovanni's Hair Stylings. In his hand, he had several pieces of paper and was inspecting them.

"So, what do you have in mind, son?" asked Enzo Romano, a bald, heavyset man with a gray horseshoe mustache.

"I'm debating about which hairstyle to select," said Israel, pointing to the images of Cristiano Ronaldo. "The textured top with short sides is a good one, or perhaps the messy wave with highlights. I might even consider a man bun. I think my hair is long enough for that."

Enzo took the papers from Israel and leafed through them. He grunted each time he flipped to a new page, shaking his head.

"Soccer's got some real pretty boys, I tell you," said Enzo. "My grandfather was a soccer fanatic. He was from Sicily. We used to kick the ball around our backyard when I was a kid, and I think he'd roll over in his grave if he saw how players look and act today."

Enzo pulled at Israel's long, bushy beard. Israel thought he saw a swarm of gnats fly away, but he couldn't be sure.

"I need to get a lawnmower to clean this up first," Enzo said, placing a towel over the back of Israel's neck and around his shoulders. "Let's take care of this mess, then see what might work best for you."

Enzo walked over to the towel warmer at his barber station a few feet away and pulled out a steaming white cotton cloth, waving it back and forth to cool it off. Then, positioning himself behind Israel, he placed it over Israel's chin and folded it upward to his mouth, rubbing his face to loosen up his pores.

"You look familiar," said Enzo. "Where are you from?"

"I live near Sunset Park," mumbled Israel as Enzo roughly massaged his cheeks.

"You don't happen to be Italian?" he asked. "You remind me a lot of my cousin Bosco."

"Nrgh," attempted Israel. "Portusheep."

"What's that? Portuguese, huh?" asked Enzo. "I knew a guy from Jersey who was Portuguese. Haven't met too many in the Chicago area. I guess that's why you like Ronaldo."

Enzo removed the towel and applied a pre-shave lotion on Israel's beard and neck.

"Ever been to the old country?" he asked.

"You mean Portugal?" asked Israel.

"Yeah, you know, to visit your relatives. That sort of thing," Enzo said.

Israel thought about this for a moment. He wasn't aware of any relatives in Portugal, given that he had just recently become Portuguese, but he thought there might be long-lost ancestors in the country. Families were constantly moving to different locations, and country boundaries changed. The more he thought about this, the more he convinced himself that there could be some sort of familial connection in Portugal.

"Never been," said Israel. "But I'm moving there soon. I hope to track down my ancestors."

"No kidding!" exclaimed Enzo, pulling out a straight razor. "Moving to Portugal, huh? Are you taking some time off school or work or something?"

"Yes, I am," said Israel, thinking about Assassin's Creed. "I've been hard at work. Need a break. To figure things out."

"Amazing," said Enzo. "Always wanted to do something like that. Travel to Sicily, track down family. I actually encouraged my daughter to take a year off college and travel to Europe. She ended up doing a semester in Paris and came home with a French boyfriend. Not exactly what I had in mind, but what can you do about it?"

Israel shut his eyes as Enzo began shaving off tufts of beard. He felt the barber stroking the razor down from his right sideburn to his chin.

"Take a look," said Enzo after a couple of minutes patting Israel on the back.

Israel opened his eyes and stared into the mirror. For the first time in months, he could properly see his face, and he looked years younger.

"All right, so the man bun and messy wave are out," said Enzo. "Let's give you a clean look. Something like the first option you showed me."

Israel rode the connector bus back from Giovanni's to the library, and from there, he had only a ten-minute walk home. It was a little past noon, and it had warmed up considerably since earlier in the day.

Israel pulled out his cell phone and took another look at himself through the camera. *Not really what I was going for,* he thought. He had a crew cut, trimmed only slightly longer than a buzz cut, and he resembled more the army recruits he had seen on videos than the international soccer superstar he had aspired to emulate. *Should have known better,* he said to himself. All the male patrons at Giovanni's walked out with the same haircut. He saw three others leave the barbershop with a slightly stunned look, like they were just initiated into basic training against their will.

"Oh well," he said aloud. "At least I won't need to go through that again for some time."

When Israel returned home, he found his brother sitting at the kitchen table in a bathrobe, blowing his nose. There was a box of tissues at the edge of the table beside a bowl of ramen soup and a small trash can at his feet overflowing with Kleenex.

"I thought you were working today," said Israel, opening the refrigerator.

"I'm sek," said Judah.

"What's that?" asked Israel, looking at the expiration date on a package of salami.

"What happened to you?" asked Judah. "Run your hair through a woodchipper?"

"Best used by December fifteenth," said Israel, sniffing the salami. "Should be edible, right?"

"You joining the Marines?" asked Judah. "I thought you needed to be in shape for that."

"Marines?" asked Israel, chewing a slice of salami. "What? No way. This is a haircut modeled after my brother from another mother, Cristiano Ronaldo."

"So, you're really serious about Portugal?"

"Like I said earlier, I'm Portuguese now. So yes, it would be good to go back to the old country."

"The old country," murmured Judah. "Like a retirement village? I know those are popular in places like Portugal and Spain. But usually you have to have some sort of income to live there."

"Not to worry, not to worry," said Israel, chewing another slice of salami and sitting down across from Judah. "What happened to you?"

Judah sighed and reached for another tissue. "I'm sek."

"Sick!" cried Israel leaping to his feet. "Why didn't you say so earlier? What do you have? Flu, RSV, rhinovirus?"

"Beats me. Just woke up today feeling bad."

"Well, I don't mean to be rude, but I need to be in tip-top shape," said Israel, backing away. "Once I get to Portugal, I'm going to be doing several rounds of job interviews and negotiations and need to be at the top of my game."

"I understand," said Judah, wiping his nose.

"I'll bring up some cough drops for you," said Israel reassuringly. "Just going to head downstairs to do a little more research on plane tickets, accommodations, a certain fashionista, et cetera, et cetera … ."

Half an hour had passed. Israel was reclining in his gaming chair and had his feet up on the desk. He held his cell phone in his hands and scrolled idly through posts from M&M.

"Sustainable, ethical and purified makeup," he said out loud. "Fermented moisturizing cream cleansers. Cruelty-free collagen serum. Amazing what they're capable of marketing nowadays."

An ad popped up on his phone with an image of two young couples holding glasses of wine while overlooking the ocean from the deck of a cruise ship. They were smiling, and their hair flowed in the breeze.

"Fifteen percent off. Passenger Immersion—Destination Portugal," Israel read aloud. "Gotta love these personalized ads. This is just the sort of thing I was looking for."

Israel clicked on the ad, and it redirected him to the Royal American Line (Dignified Destinations) transatlantic journeys site. Sailing for over 120 years!

"Join a centuries-old nautical journey across the Atlantic," he read. "Immerse yourself in Portuguese so you can mingle with the locals. Twenty-one days, from the eastern Caribbean and passage to Portugal, with intensive language instruction each morning."

Israel thought about intensive instruction. This was a novel concept and made him slightly uncomfortable. *Then again, I could benefit from a crash course in my ancestral tongue. It would make acclimating to Portugal easier.*

A detail caught his eye. He dropped the phone.

"Two thousand and forty-nine dollars?" cried Israel, his feet firmly planted on the floor now. "Are these people nuts?"

He walked over to the hammock, slipped inside and pulled the blankets over himself. *What a day! So much has happened.* He shut his eyes and exhaled, his mind drifting. *An ocean passage. A journey of discovery. A new beginning …*

Shortly after six in the evening, Israel woke to the smell of Chinese takeout. He opened his eyes and could hear his mother speaking upstairs, the occasional trumpeting of Judah as he blew his nose, the clanking of silverware.

Chinese two days in a row? Ugh. We should really try to diversify. Maybe Mexican? Or better yet, Portuguese takeout?

Israel stood up, adjusted his shirt and pants and made his way upstairs. He pushed open the door to the kitchen and saw his mother, father and Judah sitting around the kitchen table. His parents had not changed out of their work clothes. His father was wearing his navy-blue suit and tie, and his mother wore a black blouse with matching slacks.

"Then there's this Adams kid. The co-counsel discussing the matter failed to retrieve …" Estephan paused, turning to Israel.

Israel waved a hand in greeting. Judah was sitting in the same chair he had been seated in earlier, a box of tissues in his lap. Chinese takeout containers were arranged in the middle of the dining room table.

"Now this is a change," said Estephan. "You're not enlisting in the army, are you?"

"Honey, I can see your face!" cried Ida, standing up and placing her hands on Israel's shoulders. "This is a much better look."

"Go ahead, please explain," prodded Estephan.

"I've decided on my next steps," said Israel, stuffing his mouth with a spoonful of fried rice.

"Go on," said Estephan.

"Well," started Israel, swallowing. "I've decided to become Portuguese."

Estephan glanced at Ida, then loosened his tie. He stared at Israel for several moments as if trying to decide how to react.

"Portuguese? Interesting," said Estephan. "Why Portuguese?"

"You know how you said Judah and I were Spanish and Jewish. And Puerto Rican. And Sephardic?"

"You have a diverse heritage," said his mother.

"Yeah, well, it's highly confusing," said Israel.

"I don't see what's so confusing about it," said his father. "Plenty of people are mixed."

"I agree. But even understanding one side or the other is confusing. I mean, what kind of Jew are we? We were raised Evangelical. Mom converted before she had me. We never had a bar mitzvah. I mean, Judah and I don't really seem to fit the mold of anything. And since you've been asking me to make up my mind about my next steps, I've decided to become one hundred percent Portuguese, to remove any ambiguity about my ethnicity. I'm leaving for Portugal by the end of the week," said Israel.

Estephan held the fork to his lips and stared at Israel with an uncomprehending expression. Neither Estephan nor Ida said anything for some time.

"Um, I don't really understand what you mean," Ida said at last. "But if you're saying what I think you're saying, well, you can't just give up your ethnicity because you feel like it. You are what you are. It's the way it works."

"I beg to differ," countered Israel. "I believe we can decide. Why not? It's not like there is a rule book that says you have to stay the same. I've decided to become Portuguese. I look Portuguese, my last name sounds Portuguese, I feel Portuguese, so I am Portuguese."

"That's the most ridiculous thing I've heard you say, which is saying a lot," said Estephan, his face turning red. "It's insulting, really. What, are you ashamed or something? We're not good enough or something?"

"It's not that I'm ashamed," began Israel.

"People can choose different nationalities, but they can't choose who they are," said Ida.

"There are plenty of gender-fluid people changing their minds about who they are," replied Israel.

"Okay, so you're going there now? Really?" asked Estephan, placing his hand at the side of his stomach.

"Uh, if I could jump in," said Judah, standing up and blowing his nose. "There was a time when Jews and Italians weren't considered white, but now they are. Times change, and if nothing else, I kind of agree that our family history is hard to explain."

"So, you're taking sides now, are you?" said Estephan.

"Dad, all I'm saying is that it takes some courage to leave home," said Judah. "Maybe you'll disagree with his motivations, but I'm sure you can agree that his recent attention to bathing, shaving, grooming and the application of deodorant are all positive developments, thanks in large part to his pending trip to Portugal. And by the way, I plan to join him."

"Ahem," said Estephan, as if clearing his throat. "So, you're giving up your job as well? Joining your wayward brother and delaying your college education?"

"And how do you plan to pay for this trip?" asked Ida.

"I've saved up some money," replied Judah.

A chair creaked, and then there was a thud and a clattering as something dropped to the floor. Israel followed his mother's and brother's gazes. A piercing shriek rang across the room.

"Oh God," said Judah.

"Should I call 911?" asked Israel.

CHAPTER THREE

Israel Heads to the Hospital and Plays Bocce Ball

"Did I just kill Dad?" asked Judah, waving a box of tissues while pacing in the waiting room at the hospital's emergency area.

"It's a distinct possibility," said Israel, seated on a chair, sucking a raspberry lollipop he had taken from a basket at the reception desk.

A small boy, perhaps five or six years old, pushed a red toy carrier truck past Israel. The truck included several smaller emergency vehicles and a helicopter. He shuffled up to Judah, paused, then turned back and shuffled over to Israel to inspect the stick protruding from Israel's mouth.

"Over there," said Israel, pointing to the reception desk.

The boy studied Israel for a moment, then looked at Judah, who was pacing nervously back and forth. He let go of the truck, knocking out the smaller vehicles, and ran over to his mother.

"I shouldn't have told him I was joining you," cried Judah. "It was too much for him to handle."

"I was very surprised, I must say," replied Israel.

"But I want one, and I want one *now*," yelled the boy at the far end of the room.

Israel glanced at the boy's mother, who scowled at him.

"Dad's under too much stress. Dealing with criminals day to day," said Judah, staring at the ceiling.

"He really is," added Israel.

"But he's so young. This can't be it, can it? On account of five words. Five silly words: 'I plan to join him,'" asked Judah.

"Shock can provoke a heart attack," said Israel. "Life is so fragile."

"Not fair! Not fair! Not fair!" shouted the little boy.

"It's not fair. If he only knew how much money I had saved up," said Judah. "I was planning on moving out, anyway. At some point, at least. Maybe to San Diego."

"I heard San Diego has pleasant weather," said Israel. "And the Padres."

"Oh my God," cried Judah, placing his hands on his head. "Don't remind me of the Padres. How could I overlook that? How could I ever set foot in San Diego after what's transpired tonight?"

"After what's transpired?" asked Ida, returning from the restroom.

"Mother," said Judah, grasping her hands. "Can you ever forgive me?"

Israel crunched the remaining pieces of lollipop and swallowed. He pulled out another lollipop, grape flavored this time, from his jacket pocket. He undid the wrapper and placed the sucker in his mouth, watching his mother and brother intently from his chair.

"I sent him into cardiogenic shock," said Judah.

Ida stared at Judah for a moment. At the far end of the room, the boy was stomping his feet.

"I just spoke with the physician," she said at last. "They gave him an antacid."

"An antacid?" asked Judah.

"Tums," she said. "They suggested we stay away from greasy foods."

"But Dad loves Wondrous Wok," said Judah.

"Yes, I know. Just not every day," said Ida.

Amen, Mother, thought Israel. *Been overdoing it a bit there.*

"They're running one more test, and then he'll be released," said Ida. "His fall from the chair likely caused more damage than anything. He has a nasty welt on his shoulder."

"Well, that's a relief," said Israel.

Ida placed her hands on her hips and frowned. "I'm not sure which one of you I should be more concerned about," said Ida, glancing in the direction of the emergency department, then looking at Judah and Israel. "Are you really serious about moving out?"

"It's a calling, mother," said Israel. "I've been called to my homeland."

Ida sighed and turned to Judah. "And you?" she asked.

"Well, assuming Dad is still alive and well, then yes, I'll join Israel," said Judah, placing his hands in the pockets of his hooded ski jacket.

"Okay, then," she said. "I admit, you are grown now, and we could all benefit from some space. I'll speak to your dad about this when we get home."

The next day, Israel was sitting in the atrium of the Pancake House, surfing the internet on his laptop. It was one o'clock in the afternoon, and the lunch rush was subsiding. Israel looked out through the windows into the town square and took another sip of his coffee. He furrowed his brow, placed the coffee mug on the table and inspected it. There was just milk froth and a drop of coffee remaining.

"Garçon," he said, raising his hand in the air.

Judah walked over to his table. He was wearing a green polo shirt, tan khaki pants and brown penny loafers and held two coffee pots.

"Will you knock that off?" he said.

"I've run out," said Israel, gesturing to his mug.

"You're lucky you have a table. There are rules against loitering."

"I'm a paying customer."

"A lousy paying one, to be more accurate."

"Regardless, there's more work to be done. The Pancake House is an excellent venue for gathering one's thoughts. Look, I've discovered an interesting route to Portugal," said Israel, pointing to his laptop.

Judah leaned over Israel's shoulders and studied the screen. "I'm not sure what I'm looking at. Transporti Maritime Line? It's a container ship," said Judah.

"Bingo!"

"I'm at a loss, really," said Judah, looking around. "Can you hurry it up? My supervisor's not a fan of idle chitchat."

"Patience, my good sir. The Transporti Maritime Line is a *budget* cruise. I spoke with one of their representatives via chat, and they have room for two more passengers, with a departure date of this Saturday at six o'clock in the morning from Baltimore."

Judah sat down next to Israel and filled his coffee mug. He grabbed another cup and poured one for himself.

"Interesting, go on."

"Right, so this ship sails straight from Baltimore to the Azores, stopping at port for several days before making its way to Madeira, then Lisbon. Thirty days in total. Plus, the crew speaks several languages, including Portuguese. Portuguese lessons can be arranged," said Israel.

"It would be good to study Portuguese beforehand."

"I mean, Portuguese can't be all that hard. After thirty days at sea, we should be plenty conversant," said Israel. "Full immersion, so to speak."

"The last time I checked, you were lucky to have passed French," said Judah.

"Minor detail."

"How much does this trip cost?"

"Ah, now, that's the best part," said Israel. "Normally, this would be a few thousand dollars, plus extra for lessons, sightseeing, et cetera. But this is a working ship, and if we're willing to work in the kitchen and support a few errands at port, we only need to pay an initial deposit of five hundred dollars in total to secure our spots. Apparently, they're short staffed."

"Did you speak to an actual human about this or a bot?" asked Judah.

"I spoke to the venerable Signora Francesca Benedetti, head of customer relations and a colleague of the director of human resources. She gave me a job application form and a link to their trip-booking page. Oh, and before I forget, I have one other timely bit of good fortune." Israel took a sip of coffee and pointed out the window. "As we got to chatting, and I mentioned I was an American from Chicago, Signora Francesca Benedetti became excited and asked where I lived. I told her I was from Highland Park, at which point she asked me if I ever went to Highwood. 'Sure,' I said. 'Sometimes I go to Buffo's for Italian beef.' She said, 'What a coincidence—Signor Sérgio Ricardo de Carvalho, originally from Lisbon and part owner of the Transporti Maritime Line, happens to be married to an Italian woman. His father-in-law, Signor Domenico di Stefano, lives in Highwood. He immigrated to the States over forty years ago. I'm sure he would be willing to speak with you. I often hear him talking to Sérgio Ricardo de Carvalho. I am told that he plays bocce ball every afternoon at the Highwood Bocce Club, host of national championships."

* * *

"National championships in Highwood?" asked Judah. "Now this would be interesting to see."

Israel and Judah arrived at the Highwood Bocce Club on Bank Lane around four o'clock in the afternoon, where they were greeted in the hallway by a smiling, bespectacled woman with short white hair and a mild case of kyphosis. She was standing beside a plastic folding table handing out lemon-drop cookies coated in vanilla icing and sprinkles.

"Are you here for the mixed pick-up league? The games are going to start in, oh"—she held the watch on her wrist close to her eyes—"ten minutes, I believe."

Israel glanced at Judah.

"Why, yes," said Israel. "We are bocce ball enthusiasts."

"We are?" questioned Judah.

"Wonderful. The courts are just beyond the double glass doors." She motioned behind her. "Could I offer you some cookies?"

"Thank you very much," said Israel, taking the entire tray of cookies and walking up to the double doors toward the courts.

"Israel!" hissed Judah.

"These are lovely," said Israel with his mouth full. "Amazing facility."

There were four indoor bocce courts surrounded by flat-black closed picket fencing. These courts appeared to have been recently renovated. There were photos on the walls depicting competitors with one of the captions describing the "Pan American Club Championships featuring the best bocce ball players in the world." Next to the courts were a bar and seating area where people gathered to play cards, watch the games and have coffee and cocktails. The seating area was packed with at least twenty gray-haired or balding men sitting around tables and another twenty or so men standing around the fencing waiting for the games to begin. Israel was holding the cookie tray on the palm of his hand, which garnered interest among several of the members.

"Now here's a good man," said someone, walking up to Israel and taking a cookie.

"Goes well with a cappuccino," said another, taking a cookie.

"Work for the bar, do you?" asked a man, taking two cookies. "Must be new. Haven't seen you here before."

"Oh no, we're not with the bar," interjected Judah. "Just, uh, bringing some treats for the members."

"Right," added Israel, placing the tray on a nearby table being used for a game of *briscola*, much to the surprise of the players. "You don't happen to know a gentleman by the name of Domenico di Stefano?"

"Domenico? Of course, I know him," said the man, laughing. "You're standing right next to him."

Israel turned to his left and saw seated beside him a thin, bald man in a blue short-sleeve button-down shirt tucked into his black jeans. His cards were under the cookie tray, and he blinked at Israel, apparently confused by the commotion.

"Ah, what an honor," said Israel, taking Domenico's right hand and shaking it vigorously. "We were hoping to ask you a few questions, if you don't mind."

"You're not with the police, are you?" asked a man across the table, bald except for white tufts of hair sticking out from the sides of his head, giving him the appearance of an abbot. "If so, it wasn't me."

The man grabbed a handful of cookies.

"Uh ... no," replied Israel. "You see, we are about to embark on our maiden transatlantic voyage to the old country of Portugal. We've been in communication with the Transporti Maritime Line, a part Italian-, part-Portuguese-owned vessel, and we were told that the venerable Domenico di Stefano was the father-in-law of Signor Sérgio Ricardo de Carvalho and might be able to offer some insights about the ship. We are contemplating joining their crew this coming Saturday."

"That's a relief," said the man with a mouthful of cookie. "Cops these days ... always look at us suspiciously because of our origins. Meanwhile, all they need to do is look at some of these people from south of the border, bringing drugs and gangs ..."

"Thank you, Mario, for your opinion," said Domenico, gesturing toward several unused folding chairs. "And try to practice a little moderation, will you? We call him Sweet Tooth, for obvious reasons."

"So, what we wanted to ask about is the crew," said Israel, pulling up a chair beside Domenico. "Are you familiar with what it's like to work on a container ship?"

"Familiar?" scoffed Domenico. "I ran them for years before moving to the States."

"You see, we were offered a position to assist with the culinary arts as well as helping with various errands on shore."

"Well, I don't know much about that sort of thing," said Domenico, scratching his head. "It's been a very long time since I've been on a ship, but Sérgio hires the best. He's become a big name in the industry and has investments in multiple transportation companies. He flew Ginevra and me to Milan a couple years ago, where we had a chance to see our grandchildren and great-grandchildren."

"So, you would say that this is a perfectly legitimate operation?" asked Judah.

"Legitimate? Of course it is," said Domenico testily, glancing at one of his colleagues.

"I told you so," said Israel.

"Well, you never know," countered Judah. "Plus, you found this randomly online."

"Transporti Maritime Line is a carrier-owned container line offering a full-service package to customers. They control most of the transport chain across many long routes." Domenico paused and took a sip from his glass of water. "And how were you referred to me again?"

"Right," said Israel. "We've been looking at joining the Transporti Maritime Line, and one of their associates referred us to you, given your expertise in shipping and relationship with Sérgio. We live down the road."

"What a remarkable turn of events," said Domenico.

"I thought so, too," exclaimed Israel.

"Sérgio can always use a helping hand …" started Domenico.

"Courts now open!" shouted a man near the double doors.

"It's about time," said Mario. "Are you playing, Domenico?"

"No, not today. My ankle's been acting up again," he said. "Why don't you take this young man with you? What's your name, son?"

"My name's Israel, and he's Judah," said Israel, pointing to his brother. "I'm rather passionate about the game of bocce, as a matter of fact."

Judah elbowed him in the shoulder.

"A game of skill requiring expert hand-eye coordination," Israel continued. "And great feats of stamina and strength."

"Great, come with me," said Mario, standing up and wiping cookie crumbs from his shirt. He began walking toward the third court.

"Do you even know the rules for bocce?" whispered Judah as they followed Mario.

"Come on, now," said Israel under his breath. "It's bowling. What's there to know?"

Israel took his place beyond Mario and two others on the third court. Mario placed his bocce ball set at the edge of the court and pulled out the small white *pallino* and an orange bocce ball.

"You're with Dino, okay?" said Mario. "You can go after me."

Israel glanced at his brother, who was standing behind the gate to the court and gave a thumbs-up sign. He bent over, grabbed a blue bocce ball and tossed it in the air absent-mindedly while Mario began his warm-up routine, rotating his torso and shoulders from side to side.

Israel yawned, scratched his chest with his free hand and watched Mario size up the court before tossing the *pallino*. The ball bounced once, then rolled toward the far end of the court. Moments later, the orange ball landed just over a foot in front of the *pallino*.

Mario grinned and patted Israel on the shoulder, walking behind him to observe the next throw.

"Love games of athletic prowess," said Israel, mimicking Mario's upper body warm-up motions.

Israel studied the court. He held a blue bocce ball in his right hand. *Funny, this is heavier than I imagined. The ball needs a strong throw*, he thought.

Israel brought the bocce ball to his chest in a palm-down overhand grip. Then, swinging it down to his side and up, he let go of the ball, confident of the fluidity of his motion.

The ball wasn't visible on the court, and Israel, for a brief moment was confused about its trajectory. Then a cry rang out from behind him, and all was clear.

"My foot!"

CHAPTER FOUR

Israel and Judah Board a Train and Encounter a Traveling Band

Israel and Judah were standing in front of the Highland Park Metra Station at five-thirty in the morning, speaking with Ida and Estephan. It was Friday, the sun had not yet risen and it was eleven degrees outside.

Israel and Judah were bundled in insulated ski jackets. Israel wore a blue jacket with the hood and collar covering his head and neck, and Judah wore a matching red jacket. They each wore black jeans, brown water-resistant hiking boots and black mittens. Together, they looked like mountaineers preparing for an arctic expedition, not a Mediterranean excursion. At their feet, they had two large, hard roller bags, which contained all their critical earthly belongings, other than Israel's Xbox console and associated electronics.

"I'm in shock that you're actually following through with this," said Ida, her hands in the pockets of her parka.

Israel nodded his head slightly in a stoic, almost stern manner. Or perhaps he was frozen stiff on the wind-swept early-morning platform. It was hard to tell.

Estephan rubbed his bare hands in front of his face, blowing hot air on them. He hadn't dressed properly, having nearly overslept their departure and had only thrown on a Bears football sweater hoodie, pajama pants and slippers.

"It's been a tough, tiring, I'll even say, memorable week," he said, part of his mustache visibly frozen. "But I take some responsibility here. I asked you to figure out your next steps, and by God, you're on your way to doing *something*. What exactly you hope to achieve, I'm not sure. But perhaps this trip will provide you with some clarity."

"And you're sure you don't need to book a room in Baltimore?" asked Ida, for the third time that morning.

"Yes, Mom, everything's been taken care of," said Judah. "We'll arrive in Baltimore early tomorrow morning and can sleep on the train, remember?"

"And one more time," began Ida, "how do you plan to get to the cruise ship? You mentioned something about a budget cruise, which I'm not familiar with."

"Uber, Mom," said Judah. "We'll take it to the Cruise Maryland Terminal. I was also skeptical at first, but it seems legit."

"Yes, nothing to worry about," added Israel. "We met the father-in-law of the shipowner and his colleagues, and I'm more confident than ever about the operation. Soon we'll stand on our own two feet."

"The same can't be said about Mario …," said Judah under his breath.

"What was that?" asked Estephan, placing a hand on Israel's and Judah's shoulders. "Anyway, just keep an eye out for each other. Remain vigilant during your travels. There are too many swindlers out there looking to take advantage of people."

"Of course, Dad," said Israel. "We have all the important details sorted out. I'll be excited to report our progress over the next few months."

"Good. And don't forget your roots. You're a Cruz foremost," said Estephan.

"And Portuguese, of course," added Israel.

"Right, uh, well …," said Estephan, blowing hot air on his hands again. "And most importantly, don't forget to call your mother."

"We'll call at least once a week," said Judah. "That is, after we dock in Lisbon. Cell phone coverage may be spotty at sea."

"I'd like you boys to stay around the house forever," fretted Ida.

"What's that?" exclaimed Estephan.

"I just have a hard time letting you two go," said Ida, grabbing Judah by the sleeve and hugging him tightly before squeezing Israel to the point of light-headedness. "But now, it's time for you to scoot. Get inside the train station before you catch a cold. Estephan, you too. Get in the car before you get frostbite. Call us when you're in Baltimore, understand?"

The route from Chicago to Baltimore, on average, took twenty-one hours, not including the extra hour it took to travel from the Metra Station in Highland Park to the Chicago Union Station downtown. It was among the least efficient transportation options available and marginally less expensive for Israel and Judah than flying, renting a car, or taking the Greyhound bus. They were also able to avoid the costs of reserving a hotel room in Baltimore since the train served as a hotel on wheels, but that was beside the point. Israel had insisted on Amtrak as a purer form of travel that would, in literal terms, keep them on track. It was a ponderous undertaking, much like their pending transatlantic voyage. It was the slow passage through the vast everything in between that was enticing to Israel, and he couldn't think of a better way to start the trip.

Israel had been captivated by advertisements of Amtrak's grandeur, its big picture windows and its sleeper cars. The reality turned out to be a bit more mundane.

When the train rumbled through Indiana and Ohio, the only grandiose vistas Israel and Judah witnessed were frozen, powder-covered corn and soybean fields; freight train congestion near Toledo; and a squat, brown Cleveland Amtrak station. Israel and Judah had mercifully slept through much of the route, waking for lunch, then dozing on and off again as they approached Pennsylvania.

In Pittsburgh, Israel and Judah woke to several new passengers boarding their car. A group of four, carrying instruments, took seats a few rows in front of them, laughing and talking loudly as they sat down. They spoke with a southern drawl, with an odd emphasis on the last syllables of words that Israel couldn't place.

One was a tall, slender black woman with a two-level box haircut, wine-colored lipstick and mascara. Another was a double-breasted, tan trench-coat man who unzipped the gig bag containing the woman's double bass and handed it to her. In the seat in front of her, sat a brown-skinned man wearing a black pea coat and black fedora who had a red button accordion on his lap. Across the aisle from him, sat a woman with jet-black hair that fell down the back of her long, silver winter jacket. She held a guitar in her hands, which she was tuning. Behind her sat a pasty, gangly man in a black, white and gold New Orleans Saints zip-up hoodie who was holding a galvanized frottoir. He tossed a baseball cap in the middle of the aisle, where it lay upside down.

"Bertrand, are we ready?" asked the man in the Saints hoodie after a minute.

"Ti-Jean, we was born ready," said Bertrand.

Israel turned to Judah, seated near the window and pointed at the musicians. "What's this all about?"

"Looks like a traveling band," said Judah. "Didn't know Amtrak allowed these."

Bertrand stood up in the center of the aisle, the accordion hanging against his chest from its shoulder straps and bowed. The car was mostly full, and there was a murmur as passengers turned their attention to this curious development.

"Now, who's ready for a fais do-do?" bellowed Bertrand to the assembled passengers.

"A fay dough what?" whispered Israel to Judah.

"I think they're from Louisiana," said Judah. "It's like a dance party or something. I think I saw a PBS documentary about this, the mix of cultures …"

"Now, let me repeat myself, ladies and gentlemen," shouted Bertrand, playing a do-re-mi arpeggio on his accordion. "It's Saturday afternoon and dis here train is too quiet for my liking. We've come to lighten dings up."

"*Ça c'est bon*, Bertrand," said the woman with the guitar. "But why don't you introduce us to these fine folks?"

"Margo, pearl of my eyes, how could I forget?" exclaimed Bertrand. "We're gathered here today to celebrate one of life's greatest moments: da joining of hearts, da stomping of feet, da clapping of hands."

"Don't forget da giving of coins," added Ti-Jean, pointing to his cap on the aisle floor.

"… As a token of appreciation," said Bertrand. "But now, let me introduce da Bullhorn String Band, straight from da bayous of south-central Louisiana, bringing you da best of Cajun and Zydeco music on dis here train, for your traveling pleasure."

Bertrand's fingers danced across the buttons of his accordion, playing a series of rapid- fire blues runs that reverberated through the car, causing the passengers to sit up on the edges of their seats, oohing and aahing in amazement until he finally landed on a bluesy trill that he sustained as he spoke.

"You know, it's been a long time," said Bertrand, pushing and pulling the accordion's bellows. "It's been a long time since we've been on a locomotive. But if you dink about that word, if you dink about locomotion, well, dat's what we're all about. Movement! And if you're ready to move around, to stretch your legs, to lift your feet, den raise your hands in the air! Dat's right, in da air!"

"It's party time!" exclaimed a small girl, standing up in the aisle next to her mother and clapping her hands.

Israel looked over his shoulder and saw several people laughing.

"Dat's the spirit!" hollered Bertrand, launching into an accordion shake for some type of funky jig. *Push*, pull, push, *pull*, push, pull, went the bellows. Soon the frottoir joined the accordion, adding its snare-like sixteenth notes, and the music morphed into a one, two, three cha-cha, one, two, three rhythm.

"Da Zydeco cha cha, ladies and gentlemen!" shouted Bertrand. "Da Zydeco cha cha!"

The double bass and guitar joined in, and a half dozen passengers spilled into the aisle shaking their hips, bending their knees and rocking to the beat. It was a spontaneous sort of dance. The small girl forced her mother up, and she laughed as she swung the girl's arms from side to side. An elderly man with a quad cane stepped into the aisle and tapped his right foot enthusiastically. A young Latino couple leaped to their feet and began an elaborate dance, swaying to the rhythm of the cha-cha-cha.

Israel had never heard Zydeco music before. It was both strange and familiar, with its rhythm and blues sounds. The frottoir looked like a mix between a washboard and body armor, and he didn't know what to make of it. Israel wondered where this music fit in.

"Judah, these musicians," asked Israel as the band continued to play, "you said it was a mixing of cultures? Like the Creoles?"

Judah nodded, but Israel wasn't sure if he'd properly heard the question, or if he was nodding his head to the rhythm of the song.

Creole music, thought Israel. *I need to look into this. The Creole people. How do they fit in? How does this music, a mix of everything, fit in? Why are they traveling on a train? Are they like me, people on the outside, a little bit of this, a little bit of that, but not really part of any group of people? Is that why they're on the train, moving from town to town? Outsiders?*

Israel shook his head as if trying to shake unwanted rainwater from his hair. *No, I need to stop these thoughts. I'm Portuguese now. Born again. Hallelujah! No more questions about my origins pulling me in different directions.*

The cha-cha-cha ended, and the passengers shouted and applauded in delight. The man with the quad cane tossed several bills into the cap on the floor. The little girl ran up to the band and blew them kisses. The young Latino couple dropped a handful of coins into Ti-Jean's outstretched hands.

"Dank you, dank you!" said Bertrand. "*Merci beaucoup*. We hope we gave you some entertainment on dis cha-cha train! If you like what you heard, check us out on Soundcloud or da Bullhorn String Band dot com. Now, without further ado, we're off to the next car to liven dings up."

Bertrand winked at the young Latina woman who was standing next to her partner and unfastened his accordion. The other band members took a bow.

"This performance reminds me of Bob Dylan," said Judah, after the musicians had packed their instruments and left the car.

"Bob Dylan?" asked Israel. "Don't see the connection."

"It's the French connection. Some people call Bob Dylan the last surviving troubadour," said Judah. "He's been on the road for so many years, his schedule's been called the never-ending tour. Troubadours would go from home to home in medieval France, singing about love, talking about society, trying to earn a buck. Or some coins."

"And they'd sometimes try to win the heart of a maiden, I suppose?" asked Israel, perking up.

"That too. Traveling troubadours," said Judah, chuckling. "Kind of funny to think of the band that way. If we were poets or musicians, I suppose we might be troubadours. Given that we have no musical talent, our only option is poetry. And, of course, since we have no romantic interests, this probably isn't the best description of us at this time."

"Right. Of course. No romantic interests at all. Not in the slightest bit. Troubadour …" said Israel, closing his eyes and clasping his hands, his heart beating to the percussive sounds of the frottoir.

CHAPTER FIVE

Israel and Judah Arrive at the Port of Baltimore

"So, after taking a closer look at my email instructions," said Israel, inspecting his cell phone, "I may have misunderstood our rendezvous location."

Judah's teeth were chattering in the frigid early-morning chill as they stood outside the blue Cruise Maryland Terminal building. A sign on the door stated that the terminal opened at eight o'clock in the morning or two hours after the ship arrived. It was four-thirty in the morning, and there was no ship in sight. Nor was there another soul to be found.

"I must have gotten the terminal mixed up when researching other cruise packages," said Israel, scratching his leg. "We're supposed to be at the Seagirt Marine Terminal."

"I'd normally be more upset," said Judah, bouncing up and down to keep himself warm, "but I'm too tired and cold to be angry. How far is this other terminal?"

"Should only be about ten or fifteen minutes away," said Israel. "But there's one minor challenge."

"What's that?" asked Judah.

"No ride shares or taxis are in the area," said Israel.

"Wonderful," said Judah. "Can you try hailing the taxi we just rode in?"

"Yeah, that's the problem. We took a cab from the train station. I don't have his contact info," said Israel. "Nothing's showing up for me on Uber or Lyft."

"There's got to be someone available," said Judah. "People are flying in and out of Baltimore."

"BWI's twenty minutes away," said Israel. "I suppose we could walk to the terminal, worst-case scenario."

"Uh, no," said Judah. "Not an option. Haven't you seen *The Wire*?"

Israel sat on top of his roller bag and stared out at Interstate 95. There was a steady stream of cars on the highway, even at these early hours.

"By the way, didn't the security guard at the entrance checkpoint review our boarding passes and IDs?" asked Judah. "He should have noticed we were at the wrong terminal."

"He seemed a little distracted," said Israel. "We had to tap on the booth window to wake him up."

"I see. I suppose I was asleep as well," said Judah. "Well, it's deserted here. Should we walk over to the checkpoint and see if he can provide any help?"

"I suppose it couldn't hurt," said Israel.

Judah grabbed his roller bag handle and stiffly walked toward the entrance checkpoint near the highway. Israel followed, flipping back and forth between Uber and Lyft to find a ride. There was a sharp westerly wind that was unobstructed in the parking lot, and Israel was chilled to the bone.

After about five minutes, they came to the guard booth and found the security guard inside with his hands in his lap and his black baseball cap brim covering his face as he snored on his swivel chair. Judah tapped the sliding-panel service window twice. The security guard abruptly stopped snoring, then resumed a moment later, louder and deeper this time.

"Ahem!" said Judah. "Uh, sir, do you mind if we ask for your help?"

The security guard continued to snore.

Tap, tap, tap went Judah.

"Sir, sorry to interrupt you," said Judah, more forcefully this time.

The security guard continued to snore.

"Let me try," said Israel, pushing Judah to the side. "I heard they were going to trade Lamar Jackson to the Steelers!" yelled Israel into the service window.

The security guard leaped from his chair as if electrocuted. His baseball cap fell to the floor, and he looked from side to side in confusion, until he settled on Israel, who was smiling and waving at him.

"Sir, my apologies for bothering you," said Israel. "I know how busy you are. We're in desperate need of assistance finding a taxi. Any chance you could help with that?"

The security guard picked up his cap and pulled open the service window.

"Jesus lord almighty," he cried. "I thought I heard some devilish noise, but it turns out it's just you. You're not up to mischief, are you?"

"I swear on my heart and hope to die …," Israel paused and thought about that expression for a moment. *Odd saying, really. If I've prioritized one thing, it's not dying.* "As I was saying, we made the mistake of asking a taxi to take us from Penn Station to here. We're at the wrong terminal, but we can't seem to find any cabs or ride shares right now. We were hoping you might have some ideas."

The security guard settled back into his seat and placed his cap on his balding head. He gave Israel and Judah a hard look. "Y'all should know that the terminal building doesn't open for another three hours," he said. "Where you trying to go? Bahamas or something?"

"We're on a cruise to Portugal," said Israel. "We need to be at the Seagirt Marine Terminal in two hours."

"Seagirt?" exclaimed the guard. "There ain't nothing there but cargo ships."

"We're on a budget cruise," said Israel. "Through the Transporti Maritime Line."

"There's no such thing as a budget cruise," said the guard. "You'll pay for it one way or another."

"Sir, I know this sounds odd," said Judah, holding his breath momentarily as a sharp breeze blew around them. "We're going to be passengers on a container ship. They sometimes make room for a few paying customers. We just got our terminals mixed up."

"Well, I'll be," said the guard, his expression softening. "It's mighty cold outside."

He looked out the window at the white Ford F-150 parked next to the booth. There was a Port of Baltimore Security insignia decal on the driver's-side door.

"Give me a minute," he said, picking up his walkie-talkie and shutting the service window.

Israel pulled his phone from his jacket pocket as the security guard spoke into his device. He swiped for Uber and typed in Seagirt Marine Terminal. After a few seconds, Uber came up with a Black SUV as a rideshare option, forty minutes away, for seventy-five dollars.

"A'ight, fellas," said the guard, opening the service window. "I got it worked out. I can take you to Seagirt. I don't want nobody freezing on my watch. Creates too much paperwork. Step around the booth, and you can ride in the truck. Tips will be kindly accepted."

"I call shotgun," said Israel, hurrying toward the truck with his luggage.

It took only a few minutes for them to load their belongings and warm up the truck before exiting the terminal area. Soon they were on the interstate, approaching the Fort

McHenry Tunnel, which carried traffic through Baltimore Harbor.

"That's Fort McHenry," said the security guard. "You can't see it right now because we're heading under water, but that's where we fought the British navy during the War of 1812. I assume y'all aren't from here?"

"That's right," said Israel from the passenger seat. "We're from Chicago. First time in Baltimore."

"No offense, but nobody from the DMV would stand in a parking lot in Baltimore at four-thirty in the morning," said the security guard.

"I can see that," said Israel.

"I've always had mixed feelings about Fort McHenry and what it represents," said the guard. "The War of 1812 was a catastrophe for native peoples. That's often overlooked in history class, but it's impossible to ignore when you're someone like me who commutes by it every day. As a Melungeon …" He paused and glanced at Israel. "Have you heard of us?"

"I'm afraid not," said Israel.

"Some people call us the Lost Tribe of Appalachia because we were darker than others in the region. Most of us have some Native American, African and Irish ancestors. Who knows what else? My grandmother used to tell stories about the courage of Tecumseh, and his eventual downfall because of the War of 1812. It's a tragedy, really. But I suppose it led to a whole new order, a new era of peace for the white man. The end of hostilities, at least with England."

Israel stared at the lights near the ceiling of the Fort McHenry Tunnel and the way they pulsated on the walls. It produced a mesmerizing strobe-light effect on the thousands of white ceramic tiles that made Israel think how, in certain parts of the country, there were order and structure and uniformity. This was not something he was accustomed to at home. His home had always been chaotic, breaking, teetering from crisis to crisis.

Images of his father surfaced: stressed, irritable, face ragged from unmanageable caseloads. His frazzled mother, meeting a plumber one day, an electrician the next, trying to keep the home from falling into further disrepair while working as an administrative assistant for the capricious high school principal. Discussions about becoming missionaries. Meetings at the messianic church. Jews for Jesus. Financial troubles. Should they divorce after all? Was everything just chasing after the wind?

The oddness of their relationship to the community seemed to be symbolized by a brown wall tile amid the gleaming whiteness. A round hole among square pegs. A large gray cygnet among yellow ducklings.

Two sons, failing to live up to expectations. Unmoored. Aimless. Drifting.

The truck exited the tunnel, and the security guard got off at the first exit toward Keith Avenue and the Seagirt Marine Terminal. It was still dark and poorly lit, but Israel could make out the industrial orderliness, an Amazon warehouse, railroad tracks and semi-trucks.

"You know where you're going?" asked the security guard. "Where exactly is the meetup point?"

"We were told to meet at the ship by five o'clock in the morning," said Israel, pulling out his phone and scanning the email he had received. "The ship is scheduled to depart at six, and we're supposed to meet someone by the name of Dantel Paña Montilla at the dock."

"A'ight. Let's hope we don't have any trouble getting through the gate," said the security guard, pulling into the terminal.

Israel could make out the rows of multicolored containers stacked neatly on top of each other as they entered the complex. They passed assorted semitrucks, truck-mounted cranes, pickup trucks, bucket trucks, dump trucks, flatbed trucks, front-end loaders, bulldozers, road rollers, skid steer loaders and sedans. They crossed over a railroad track and saw a sign with the words Point Breeze and were now driving along a vast area with thousands of shipping containers.

"What's that over there?" said the security guard, pointing to a large ship in the distance.

"Yes, I can see the white letters TML on the hull of the ship," said Israel "That must be the Transporti Maritime Line."

"That's enormous," said Judah, sitting up from his seat in the back of the truck.

"Looks like a Panamax. That's a good-size ship," said the security guard. "This terminal can actually handle super-post-Panamax vessels. Can you see those giant cranes? That's what makes the Port of Baltimore so special. It's one of the few ports in the country with a fifty-foot shipping channel and a fifty-foot container berth."

"Did they give us any more information on where to meet this Dantel guy?" asked Judah. "Are we just supposed to walk onto the ship?"

"Not sure," said Israel, scanning the area for clues.

After another couple of minutes, they pulled directly up to the container ship anchored at the dock. The cranes towered over them twenty stories high. There were trucks moving in and out of the area, and the ship was fully laden with cargo.

The security guard rolled down his window and waved at a passing silver Jeep Cherokee, which came to a stop. "We're looking for a man by the name of Dantel," shouted the security guard to a longshoreman. Then, turning to Israel: "What's his last name?"

"Montilla," said Israel.

"Dantel Montilla," said the guard. "You happen to know who he is?"

"No," said the man, shaking his head from the open driver's-side window. "Ask the man in that van."

Israel turned and looked out the window in the direction of the ship. There was a white van idling by the heavy-duty truss gangway. Two men dressed in winter jackets were ascending the platform toward the upper deck.

The security guard spun the truck around and drove the short distance to the white van. The truck's passenger-side window faced the van, and Israel rolled down his window.

"We're looking for Dantel Montilla," he shouted.

A man in an orange hooded bomber jacket, orange cargo pants, black rubber boots and a hard hat stepped out of the van. He was not a tall man, but he had a gruff, do-not-trifle-with-me expression. He had a thin goatee and was smoking a cigarette.

He walked up to the truck, inspected Israel for a moment, then took a deep drag of his cigarette before tossing it on the ground, where it tumbled away in the wind.

"I thought there were two of you," he said.

"Are you Dantel?" asked Israel.

"That's right," he replied, crossing his arms. "First Officer Montilla."

"Got it," said Israel, hesitating. The man's demeanor threw him off. "Uh, my brother is in the back seat. We were told to meet you so you could take us on the ship."

"You sure this is legit?" whispered the security guard. "I don't like the look of this."

Israel glanced at the security guard. "Yes, perfectly legit," he said under his breath, his confidence in the trip beginning to wane.

"You ready?" asked Dantel.

"Yes, we're all set," said Israel. "Just give us a minute to collect our stuff."

Israel shut the passenger-door window and turned to Judah. "This is it, I guess," he said.

Judah yawned and unbuckled his seat belt. "I couldn't see Dantel," said Judah. "We're good, right?"

"Sure. Everything's good," said Israel. "Everything's just fine."

"Look, son," said the security guard, "you sure you want to go through with this? Have you done your proper research? Like I told you earlier, there ain't no such thing as a budget cruise. You look like good kids, but if you was my sons, hell, no, you wouldn't be getting on that ship."

"What do you mean by that?" asked Judah.

Israel cut the security guard off before he could elaborate. "Sir, we're committed," he said. "And we can't thank you enough for your assistance."

Judah tapped Israel on the shoulder and handed him fifty dollars. Israel looked at the cash and sighed. *We have little to spare, but he really did us a mitzvah*, he thought.

"For you, sir," he said.

The security guard looked at the cash and shook his head. "I have a feeling you're gonna need that," he told them. "Like I said, I was hard at work when you arrived and wanted no trouble dealing with two frozen corpses in the terminal parking lot. You just take care of yourselves, got it? Keep your wits about you."

Israel and Judah gathered their belongings and stepped out of the truck while Dantel stood a few feet away, staring past them, indifferent yet impatient. Israel pulled his hood over his head and turned to wave goodbye to the security guard, but he was already gone, making his way among the maze of containers. *We're committed*, thought Israel as a gust of frigid, salty air whipped him in the face. *No changing course now. No turning back.*

CHAPTER SIX

Israel and Judah Embark on a Journey and Are Tested in the Galley

"The Transporti Maritime Line has a twenty-six-man crew," said Dantel, leading Israel and Judah up the truss gangway. "There are no women on board the ship and no pleasure-seekers either."

Judah elbowed Israel in the rib cage.

"Ow!"

"Is something wrong?" asked Dantel.

"Everything's great," said Judah. "*Just perfect.*"

"This is a working ship," said Dantel, emphasizing the point. "It's nearly one thousand feet long, with a one-hundred-foot beam and a bulbous bow. It's designed for transatlantic voyages."

"Ah yes, a Panamax. Just the ship we need," said Israel.

They walked in silence for a moment. Israel was out of breath, and they were barely halfway up the walkway.

"Geez it's freezing!" exclaimed Judah as a brisk wind shook the aluminum steps.

Dantel grunted.

A light flashed from the steps above, and Israel could make out a man in an orange uniform. They continued climbing and when they were near the top of the gangway, Dantel pulled out his walkie-talkie.

"Permission to come aboard," said Dantel, speaking into the device. "First Officer Montilla here with new joiners."

Israel panted, grateful for a moment to recover. The static from the walkie-talkie crackled in the cold early morning air.

"Permission granted," came back the reply.

The next thirty minutes were a blur. Dantel and the security guard had done a thorough (Israel thought rather intrusive) search of their belongings prior to boarding, in coordination with a port official who was with him in the van. Once they cleared security, Dantel handed them off to João Abreu, an affable, pot-bellied man with a receding hairline, who was eagerly waiting for them onboard. João took them to their quarters to drop off their luggage, speaking rapidly to them in a combination of Portuguese and English, then immediately escorted them to the bridge per the captain's orders.

Israel, Judah and João were the last of the crew to arrive at the bridge. The seamen were standing around the various navigational and communications controls, talking to each other in small groups, when they entered the room. Master Capurro, who was in mid conversation with Chief Officer Russo, motioned for Israel and Judah to stand beside him.

"The positioning is fine on account of the tides. We should be all set then," Israel heard him say to Chief Officer Russo in perfect English, with the slightest Italian accent.

"As you know, we have two new joiners. Your attention, please," said Master Capurro, raising his hand in the air from his pedestal-mounted marine chair. He was a stern, bespectacled, clean-shaven man of slim build, who bore a natural air of authority. "They will be reporting to Chief Steward Abreu in the steward's department."

This comment elicited a chuckle from two seamen. Israel heard someone call them "our unfortunate cooks."

"I expect this to be a beneficial addition to our crew, so please welcome aboard Israel and Judah Cruz," said Master Capurro, lightly clapping his hands. "They may also take special remedial assignments from First Officer Montilla, as needed."

Israel glanced at Dantel, whose severe expression had hardly changed since they first met. He was glad they would primarily be reporting to João in the galley.

"As always, I want to review safety procedures, which I expect you will all follow to the letter. No deviation from policies and procedures will be tolerated, including during shore leave," said Master Capurro about to read from the International Ship and Port Facility Security Code: "You are to report any warning signs of illicit behavior, such as, but not limited to, narcotics trafficking, stowaways, piracy, terroristic activity and any other nefarious conduct. Failure to do so may cause you to be referred to local authorities, customs, the police. You are to adhere to all policies and procedures around personal safety, including fire prevention and firefighting, elementary first aid, survival techniques for craft and rescue boats." Capurro added his own bit at the end: "Container shipping is the lifeblood of the global economy, and we play an important role in transporting goods to regions around the world. Your personal well-being and the safety of our cargo are my number one priorities. I will now turn it over to Chief Officer Russo to review our passage plan."

"*Grazie*, Master," said Chief Officer Russo, rising from his seat, his Italian accent more pronounced. "We will be at sea for eight days from Porta of Baltimore to Ponta Delgada. *Navigazione* details can be found in ECDIS, and ECDIS charts will be updated daily and shared by email. We will be traveling north of the fortieth parallel, and the weather shoulda be good, except for a *disturbo* north of Bermuda that we will monitor."

The word *disturbo* caught Israel's attention. *Did he mean disturbance? Like a storm? Well, I'm sure it's nothing to be concerned about.*

"Once at the Azores," continued Chief Officer Russo, "we will bertha and partially offloada at Ponta Delgada, before heading to Funchal. Because of scheduling constraints, we will be at Ponta Delgada for two nights before heading out to sea for a day and then will bertha and partially offloada at Funchal. Again, because of scheduling constraints, we will remain at Funchal for two nights before leaving for Lisbona. We shoulda reach the Port of Lisbona by January twenty-seventh, where we will offloada the remaining cargo."

"This sounds great!" whispered Israel into Judah's ear.

"Yeah, seems fine," whispered Judah. "But I thought we were mainly going on a cruise versus joining a shipping crew. Like a seventy-thirty split: mostly sightseeing, then some work."

"Oh, it's just minor work, here and there," said Israel reassuringly. "There's going to be so much to see and do. I feel much better about this than I did earlier this morning."

Shortly after the all-hands meeting on the bridge, as the ship was preparing to set sail, Israel and Judah met João in the galley, not far from their cabin.

"Come in, come in," said João enthusiastically, ushering Israel and Judah inside.

"Welcome to my steward's department," he said enthusiastically and quickly gave them a tour of the austere galley, a square stainless-steel room used for food storage, food preparation and cooking. The primary appliances were the stoves and microwaves. The stoves were gimbaled and fitted with guardrails to prevent the spillage of hot liquids while also helping protect the cook from falling into the stove during rough waters. The microwaves were secured above the stoves and surrounded by cabinets. At the far end of the cooking area were two refrigerated rooms filled with produce, fish and meat.

"So you are new to sailing?" João asked.

"I've had some experience in open waters," said Israel.

"You have?" asked Judah.

"Yes. I've ridden the Wendella down the Chicago River. You also might recall my kayak expeditions this summer."

"Kayak expeditions?" questioned Judah. "You mean fishing for bluegill, stocked by the city, in the streams behind the Chicago Botanical Garden?"

"If I might interrupt," said João, "what I meant was if you had any experience on a container ship."

"Well, in that case, no," said Israel.

"That's right. We've never even been on a cruise, which was supposed to be part of this trip," said Judah.

"Ah, I see," said João. "Not a problem. You will learn from me the ins and outs of container shipping. And there will be much to see in this, er, cruise."

João paused and placed his hands on his hips and stared intently at Israel and Judah.

"If you don't mind me asking," he began. "You are brothers, yes?"

"I'm sorry to say we are," replied Judah.

"Good, I can see the resemblance," said João.

"Uh, I beg to differ," said Israel.

"Right, I have to agree with Israel on that," added Judah.

"I've always been called the tall, dark and handsome one," said Israel.

"You look Portuguese," said João. "You have a Portuguese last name. But did you not learn Portuguese at home? On your job application, you mentioned you would like to improve your Portuguese. Is that correct?"

"Yes, that's correct," said Israel. "You see, we are Portuguese Americans, looking to reconnect with our roots in the motherland."

"The word *improve* may be a bit of an exaggeration," replied Judah.

"And by motherland, you mean Portugal?"

"Yes, we are planning to immigrate to Portugal," said Israel. "In the meantime, we would very much appreciate any assistance in studying the language of our ancestors."

"Ah, I see," said João, rubbing his forehead. "We can arrange this. I will teach you while we work in the kitchen. *Certamente vocês não são tolos e sabem un pouco de português, não é?*"

Israel and Judah stared blankly at João.

"Okay, so we will start at the beginning," said João, breaking an awkward silence. "I'd like to see what you can cook. Follow me."

João led Israel and Judah to a refrigerated room stocked with perishables on metal racks. There were cartons of milk and juice, bags of apples, beets, broccoli, cabbages, lettuces, mushrooms, sweet peppers, turnips, radishes and assorted squashes. There were large cases of butter and eggs. João bent over, picked up a small empty cardboard box from the floor and handed it to Judah.

"I'd like you to cook an omelet," said João. "Judah, you can go first."

Israel watched as João started placing items in the box. "*Os ovos,*" João said, putting three eggs into the box. "Repeat after me."

"*Ooz ovooss,*" said Israel and Judah, in unison.

"No, no, no," said João, waving his hand in the air. "European Portuguese is not like the Spanish you hear in the US. You pronounce *s* with a *sh* sound at the end of a word, unless it's followed by a word starting with a consonant or the silent letter *h*, in which case it's pronounced like a *z*. Say it again. *Os ovos*."

"*Ooz ohvoosh*," said Israel and Judah.

"No, the *o* sound is off now," said João, sighing, and placing shredded cheese in the box. "You pronounce it from the back of your mouth. Now, follow me."

João led Israel and Judah to the countertop, where he instructed Judah to place the box. He pulled down an eight-inch nonstick skillet and lid hanging from the wall and placed them on the stovetop.

"This is an electric stove. You work it like this," he said, turning the dial clockwise, then turning it in the opposite direction to shut it off. "For me, cooking is not a job, it is a passion. It is poetry. There is skill required. An understanding of rhythm and sound and balance. But there is also feeling and emotion. That cannot be taught. The omelet is the perfect representation of poetry. Simple to make but difficult to master. We can all write a sonnet, but how many of us can do it expertly? Do you get my point?"

Israel thought of the haiku he had worked on for M&M. He had scribbled lines of verse on the back of a *Modern Cat* magazine he had found on the train, but they didn't seem to properly convey his attitude toward her. He may have imbued them with a bit too much feline imagery.

"Do you have any women in your life?" asked João, more as a statement than a question. "Tell me, what better way is there to a woman's heart than through the poetic power of food?"

Israel was now becoming very interested in this cooking challenge. *I am an expert at making ramen. I am great at pouring cereal. What is an omelet but a large, scrambled egg?*

Judah picked up the skillet, walked over to the stove and placed it on the burner.

"French omelet?" asked Judah.

"A French omelet? Yes, of course," said João. "Now you are speaking my language. The *zone culinaire*, *Mastering the Art of French Cooking*."

"I cannot guarantee an omelet in the style of Julia Child or Wolfgang Puck," said Judah, turning on the burner and adding butter to the pan, "but I recall a recipe from Chef Jacques Pépin, if that will do."

"*Chef cuisinier* Pépin?" exclaimed João, his eyes widening. "Why, yes, of course. Show me."

Judah cracked the three eggs into a small glass bowl, tossed in a pinch of salt and pepper, then began mixing vigorously with a fork.

"I usually try to remove strands of white," said Judah. "At least, on occasions when I am making an extra-special omelet."

"Go on," said João excitedly.

Judah lifted the skillet from the burner and swirled the bubbling butter so it fully covered the hot surface of the pan.

"I then add the eggs," said Judah, pouring the egg mixture into the pan. "If I have herbs on hand, I may also add them."

Judah shook the skillet and began stirring the eggs with his fork, scraping bits from the side of the pan to the middle. After about a minute of this, he turned off the heat and smoothed the surface of the eggs.

"I add cheese," said Judah. "Shredded Gouda will work just fine."

Judah placed the shreds of Gouda in the center of the omelet. He put a lid over the skillet to allow the cheese to soften.

"Once the omelet is set, I move it to the far side of the skillet, like this," said Judah, sliding the omelet to one side. "This is the trickiest part, when I fold one side of the omelet partway over the filling, then I roll it over onto a serving plate."

Judah rolled the steaming omelet onto a plate and added another pinch of salt and pepper. "And *voilà! Bon Appétit!*" said Judah, handing João the dish.

João examined the omelet, poking at it with his fork. He lifted the dish to his nose and breathed in the aroma. He cut the omelet down the middle and inspected inside, then scooped a large piece and took a bite.

"*Maravilhoso!*" cried João. "Tender. Savory. Firm. What a revelation! You know how to cook."

"I dabble here and there," said Judah, crossing his arms and leaning against the counter.

"This is excellent," said João. "You are a strong candidate for my sous chef. I am very curious to see what your brother can prepare."

Israel stepped forward, turned on the burner and placed the skillet on it. He cut a piece of butter and placed it in the pan like he had seen his brother do to prepare for the omelet.

"My version of the omelet," said Israel, rubbing his hands together, "is what the culinary experts might call fusion. It is a mix of the American and French varieties. I would love to serve you a Portuguese omelet, given my proclivity for all things Portuguese, but alas, I was not aware of this challenge beforehand. Otherwise, I would have been more prepared."

Israel cracked three eggs into a bowl and began whipping them vigorously with a fork, causing some egg mixture to splatter on his shirt.

João appeared aghast but said nothing.

"As you can see, the butter is now beginning to bubble and brown," said Israel.

The butter was simmering, giving off a pungent, metallic aroma. There was black debris floating in the sea of brown liquid.

"I will add the egg mixture to the pan, like this," said Israel, pouring the mixture into the skillet and causing the eggs to roil and sizzle violently. The omelet mixture had an unsavory brown-and-yellow color.

"I like to stir like so," said Israel, stirring the mixture around the pan in a clockwise manner. "Oh, and let me add some salt and pepper." Israel added salt and pepper to the pan.

"Aye yai yai!" cried João. "That's a lot of salt."

"No worries," said Israel. "Restaurants are known for adding extra salt to their dishes. Plus, you might say a little extra salt is appropriate. We are sailors. Seamen. The salt in the sea is the salt in our blood!"

Israel prodded the omelet, and it was firm. He tried moving it to the side of the pan, like Judah had, but the high heat had caused it to stick to the nonstick surface.

"Eggs can be such fickle things," said Israel, shaking the skillet. "I will fold it over now."

Israel tried to fold one side of the omelet partially over the middle of the mixture, but it broke.

"Ah, before I forget, let me add some cheese," said Israel, grabbing a handful of Gouda shreds and tossing them haphazardly into the pan. "The lid, when placed over the skillet, allows the cheese to melt." He covered the skillet with the lid.

João stared wide-eyed at the operation, as if witnessing the murder of Julius Caesar.

"Okay, so let me scrape this off the pan now," said Israel after a minute.

He could not fold the omelet, so he scraped chunks of the black, brown and yellow mixture onto a serving dish in the manner of scrambled eggs. The eggs appeared dry and charred and looked a bit like the splattered brain from a crime scene.

"*Voilà! Bon Appétit!*" said Israel proudly, handing João the plate.

João was white with shock. He held the dish in his hand, motionless for a moment.

"Allow me to serve you," said Israel, picking up a fork, stuffing the mixture into João's mouth.

João chewed it gingerly, sweat materializing on his forehead as the egg-and-cheese mixture swirled over his tongue. He glanced at the sink and appeared to hesitate, as if deciding whether to swallow or spit out the contents of his mouth.

"So, what do you think?" asked Israel, patting him on the back, which caused João to swallow his mouthful. "Speechless?"

João nodded his head weakly, then placed his hand against his throat.

"Water," he hissed. "Please, water!"

CHAPTER SEVEN

Israel Refines His Poems and Speaks with an Engineer

Two days later, during a break in the afternoon kitchen duties, Israel's madness was becoming clear to all. He was moody and had slept poorly for several days. He was unsteady on his feet as if drunk, although he hadn't touched alcohol. The movement of the ship made him clumsy, and he was constantly queasy. He often appeared lost in thought and confused. On several occasions, he ended up in the engine room, even though it was a restricted area that one needed special permission to access.

The voyage was an abrupt change to his routine. He had spent months doing nothing at home, other than scrolling through his phone and playing Xbox. The recent excursion seemed to have caused a rewiring of his brain. It was impossible to say precisely what was happening to the evolving physiological characteristics of his mind and the impact this had on his reasoning and IQ but suffice it to say that he was in a serious state of digital technology withdrawal.

The most troubling and telling sign of this was his sudden passion for haikus. He was consumed with them.

Dear M&M (version one),
A short poem, for you.
Warmest regards, Israel Cruz

> *I peel potatoes*
> *In the bowel of the ship*
> *Carbs to fuel my love.*

Dear M&M (version two),
A short poem, for you.
Deepest regards, Israel Cruz

> *I rock back and forth*
> *Floating on dreams of our love*
> *Refusing to wake.*

Dear M&M (version three),
A short poem, for you.
Utmost regards, Israel Cruz

> *In a vast ocean*
> *The salt water tempts my thirst*
> *But then I see you.*

João had taken Judah aside in the middle of the day with a concerned look on his face.

"This brother of yours," he began, "is he all right?"

"What do you mean?" replied Judah. "He should be in good health."

"Er, no," said João. "That's not what I meant. What I meant, and I hope this doesn't cause offense … Is he right in the head?"

"He's a little eccentric, I'll give you that," Judah said. "Not sure he has any natural abilities, to be honest. I figured you noticed that with his cooking, which is why I assumed you relegated him to washing the dishes."

"But he is moving in a—how should I say it?—way that looks looney, I think that's the word," said João.

"Now that you mention it, he is acting a little differently," said Judah. "But you have to understand, he was in isolation the past several months. It takes time to adjust to a new routine."

"Ah, yes, that must be it," said João. "Do you think he's still reliable? There are some deliveries that we'd like him to run during our port of call, assuming he is mentally capable."

"I wouldn't worry about him being reliable," said Judah. "He's generally good at taking direction. It's more the taking initiative part that is lacking. Although, I give him credit. It was his idea to go to Portugal."

Later that evening, an engineer pulled Judah aside in the ship's mess.

"You're Israel's brother, right?" asked the engineer.

"Guilty as charged."

"Tell that crazy man to stay out of the engine room," he said. "It's not safe. He's not trained."

The following day, during Israel and Judah's afternoon break, Judah attempted to speak to Israel about the feedback he had been receiving. They were headed back to their quarters, and Israel was distracted, scribbling notes in a small spiral-bound notepad.

"Are you composing a letter to Mom and Dad?" asked Judah.

"Huh? What was that?" asked Israel distractedly.

"A letter. Are you sending a letter to Mom and Dad?" asked Judah. "We didn't get to speak to them properly in Baltimore. The reception was bad."

"We are joined in love …" murmured Israel.

"Come again?"

"Your dun-colored breasts …"

"My what?"

"Huh."

"Will you look at me and stop your weird mumbling?" exclaimed Judah, grabbing Israel by the shirt collar.

Israel stared at Judah as if for the first time all week. He dropped his notepad to the floor and looked down at Judah's hand on his collar, then back up at his brother's face.

"What's the meaning of this?" he said hotly.

"You weren't listening to me," said Judah. "I need to give you some feedback."

"Feedback often tells you more about the person giving it than the feedback itself," said Israel, slapping Judah's hand away and then bending to retrieve his notepad.

"Take it any way you like," said Judah. "You've been acting strange lately. You're scribbling nonstop. It's like you're uninterested in this quote-unquote cruise we're on."

"I can assure you I have full command of my faculties," said Israel.

"Just stay out of the engine room," said Judah. "People are starting to notice, and I don't want to upset this crew. We're stuck on this ship for the next few weeks."

Ten minutes later, Israel wandered into the engine room.

"The color of love …" he muttered to himself, scratching out a line of poetry in his notepad.

He bumped his foot against a drain.

"Watch your foot," said a voice from the corner. "That's a hazardous place to step. Also a critical piece of machinery. The air condensate drain is essential to the safe operation of the engine."

Israel awoke from his literary reverie and spun around, trying to locate the voice. He wasn't sure how he had entered the engine room again.

"I recognize that look," said the voice. "Your eyes are out of balance with your inner senses. You're confused. The sea will do it to you."

"Uh, the sea will do what to you?" asked Israel, still trying to locate the voice.

"It will mess with your sense of place. Your equilibrium. It can cause sleep deprivation and hallucinations. This most commonly occurs with landlubbers who have yet to experience the open ocean," said the voice.

"I see," said Israel.

"Mental impairment usually sets in after twenty-four hours of lack of sleep. It will affect a sailor's ability to think logically, to solve problems," said the man, coming into full view of Israel. "In some cases, people may sleepwalk. After a couple more days of extreme fatigue, individuals may experience slurred speech, extreme lethargy and erratic behavior. This is very dangerous on a ship. Accidents can and do occur, often with fatal consequences. That's why it's so important to get proper sleep, or else you may inadvertently wander into an engine room on multiple occasions and end up in the auxiliary engine turbocharger drain."

Israel blinked several times and stared at the man. He was about Israel's height, with a neatly trimmed black beard and short, curly hair. He was wearing the standard-issue orange hooded jacket, orange cargo pants and black rubber boots.

"My name's Moshe, by the way," said the engineer. "I'm on watch duty and couldn't help but notice you wandering about."

"I have been feeling a bit out of sorts lately," said Israel.

"I'd recommend getting some sleep," said Moshe. "I'm sure João can last a day or two without your services. It's not like he had any help before, and we managed just fine."

"You think so?"

"Certain of it," said Moshe. "By the way, if you don't mind me asking, before you take your leave, you don't happen to be Jewish?"

This question stirred in Israel all the currents and countercurrents of knowledge about his identity. He had so convinced himself of his new Portuguese heritage over the past week that his previous sense of self was slipping into the recesses of his mind, although it hadn't disappeared entirely. The question had the effect of surfacing the remnants of his old identity, and he was even more confused and disoriented than before.

Israel shook his head, trying to shake off his dizziness. He placed his hand behind his head and rubbed the nape of his neck to relieve the sudden pressure.

"Cruz must be a Portuguese or Spanish name then," said Moshe, misinterpreting Israel's head shaking. "I have some cousins who look like you. The names Israel and Judah are of Hebrew origin, if that wasn't obvious to you. I've met some Hispanic Americans, though, with long Catholic lineages who had the name Israel, so I suppose I shouldn't read too much into your first names. Just curious, since I happen to be Israeli. I have a bunch of relatives who live in the US. Where are you from?"

"I'm from Chicago."

"Never been there," said Moshe. "I have family in New York and Philadelphia. I've been to the States a few times. It was a good place for Jews, but it's been getting worse over the years. The shooting at the L'Simcha Congregation in Pittsburgh was a low point, although sadly, not an end point. Just a long continuum of hate that doesn't seem to go away.

Then again, we Israelis have our troubles as well. The Palestinians, as I'm sure you know."

"Yes, I'm familiar with the conflict," said Israel.

"You should be," said Moshe, "especially with a name like yours. But it goes beyond the Palestinians. We Israelis can't even agree on what constitutes a Jew. There are some hard-liners who want to change the Law of Return. That was a foundational doctrine concerning Jewish citizenship and how it could be granted to anyone with Jewish parents. The law was later expanded, allowing people with only one Jewish grandparent the right to return to Israel. But imagine if that law were to be rescinded? It would have far-reaching implications, not just in Israel but in the entire diaspora."

Israel thought about the word diaspora. *A dispersion of people. Disconnected from their place of origins.*

"People's understanding of Jewishness would be fundamentally altered," Moshe continued. "I mean, there are arguments for reforming determinations of status, but one way or another, changes to the law would create mass confusion about who is Jewish, potentially creating a rift with American Jews and even dampen interest in Aliyah. And what would it say to people of Jewish heritage who perhaps don't practice Judaism but are nonetheless viewed as Jews by societies outside Israel? What would happen to them if they were persecuted? What would be their safety net? Our identities are no small matter. But like so many things in this world, so much is affected by geography. Take the fatigue you've been experiencing lately. That's because of geography. It's because you are in the middle of the ocean, cresting wave after wave, miles away from land in every direction. Not being on firm ground is disorienting. It's unmooring."

"That's why I'm going to Portugal," interjected Israel.

"That makes sense," said Moshe. "You should connect with your roots. Riding a container ship is an unconventional way to get there, I must say, but the path you take is perhaps more important than the destination. There's a quote from one of your great writers, James Baldwin, that comes to mind: 'People can't, unhappily, invent their mooring posts, their lovers, and their friends, any more than they can invent their parents.' I'm a great fan of American literature, especially the writers representing the oppressed, the downtrodden. You'll soon learn that reading is one of the few pastimes to keep you sane on these long voyages. Internet access is spotty at best out at sea, and there are also company constraints with usage."

"It has been difficult accessing Instagram," said Israel, steadying himself as the ship crested a large wave.

"What I see, if you don't mind me being so forthright, is a man who's wobbly on his feet, looking for the security of a firm identity," said Moshe. "Fasten yourself to your community. If it's Portugal and the Portuguese people, then tie yourself to that mooring post, and let the waters of that culture wash all over you so you are immersed in your heritage and have a better understanding of who you are. Perhaps I am biased. We Israelis came from all over the world to settle in the Promised Land, for better or worse. Planting firm roots in Israel is the basis of our existence as a state. But I do very much believe that without an anchoring in your culture, you risk being battered by the whims of the sea, without the stanchion of people who can support you."

The lights in the engine room flickered momentarily, and Moshe grabbed a guardrail near one of the auxiliary engines. The ship heaved, and Israel heard an eerie creaking sound as the angle of the floor shifted, causing him to slip and slide down several feet.

"Rogue wave!" shouted Moshe. "Rough waters ahead!"

Israel struggled to get to his feet as the ship slowly heaved in the opposite direction. His notepad had slid into a drain at the far end of the room.

"Forget the notebook," said Moshe. "I'll give it to you later. Just get the heck out of here. Get back to your quarters, and don't leave until someone tells you to, okay?"

CHAPTER EIGHT

Israel Experiences Rough Water and Loses His Marbles

Israel didn't need anyone to tell him to stay in his quarters. He was in no condition to move. The day after the ship's first encounter with the rogue wave, the weather rapidly deteriorated. Rogue waves were rogue no more. Now, they were common waves of immense proportions that churned Israel's insides and saddled him to the bed.

The first day was the worst. He lay in the bottom bunk of their beds in a fetal position, his eyes closed as the ship rocked back and forth. Their quarters, which under normal circumstances resembled a typical hotel room with a small kitchenette and TV, now looked like a room stuck on a swinging pendulum. It was as if he had entered a fun house where the floor played tricks, moving from side to side, depending on where you stood.

When he opened his eyes, he saw the room move up and down at severe angles. An unopened water bottle rolled from one end of the room to the other. The shirts in his closet spilled out, clinging desperately to their hangers each time the ship crested a wave. At one point, Judah's phone flew off the top bunk and landed on the floor with a thud before sliding away.

"Rats!" cried Judah, gingerly leaving his bunk to retrieve the phone. "Ugh, the glass is cracked, and it won't turn on."

Amazingly, aside from the damage to his phone, Judah was unfazed by the rocking motion. He cooked pasta for dinner while the stove swung with the ship. He poured himself a glass of prosecco from a mini bottle and worked on a crossword puzzle. He practiced Portuguese greetings, focusing on his pronunciation. He surfed through TV programs, eventually settling on a Blu-ray of *Life of Pi* that he had checked out of the ship's library.

Meanwhile, Israel groaned from his bed. He had visited the porcelain throne four times before noon, and his stomach had little left to give. He was delirious and couldn't sleep, his madness intensifying, but when he opened his eyes, he became nauseous. He would curl in a ball and keep his eyes closed to the extent possible, squinting here and there to inspect the room or to relieve himself. By the afternoon of the first day, he was too weak to move, and he was beginning to see things.

Judah tried to get Israel to chew on ginger to settle his stomach, but the merest whiff of any edible substance turned his face a sickly green. In their rush to leave for Portugal, they had not packed motion sickness medicine, and with the storm outside raging, the master had instructed all nonessential personnel to remain in their quarters until further notice.

When Judah tapped Israel on the shoulder after dinner to see if he needed anything, Israel shouted in terror, "Let me be!"

Judah stood back, startled. Israel had pulled the covers over his head and appeared to be shivering.

"Uh, are you all right?"

"Your ghastly powers, get out of my mind," said Israel, his voice muffled by the covers. "I see your tentacle-like face, your hideous body that parodies human form."

"Right. I'll just be moving along, then."

"Cthulhu!" hissed Israel.

The following day wasn't much better. The waves were still large, and the ship rose and fell with each swell.

Israel, who had barely slept for yet another night, was now beyond the valley of nausea. When he wasn't groaning and squirming in his bunk, he was muttering something incoherent.

"T-t-t-t-t-t-t," said Israel, repeating the *T* sound in rapid succession, rehearsing an exercise he had practiced as a child to improve the way he pronounced the *S* sound.

"The shea shounds shloppy from my *sh* shound. But ish thish okay in Purtuguesh?"

The rabbit hole was another common topic.

"Down the well we go. In *that* direction lives a Hatter. In *that* direction lives a March hare. Visit either you like: they're both mad!"

And the raven.

"While I nodded, nearly napping, suddenly there came a tipping. The ship is tipping!"

By the third day, the ship had passed the disturbance, and the violent rocking had largely subsided. The master ordered all crew members back to their posts, and Judah and Israel were called back to the galley.

"I'll tell João you're unwell," said Judah as he was preparing to leave.

Israel, who had had another sleepless night and hadn't eaten anything the day before, was feverish. He opened his eyes wide and stared at Judah intently.

"We've been hired by a merchant of ambiguous origins named Elpenor, and he has given us instructions to assassinate the Wolf of Sparta," said Israel.

"Uh, you've really lost your marbles," said Judah, placing his hands on his hips.

"We will take a port of call at Kefalonia, and we must find a naval captain named Barnabas," continued Israel.

"And I assume that you, the Eagle Bearer, will soon uncover the identity of this Wolf of Sparta?" asked Judah.

"Yes! Yes, I will!" cried Israel. "It is destined to happen."

"Just like the video game."

"Just like the author of our fate."

Judah walked up to Israel, got down on his knees and stared into his brother's face, which was gaunt. Israel smelled like overripe onions.

"Ow!" cried Israel, sitting up straight and hitting his head against the bunk frame.

"I gave you the sternal rub," said Judah.

Israel was rubbing his head and chest, frowning. "That hurt like hell."

"Good," said Judah. "I hadn't used that on a real person before, just on dummies during CPR training. I suppose you might be considered a type of dummy."

"What did I do to deserve that?"

"Do you recall what you were saying a minute ago?"

"I didn't say a thing," said Israel. "I was just lying here, trying to get some rest."

"That's what I thought," said Judah. "The sternal rub is for patients who need to snap out of it. You're still not right. I'm going to head to the galley and bring back some food for lunch. You need to get some rest and eat."

Judah stood up and headed to the door. "Oh, and by the way," he said, "you're gonna take a shower tonight. You stink."

"Bastard," huffed Israel to himself as his brother left the room. "That's no way to treat a sibling."

The sudden jolt of pain did seem to reorient some of the neural circuitry in Israel's brain, and he became suddenly more aware of his physical surroundings and felt his stomach grumble. Slowly, with a great deal of effort, given his depleted energy reserves, he stood up, holding the wooden bunk bedpost. His knees wobbled as he swayed with the ship. He sniffed his armpit.

"Argh!" he cried.

He let go of the bunk bed, crossed the room unsteadily and made his way to the refrigerator. He dropped to his knees before the refrigerator, opened it and pulled out a can of Dr. Pepper, which he drank ravenously. When he had finished, he pulled out a Tupperware container with leftover pasta and olive oil that Judah had made and shoved noodles in his mouth with his hands.

"Why didn't Buddha cook more at home?" mumbled Israel, his mouth full. He swallowed and stared at the Tupperware container for a moment, chuckling. "Buddha!" he laughed. "He does have a Buddha belly. He does act holier than thou."

Israel slept for the rest of the morning. He got up briefly when Judah returned to the room with a ham sandwich, then fell slept again for most of the afternoon and through the night. He woke early the following morning, around five-thirty, and took a long, hot shower. When he exited the bathroom about twenty minutes later, Judah was up and putting on his shoes. Israel wore a towel around his waist and had a toothbrush in his mouth.

"You've emerged from your ritual purification," said Judah, tying his shoelace.

"I do feel renewed," replied Israel.

"I was starting to worry, I have to admit," said Judah.

"I appreciate it. You've always been ..."

"Worried about your safety?" interrupted Judah.

"Don't be ridiculous."

"You mistook me for Cthulhu."

"Did I really?"

"Tentacles and everything."

"These things can happen ..."

"I'm glad you're feeling better."

"I think I'm going to head in to work with you."

"That won't be necessary," said Judah, shaking his head.

"What's that supposed to mean?"

"João wants you to rest until we get to Ponta Delgada. He has jobs for you onshore." Judah yawned, picked up his belt from the bedside and pushed it through his belt loops. "He said that you are not to leave our quarters other than for the mess hall. We'll be in the Azores soon."

The next four days presented a different sort of challenge for Israel. Stuck in his cabin with nowhere to go and nothing to do, he quickly grew bored. The vast ocean vistas, the dark blues visible from his porthole, lost their novelty after the first hour. The sky and the waters seemed to blend into one big, runny watercolor painting.

The relative stillness of the ocean made him feel alone and forgotten. Insignificant. He attempted to watch *Life of Pi* to pass the time, but the images of Pi drifting in the Pacific Ocean with a Bengal tiger were unsettling, and he could not finish the film.

His passion for haikus seemed to have been swept away with the storm, and Moshe still hadn't returned his notepad. Perhaps this was a good sign. A return to normalcy. But boredom introduces its own set of difficulties, some of which are nearly as dangerous as the steepest waves.

This isn't what I had in mind for a cruise, thought Israel to himself. *There's just emptiness.*

Images of Lethargians came to mind. They were difficult to see, blending into the blues of the ocean or the browns and whites of the furniture. They looked like each other, camouflaging into their surroundings, dissipating like salt in water or scattered, vanishing thoughts as the hours went by.

"You see, it's really quite strenuous doing nothing all day," said one, and Israel agreed.

"Tell me," said Israel, yawning at one point, "does everyone here do nothing all day?"

"Nothing at all," they replied. "Nothing but the terrible watchdog."

Out of the corner of his eye, he could make out the watchdog, with its body of a clicking alarm cloud. It was trying to get his attention, being so distant and difficult to see and hear.

"Beware that malignant kind of boredom," he heard it say through the sloshing of the waters against the ship. "It's an insidious thing that causes people to behave in ways they never intended. Sailors walk over the edge of the deck. Engineers deliberately burn their hands in the engine room. Navigators run their ships aground."

After two days of extreme boredom, Israel had had enough.

"I will study Portuguese!" he exclaimed, reviewing a Portuguese dictionary he had found in the library after returning from lunch. "There's still much to do."

There was, in fact, much studying to do. Israel's four-hour intensive examination of Portuguese nouns over a two-day span, which included frequent naps, snack breaks and daydreams of the gallant courtship of a particular fair maiden, didn't do much to improve his fluency. Memorizing *casa de banho*, while a useful noun when stopping at a Portuguese gas station after a long drive and two cups of coffee, could only progress a conversation so far. He did discover, during this period of scholarship, a Blu-ray in the library about a man from the Brazilian northeast who returns to his humble village intent on chasing unsavory characters out of the community. This caught Israel's imagination, and he thought about what he might do in such circumstances.

"As is tradition," said Israel to himself, "I return the hero, transformed after a long and arduous quest. None can stand in my way."

He envisioned engaging in hand-to-hand combat with his former professor of statistics, who had a habit of torturing students through various mental devices and needed to be vanquished. These thoughts were fleeting, however, and mostly Israel did his best to distract himself with food and naps in between his studies.

In the mid-afternoon of the day before they were to dock at Ponta Delgada, João asked to see Israel. Judah had just returned to their quarters to take a break from kitchen duties following the lunch hour.

"He wants you to meet him in the galley so he can provide instructions for our port of call," said Judah. "We both need to run some errands. I'm supposed to stop by the market to restock fruits and vegetables."

Israel met João in the galley thirty minutes later. João was sitting on a stool near one of the stoves, smoking a cigarette under a ventilated ceiling.

This is odd, thought Israel. *I thought smoking wasn't allowed in the galleys of ships with dangerous cargo.*

"Ah, the brother of Judah, the sous chef, is alive," said João, pressing the butt of his cigarette against a small dish. "Please sit down."

"I'm okay," said Israel. "Been sitting ... well, lying around ... a lot the past few days."

"Yes, I understand," said João. "The waters can be harsh. But I have good news. We will be on shore soon, and you can move about freely."

"Yes, I'm looking forward to that," said Israel. "This will be the first time we set foot in Portugal."

"You will not be disappointed. *Como vai o teu português?*" asked João.

Israel stared at him blankly.

"How is your Portuguese?" repeated João. "Judah told me you've been studying."

"Yes, dabbling here and there, although less than I would have liked," said Israel. "My illness and convalescence delayed my studies, unfortunately."

"No worries. You will be fine," said João. "You will have plenty of time to practice tomorrow. Once we arrive at port, I would like you to run an errand for us, as we discussed."

"Yes, I agreed to support you with these errands," said Israel.

"They are not for me," said João quickly. "They are in support of First Officer Dantel Montilla. I am just a humble cook."

Israel narrowed his eyes. Dantel had a certain look to him that did not inspire confidence.

"What did Dantel have in mind?"

"First Officer Montilla," corrected João, "has instructed me, the chief steward, and now I delegate this to you, to retrieve packages from a dairy farm on São Miguel Island. This is a special farm that produces some of the finest milk in the world. The milk is typically freeze-dried and exported. All you need to do is deliver an envelope and then pick up the boxes from the farmer. They will wait for you, and you can tell them that First Officer Montilla sent you. Their English is not great, but they can speak enough to get by, and I'm sure your knowledge of Portuguese will be sufficient. They will give you several boxes of the milk—the freeze-dried variety and fresh milk—that need to be taken back to the ship immediately because the fresh milk is highly perishable."

"Would I be able to bring Judah with me?" asked Israel.

"Yes, Judah is fine to go with you," said João. "I asked him to pick up some produce, but he can do that after your trip to the farm. I normally run these types of errands myself, but they take time, and I have other duties assigned."

"And you will give me directions?" asked Israel.

"I'm happy that you asked," said João, pulling a map of the island from his jacket pocket. "This map shows the way to the farm. You will take a taxi from the port to São Brás. It is only thirty minutes away. São Miguel Island is small. From there, you will travel down the dirt road that I have marked. You will meet a boy along this road, perhaps thirteen, fourteen years old, named Lourenço, who will take you to the farm. He will wait for you at eight o'clock in the morning. Because the roads are uneven, you may ride with him on horseback—I am not sure. Can you ride a horse?"

"I was on a pony ride as a child."

"Then it will be like that," said João. "There is nothing to it. The Azorean people are very traditional. You will feel like you are entering a different time period. That is also why they make some of the best milk in the world. This is considered precious cargo. The milk is very expensive, so I ask that you handle the packages with great care."

"Understood. Handle with great care."

"Treat them like your unborn child."

"This must be some really precious milk."

"It is," said João, pulling out another cigarette. "Very precious indeed."

PART II

CHAPTER NINE

Israel and Judah Disembark and Collect Milk

Ponta Delgada. Terra firma. A blessed oasis in the big blue sea.

Israel, lips planted against the sidewalk pavement in a downward dog pose while pedestrians and cars passed by, was in a state of reverie. The land was unmoving. There were no stomach-turning rocking motions.

It was seven o'clock in the morning, and Israel and Judah were next to the Avenida Infante Dom Henrique, preparing to hail a taxi.

"I don't know him," said Judah, whistling to himself as a man with a cane walked by.

Israel stood up and stretched his arms to the sky, inhaling deeply before slowly expelling his breath.

"Paradise!" he exclaimed. "Welcome to our native homeland."

Judah rolled his eyes.

"I am already connected to this magnificent country," said Israel swiping his iPhone.

"Let's not get ahead of ourselves," said Judah. "We've barely been here for fifteen minutes. We know nothing about it."

"I know more than you realize," said Israel. "Such as the fact that they have an advanced internet infrastructure despite the island's small size."

"Oh, I see," said Judah, forlornly. "I need to take my phone in at some point. It won't turn on. We need to call Mom and Dad."

"That can wait."

"True. We're four hours ahead."

"The main thing is …" said Israel typing furiously on his cell phone. "There you go."

"Not following."

"I just posted my first of hopefully many haikus to M&M's Instagram feed," said Israel, grinning.

"Oh God."

"It was one of my best."

"*Best* is a relative term."

"I discussed, in philosophical terms, the rocking motion of a vessel in the sea, equating it to our love. And not just any love, but a divine one where the vessel, undulating in the grandeur of the endless sea, causes us to be agape in wonderment and ecstasy."

"Please stop."

"Floating on the deep ocean, we are not in some kind of shallow, infatuated relationship, driven by eros, but we have a more profound sense of joy and adoration: agape."

"I'm developing acid reflux," said Judah, placing his hand on his stomach. "And what do apes have to do with love?"

"*Agape*. Not ape."

"I'm pretty sure you said ape."

"There is an affective, volitional distinction here with the type of love I speak of," said Israel, staring at the orange-and-red streaks in the sky from the rising sun. "I'm talking about the purest form of love."

"Good grief, you know nothing about M&M. She doesn't even know you."

"I know all that I need to know," said Israel, primly. "These haikus of mine are an opening salvo. Soon, I am sure, she will swoon in my arms."

"So, is that what this trip is all about? To stalk this scantily clad Portuguese model?"

"How dare you insult the glorious anatomy of my beloved!" said Israel. "This trip is most certainly not *all* about M&M."

"Is that so?" said Judah, crossing his arms and frowning.

"This is a voyage of discovery. We are adventuring knights."

"Adventuring what?"

"Well, at least I am. Given your temperament and height, perhaps you are more appropriately described as a squire."

"I think I might punch you in the face."

"We are traveling to reconnect with our heritage, to cast away the ambiguities of our past life and begin anew in the bounteous land of Portugal."

Judah sighed and hailed a passing taxi, which pulled to the side of the road.

"Israel, I'm fine with a little crazy talk from you. But I don't want to get arrested for stalking, okay?"

"Arrested? Me?"

"Yeah, you, you knucklehead!"

"For what?"

"For being a creep. I don't know. Just tone it down with the crazy talk in public, will you?"

"I will do my best to follow the norms of Portuguese society."

"Good. That's right, follow the norms of society. Including social media."

The taxi driver rolled down his window and waved at them to get in.

"Now, Israel, focus. Do you have the map João gave us of São Miguel Island?"

Forty minutes later, close to a tea plantation, Israel and Judah found themselves on a dirt path in a lush meadow filled with ryegrass and white clover that came up to their knees. All around them, the air had the smell of rain. Israel, dressed in a long-sleeved flannel shirt and khakis, brushed his hands against the grass. Judah wore a short-sleeved Comic-Con T-shirt and jeans and shivered beside his brother.

"We're in the middle of nowhere," said Judah, his hands in pants pockets as he watched the white Volkswagen taxi disappear around the bend in the road.

Israel held the map in both hands and began walking in a southerly direction along the path, heading away from the taxi.

"The farm is this way," said Israel.

"I don't understand why João isn't with us," said Judah. "The map is in Portuguese, and we've never set foot on this island."

"It's no matter," said Israel. "You might recall that I'm a geography major."

"My main recollection is that your major is a work in progress."

"We should revisit that subject at some point," said Israel, placing his finger on the map. "I don't believe you've made much progress on the academic front."

"Well, if I'm being candid," said Judah, plodding along the path behind Israel, "that was one reason I joined you on this trip. While the Pancake House was a rousing occupation, it's not for me. I needed to get out of Highland Park and think things through. After sailing the high seas, all I can tell you is that I won't be going back to work there."

"It's not uncommon for youths of your age to take a gap year before college."

"We're two years apart," said Judah, kicking aside a stone on the path. "I don't think I can work as an attorney. At least, not as a public defender. Dad is always stressed."

"There are plenty of other career options."

"Right, but I don't want to jump into a major without having a sense of where I'm going. I see too many people spending five years or more at college, switching majors, ending up with a degree in English literature or biology, only to find themselves as a telemarketer for an advertising company while spending the next fifteen years trying to pay off the debt they accrued at school. It seems like the only reasonably employable fields these days are in STEM, but that's not my strong suit."

In the distance, a cow mooed. They were hiking uphill now, and Israel and Judah were panting from exertion.

"Things could be worse," huffed Judah. "We didn't grow up in the inner city like Dad and our aunt and uncle. Some of our cousins—take Edwin, for example—view us as rich white boys."

"He's mistaken on that front."

"Yeah, *we* know that," said Judah. "But I can see his point of view. We're living on the North Shore with a white mother, our father's a lawyer, while he's living in Humboldt Park, and his black father's in jail. We're privileged, there's no denying it ... even if we don't look white to people in Highland Park."

"These definitions of race are artificial," said Israel, swatting a fly away from his face.

"Real or unreal, these definitions have a way of imprinting themselves on society. The issue for people like us is that we don't fit into a neat definition of race or ethnicity. It's all in the eyes of the beholder. I hate to admit it, but you made an excellent point to Dad about the ambiguity of our mixed heritage."

They turned a corner, and then Israel stopped abruptly, causing Judah to stumble into him. They staggered further up the path for a moment before Israel raised his hand and waved.

A hundred feet away, a thin boy sat on a donkey, which was tethered to two horses near hydrangea bushes. He wore a brown-plaid newsboy cap, an oversized brown wool sweater, mud-stained jeans and black boots. He nodded in acknowledgment and spurred his donkey toward them.

"*Olá!*" cried Israel, approaching the boy. "Lourenço?"

"*Sim.*"

"Do you speak English?"

"*Não.*"

"*Chamo-me Judá, e ele é Israel,*" said Judah, eyeing the animals.

"Lourenço," said the boy, whose dark brown eyes seemed to have seen too much.

"Oh, I nearly forgot," said Israel, reaching for a small envelope in the back pocket of his jeans. "This is for you. From First Officer Dantel Montilla."

The boy dismounted from his donkey and took the envelope from Israel and placed it in his sweater's pouch pocket. He mumbled something quietly in Portuguese.

"What's that?" asked Israel, not understanding what the boy had said.

"I think he wants us to get on the horses," said Judah.

Israel looked at the boy and pointed to the chestnut mare closest to him.

"*Sim,*" said Lourenço, holding the mare's head to keep her still.

"Okay, then," said Israel, trudging up to the horse. "João mentioned this."

"You didn't tell me we were going horseback riding," said Judah.

"It slipped my mind," said Israel, gingerly placing his left foot in the stirrup.

The horse moved a step forward, and Israel bounced along on his right foot, nearly twisting his left ankle before leaping up into the saddle.

"Just like riding a pony at Goebbert's Farm," he exclaimed.

"Oh God," said Judah. "Why did you bring that up?"

"Bring what up?"

"Don't you remember the time my pony galloped to the other side of the farm while I clung on for dear life?"

"I don't recall a galloping pony."

"It may have been a trot, who knows?" said Judah testily.

"Oh," said Israel, rubbing his chin. "Now I remember. There was a black stallion. That was the estrus incident, wasn't it?"

"Call it whatever you like. It was highly traumatic," cried Judah. "I distinctly remember saying twenty Ave Marias, and we're not even Catholic!"

"That happened a long time ago. Weren't you six years old?"

"It left a deep scar on my psyche," said Judah, wringing his hands. "Haven't ridden a horse since. Nasty creatures."

"Oh, just get on, will you?" said Israel, pointing to the young gray mare behind him.

Lourenço walked over to the mare and placed his hand on its head as before. Judah approached the mare reluctantly, but the horse, sensing Judah's apprehension, squirmed, stomping its front left hoof on the ground. Lourenço placed both hands on the mare's head and whispered into its ear, which seemed to calm the horse momentarily, until Judah attempted to place his foot in the stirrup.

Not being practiced in the art of mounting a horse, Judah was awkward in his movements and inadvertently elbowed the horse in the ribs, which startled it and caused it to rear up slightly. Lourenço grabbed the reins, pulling them firmly to calm the horse. Judah, having lost his balance when the horse reared up, fell to the ground and rolled several feet downhill, staining his T-shirt with green and brown streaks.

"Like I said," cried Judah, pulling himself up to his knees, "they're nasty creatures!"

Lourenço rubbed the mare's cheeks then hurried over to Judah and helped him off the ground. Judah was red in the face and not shivering anymore.

"*Vamos*," said Lourenço, taking Judah by the hand and leading him to the donkey.

The donkey, a hinny, was of the mammoth variety, standing at fourteen hands at the withers, although still several hands shorter than the two mares. It was carrying two half-size demi-barrique wine barrels that were attached to each side of the saddle. The donkey was chewing clover and swatting its tail at flies, unconcerned about any commotion.

Lourenço led Judah to the donkey and kneeled down beside its saddle.

"How about I just walk?" asked Judah.

The boy stared at Judah, uncomprehending. Judah gritted his teeth and stared at the sky as if searching for a guardian angel.

"Not all of us are suited for thoroughbreds," said Israel, breaking the awkward silence. "You need to have a certain level of experience and skill with equines to mount one such as mine."

"Shut up, will you?" said Judah, slipping his foot into the stirrup. "Fine. Let's just get this over with. Where are we headed anyway?"

Lourenço helped steady Judah as he lifted his right leg over the saddle. The donkey, being much calmer than the mare, allowed Judah to mount it, this time without incident.

Lourenço untethered the neck strap connecting the donkey to the horses, then deftly mounted the gray mare.

"*Vamos, por aquí,*" said Lourenço, spurring his horse up a steep grassy hill.

Israel and Judah spurred their mounts, and soon they were moving single file through the meadow, with Lourenço taking the lead, followed by Israel and Judah. The sky was filled with sheetlike stratus clouds interspersed with patches of blue, and although the land was lush, it had a somber quality.

For Israel, this was the beginning he had been looking for, even though he hadn't expected this type of excursion as his introduction to Portugal. He felt a connection to the land. He could smell the grasses and the clover, he could feel the horse planting its hooves in the earth, he could taste the saltiness in the air, and he was invigorated.

"Can't this thing go any faster?" shouted Judah as Lourenço and Israel crested the hill.

Israel ignored his donkey-riding sibling and exhaled deeply.

Is this what knights-errant experienced as they traveled across the land in search of adventure and love? he wondered. *Sure, there may be some gloom, but here we are, riding through the mist, ready to vanquish any foe bold enough to stand in our way.*

He thought about the haiku he had posted to M&M's Instagram feed. *What a day of progress! But could I do more? Could I perhaps do more to stand out among M&M's legion of admiring fans? Should I, besides posting to social media, send a letter the old-fashioned way? There is something undeniably intimate about a physical letter.*

"For crying out loud, that stinks!" shouted Judah, spurring his donkey forward after it stopped to relieve itself.

"Judah," said Israel, glancing over his shoulder, "do make an effort to hold yourself together."

"What was that?" shouted Judah, again spurring his donkey, which was walking so slowly, he could have done laps around it.

"Try to enjoy the bucolic setting. This sacred land, the home of our ancestors, born from volcanic fire, is where we start anew," said Israel, staring into the distance dreamily. "*Igne natura renovatur integra*, as the expression goes. Through fire, nature is reborn whole. And here we stand, our personages reborn in this land of earth, wind and fire."

"I can't hear what you're saying!" shouted Judah. "Did you say something about Earth, Wind and Fire?"

"What I am trying to say," said Israel, calmly, "is that after extensive planning, we are in the land of our ancestors, and we should embrace this new chapter in our lives."

"Did you say extensive planning?" asked Judah. "What extensive planning? Is that a windmill in the distance?"

Israel placed his hand over his eyes and scanned the horizon.

"It appears to be a windmill," said Israel.

Lourenço led them down a small knoll, so the windmill was momentarily out of sight, then back up a steep hill until they reached a grassy promontory where a small, two-story whitewashed cottage stood. The cottage was off the grid and had a small wind turbine next to it to provide electricity. Moss and vines grew over its stone steps, and the walls were smudged with green.

There were at least a dozen donkeys of the standard Azorean variety, much smaller than the one Judah rode, grazing beside the house. A semicircular hedgerow of mostly green hydrangea bushes formed a natural boundary around the hilltop. A thirty-foot-tall rubber tree, with a nearly five-foot-diameter trunk and buttress roots, functioned as a gateway into the pasture.

Lourenço dismounted and guided his horse around the cottage, near the grazing donkeys. Israel and Judah sat on their donkeys, side by side, and stared at the cottage and the windmill.

"This farm seems kind of isolated," said Judah after a minute.

"The better pastureland is probably outside the major towns."

"I wonder where the cattle are. This is a dairy farm, right?"

"It is. Some of the best dairy in the world, as a matter of fact."

"Got it. Well, the cattle must be grazing elsewhere."

Lourenço emerged from around the cottage with a wheelbarrow filled with white shipping boxes measuring approximately two feet by two feet. A moment later, a man came down the cottage steps holding a thermos in his hand. He was a large man, over six feet tall, with a slightly protruding belly and broad shoulders. He had a long red lumberjack beard, greasy light-brown hair slicked back behind his ears and piercing blue eyes. He wore tan-colored, mud-speckled overalls, black work boots and a plain, dirty white T-shirt that showed his prominent biceps.

"You're the Americans?" he asked, with only the slightest Portuguese accent.

"We are," said Israel. "We were asked to deliver an envelope and pick up packages of dairy for First Officer Dantel Montilla."

The man walked toward Israel and Judah, smiling, and eventually placed his hand on the mammoth donkey's muzzle and rubbed it. Judah attempted to dismount, but the man waved his hand.

"Stay on," he said, more a command than a request. "We're going to load you up soon. Have you tried our products?"

"This is our first time here," said Judah.

"Ah, good," said the man. "*Bem vindo*. Welcome. My name is João."

"Our boss' name is João," said Judah. "We work for a shipping company."

"Yes, I know. João is a common name in Portugal." He held out the thermos, handing it to Judah. "Take a sip."

Judah sniffed the thermos.

"Milk?" he asked.

"Try it."

Judah took a sip, then handed it to Israel, who took a long drag from the thermos.

"I'm parched," said Israel, taking another sip. "This is excellent milk."

"Yes, it's not bad," added Judah.

"Donkey milk," said João. "Best in the world."

Judah's face turned white, and he held his hand over his stomach.

"*Equus asinus*," said João. "Because of our location, we can produce milk with unmatched polyunsaturated fatty acids. We milk our donkeys twice a day."

"Ass milk?" said Judah, in a whisper. "That would explain why we didn't see any cows."

"This is a donkey farm. We sell milk in liquid and freeze-dried forms. It's a good business, and we have certain ways of supplementing the margins," said João, glancing at the packages. "Okay, let's load you up and get you back on the road. Lourenço ..."

The boy walked over to João, and they spoke briefly in Portuguese. Israel looked at the thermos and took another sip.

"Want any more?" asked Israel. "It's really quite satisfying."

"I'll pass," said Judah.

João walked to the side of Judah's donkey and began unfastening the wine barrels attached to the packsaddle.

"Lourenço picked up some wine from one of our neighbors who grows pineapples, among other crops," said João. "The barrels are only partially full. He makes wine as a hobby but is skilled at the craft. His wine is of the Arinto dos Açores variety. Have you tried it?"

"No, you see, we just arrived," said Israel.

"You must try it," said João, turning to Lourenço, who was unpacking the boxes from the wheelbarrow.

"Grab a bottle, will you?" asked João, repeating himself in Portuguese. "*Obrigado*."

João retrieved two sisal sacks from the wheelbarrow and began stuffing them with the shipping boxes.

"When you deliver these to João and Senhor Montilla, give them my respects," said João. "But please handle with great care. This is the best donkey milk in the world."

"The *only* donkey milk in the world," muttered Judah to himself.

"If you damage it, I can't be held accountable," continued João. "From here on, the responsibility is yours."

Lourenço emerged from the house with a wine bottle in his hand.

"Good, he found it. You will try some, for the road," said João. "You know, I used to travel often when I was younger. I have been to the States many times, although I traveled to Brazil more often than anywhere else."

Lourenço handed João the wine bottle, which had been opened.

"We had some last night," said João, sniffing the bottle. "Take it, please."

"Oh, I don't know," said Israel. "It's a little early for wine, and I'm not sure it goes with the milk."

"It goes just fine," said João, thrusting the bottle into Israel's free hand. "Try some."

Israel took a sip of the wine.

"This is, again, excellent," said Israel, taking another, deeper drag. "You should try this, Judah."

João took the bottle from Israel and passed it to Judah.

"Yes, this is very good," said Judah. "It has a tropical, almost salty overtone."

João and Lourenço began attaching the sisal sacks to each side of the donkey's saddle pack.

"I have only two of the American Mammoth Jackstock. They are not common in Portugal but are good working animals," said João as he finished securing the sack to the donkey. "They are like mules, you might say. You should get to the ship shortly. Trafficking is uncommon on the island."

Judah glanced at Israel.

"Did you say trafficking is uncommon on the island?" asked Judah.

"That's right, traffic is uncommon on the island. You should get back to the ship soon. We will call a taxi."

"I see."

"Enjoy your voyage to Lisbon."

"We will."

"*Boa viajem.*"

CHAPTER TEN

Israel Wears the Chapéu of Mambrino

Lourenço mounted the gray mare and led Israel and Judah away from the farm, down the steep grassy hill and up the small knoll. As they crested the knoll, they came upon three men in sleeveless tank tops, work pants and boots, who were laughing and passing around a bottle of what Israel thought was cherry-colored brandy.

"Lourenço!" cheered one of the men, who was holding a mesh feed bag filled with hay.

The boy flinched.

"He knows these guys," whispered Judah to Israel.

Israel glanced at Lourenço and then looked at the men, who were ambling up the hill. They were speaking rapidly in Portuguese in between their swigs of drink.

"An introvert," said Israel. "He's a quiet young man. Not inclined to speak unless spoken to."

"Well, he doesn't know English, so we didn't have an in-depth conversation with him, if that's what you mean?" replied Judah.

"The sight of revelers at this early hour can be jarring for the introspective type," said Israel.

"Look at the tattoos on those guys!" hissed Judah.

"Such are the customs of our people," said Israel.

"Clowns?"

"Ornamental images, emphasizing their zest for life."

"They look like *bad* clowns."

"Lourenço!" said the man again with the feed bag as they approached the riders.

The group spoke with Lourenço in Portuguese for a moment, gesturing toward Israel and Judah. One of the men, who was built like a rugby player and had a bushy black beard and long hair, reached for the gray mare's saddle. The boy dismounted.

"Good morning my dearest Americans," said the man with the feed bag, who appeared to be their leader. "We will escort you from here."

The man with the beard slapped Lourenço on the back, nearly causing him to stumble. When he recovered, he shot the leader a dirty look, before trudging away from them and down the knoll toward the farm.

"He doesn't like to be teased," said the man with the bag. "But that is what older brothers do! It builds character, don't you think?"

"A brother's bond is unbreakable," said Israel.

"Exactly! Now let me introduce myself," said the man with the bag. "My name is Martim. The big guy, we call him Macho Man. Can you tell?"

"I see the resemblance," said Judah.

"The short guy with the buzz cut," said Martim, pointing, "his name is Martelo, also known as The Hammer."

"Of course," said Israel, pointing to Martelo's shoulder tattoo of a clown with a sledgehammer.

"Right," said Martim, glancing at his men. "He likes to pound things … I mean, excuse my poor English, he does fence posting and other work around and outside the farm."

"We closely monitor our mules," said Martelo.

"Donkeys," corrected Martim. "Now, Lourenço briefly filled us in about your background. It's my understanding that you will be delivering these goods to the ship. Is that correct?"

"Our first officer's expecting it," said Israel.

"Wonderful!" exclaimed Martim. "It's customary for us to take travelers out to breakfast. You do have some cash, I hope?"

"We have enough to get by," said Israel. "There is much to do and much to see in Portugal."

"It's a remarkable county," said Martim, walking over to the gray mare. "Is this your first time?"

"We just arrived," said Judah.

"You must see this beautiful island from the eyes of a native," said Martim.

"That is our hope!" said Israel, excitedly. "Our dream is to experience the land of our ancestors in the most authentic way."

Martelo laughed, spraying some of the liquor he was drinking on the grass.

"He laughs because he understands your desires," said Martim. "But he finds it comical that you don't speak Portuguese."

"Alas, we have been long estranged from our homeland," said Israel.

Judah sighed.

"I see," said Martim, glancing at the other men. "In that case, let us take you out to breakfast, to reacquaint you with your heritage."

"It would be our honor," said Martelo, bowing, unsteadily.

"But first, you must follow the tradition of Azorean travelers," said Martim, dumping the hay out of the feed bag. "By donning this hat. *O chapéu de Mambrino*!"

"That doesn't look like a hat," said Judah.

"But it is! I assure you," said Martim. "Traditional but modern at the same time. A replica. Packaged with hay to infuse the essence of this land."

"Don't listen to my ignorant brother," said Israel, crossly.

"Ignorant!" scoffed Judah.

"No need to quarrel," reassured Martim. "The hat may appear unusual, but I swear, it is based on Portuguese legend."

"Let me have it," said Israel, reaching for the feed bag in Martim's hand.

Israel slipped the bag over his head, causing the padded neck strap to dangle down his chest. His nose pressed against the nylon mesh and he inhaled an earthy musk that reminded him of his horse. A strand of hay tickled his nostril.

"It may take some getting used to," said Israel.

"A replica of the hat used by none other than the great Portuguese seafarer and navigator Mambrino Alonso da Rúa," said Martim, mounting the gray mare. "We will ride slowly, seeing that you are saddled with cargo. This will allow my companions to keep up."

"Pass me your wine," said Martelo, pointing to Judah. "If I must walk, then I must be refreshed."

Judah handed Martelo the wine bottle. Martim led the group slowly down the knoll.

"Legend has it that Mambrino, while in Cuba during the first voyage of discovery with Columbus, had come across this hat among the natives," said Martim. "After trading for it with a knife and scabbard, he brought the hat back with him on the return voyage to Spain. When the Santa Maria encountered a storm and had to make an emergency stopover in the Azores, it was said that Mambrino, who was navigating the ship, was wearing the hat.

"'The hat has power,' said the great Mambrino. 'I could see in and around the waves. I knew exactly where to take us to safety!' And so, ever since, there has been an Azorean tradition to wear replicas of the hat of Mambrino. It is, you might say, our good luck charm."

"And very traditional," said Martelo.

"An unusual story," said Judah.

"I wish for nothing more than to blend in," said Israel.

"Then it is settled," said Martim. "To breakfast we go!"

"In traditional Portuguese garb!" added Israel.

"For friends who foot the bill," slurred Martelo.

"To a party which has yet to end," added Martim. "As the Americans say ... let the good times roll!"

CHAPTER ELEVEN

The Rite of Passage for the Portuguese Brotherhood

"Let me take another sip of that brandy," said Israel, lifting the feed bag up just enough to free his lips.

Martelo handed Israel the brandy. A short distance away, Macho Man was loading the first bundle of cargo into the back of a white van, parked on the side of a road.

"I can't place the flavor," said Israel.

"We're your taxi service," said Martim. "The only gratuity required is a little breakfast."

"It's passion fruit," said Martelo. "We'll need another bottle!"

"Our venerable João was unclear on the rendezvous point, but as good fortune would have it, we arrived just in time," said Martim.

The donkey whinnied. Israel heard a sharp yelp and a then dull thud.

Martelo topped off the wine bottle and placed his right hand over his eyes.

"Where'd your brother go?" he asked.

"Down here," said Judah, sprawled out on his back in the grass.

"Judah, this is no time for games!" chastised Israel.

"I was trying to dismount," said Judah. "The stupid thing bucked me."

"No need for name calling," said Martim, walking over to him. "Donkeys are sensitive creatures."

Martim extended his hand to Judah.

"My backs' no worse for wear, I suppose," said Judah.

"That's the spirit," said Martim.

Israel hopped off his mare and walked over to Martelo, who was peering into his wine bottle as if through a telescope.

"You can finish this," said Israel, handing Martelo the brandy bottle.

"They never fill these up properly," bemoaned Martelo.

"What do we do with our mounts?" asked Israel.

"We'll tie them up at that tree, then we can be on our way," said Martim, pointing to a juniper.

Martim grabbed the reins of the chestnut mare.

"If we want to stay traditional, we could have them follow us on horseback," suggested Martelo.

"How far is the nearest breakfast establishment?" asked Israel.

"Enough of that," said Judah, hurriedly grabbing the donkey's reins. "You pointed to that tree, right?"

Twenty minutes later, Martim said, "We'll stop first at Afonso's."

He was seated in the passenger seat of the van. Macho Man was in the driver's seat, and they were heading west along a two-lane country road.

"Do you like *chouriço*?" asked Martelo, leaning in from the third row and tapping Judah from behind.

Judah shrugged.

"And who is this gentleman you speak of?" asked Israel.

"Afonso has the best coffee in São Brás," said Martim.

"And *chouriço*," said Martelo. "Best coffee and *chouriço*."

"We haven't had anything to eat," admitted Israel, glancing at Judah through his mesh bag.

"You must eat!" exclaimed Martim. "And seeing that you are looking to reconnect with the traditions of your ancestors, we have another custom in store for you."

"Yes, please tell us more," said Israel.

"Do we want to learn more?" questioned Judah.

"The *chamarrita*!" said Martim. "It is customary for those who wear *o chapéu de Mambrino* to lead the dance. It is a dance of sunrise."

"Ahh, yes. I've heard of such things," said Israel. "The Midsommar maypole dance comes to mind."

"This tradition's the same," said Martim.

"The sun's already up," said Judah.

"It is up, but it hasn't been acknowledged," said Martim. "Us Azoreans aren't too concerned about punctuality."

"Well in that case, I'll watch Israel dance as I eat *chouriço*," said Judah.

Macho Man pulled the van into a small parking lot in front of Afonso's Coffee and Bar, a two story, white plaster building with outdoor seating under the entrance awning. A wrinkled man with a white beard stood near the front door, smoking a cigarette.

"Germans," said Martim, pointing to a Mercedes-Benz G-Class beside them. "Do you happen to speak the language?"

"I'm afraid we don't," said Israel.

"Still working on the basics of Portuguese," added Judah. "If you hadn't noticed."

"Yes, of course," said Martim. "They are quite common here. Germans. Brits. Azores is popular for the adventurous. And those seeking luxury."

"Do the Azores attract Portuguese from the mainland?" asked Israel, an idea germinating in his mind.

"Yes. Many people," said Martim.

"Like famous people, too?" asked Israel. "Actors, models, that sort of thing?"

"Why of course," said Martim. "There was a fashion shoot last month in Ponta Delgada featuring local designers and models."

"It was a tragedy when it ended," lamented Martelo.

"He's had a hard time getting over a woman in a clam shell bikini," said Martim, opening the passenger-side door. "Most of the fashion shows are held in Lisbon."

"There's always something going on there," said Martelo.

"The bustling heart of Portugal," said Israel.

"The pace of life is much slower here," said Martelo.

"It's why we like it here," said Martim. "You're out of sight, out of mind, so to speak."

"Good for the dairy business," added Israel. "Lots of pasture."

"It simplifies operations," said Martim.

"But we have to get creative with entertainment," said Martelo. "Otherwise, it can be a bore."

"And that's why we're here," said Martim. "To show our Portuguese Americans a good time."

Israel pulled open the van's sliding door and stepped out. He could hear the murmur of conversations from inside the café. The man with the cigarette stared at Israel.

"*Olá*," said Israel, briefly raising the bag on his head in salutation.

The man let out a puff of smoke.

"*Bom dia, Senhor* Nunes!" said Martim, exiting the van.

Senhor Nunes shook his head from side to side.

"Is Benedita here today?" Martim asked.

Senhor Nunes took a deep drag from his cigarette, then slowly let out a stream of smoke. Martim smiled, broadly.

"This seems to be a popular destination," said Israel.

"*Bom dia, Senhor* Nunes!" said Martelo, staggering out of the van. "I'm starving."

Martim walked over to the front door and opened it, just as a young woman came out. She wore a black apron over her work clothes and had her brown hair pulled back in a ponytail.

"Martim!" she cried, placing her hands on her hips. "What games are you playing today?"

Martim leaned forward and kissed her, cheek to cheek.

"Benedita, my dear," he said, "we have nothing but the purest intentions!"

Benedita glanced at Israel and frowned.

"Isn't it a little early for this sort of thing?" she scolded.

"Bendita, we're here for work," he said as Macho Man nodded, and entered the café.

"Allow me to introduce myself," said Israel, approaching. "I am Israel Cruz, and I'm here with my brother, Judah."

Senhor Nunes blew smoke into Israel's face, causing his vision to become even blurrier.

"We're sailors, and having arrived at port today, are running some errands onshore for our First Officer," said Israel. "You have a lovely establishment."

"Ah, what?" she asked, confused.

"If you'll forgive my appearance," said Israel, stretching the section of the bag away from his nose. "This particular headgear wasn't appropriately sized for someone of my stature."

Benedita stared at Israel, then slowly turned to Martim.

"Would you mind placing our order, love?" asked Martim. "Same as always?"

"We need to have a conversation about this," said Benedita. "Later."

"Let's go," said Judah, grabbing Israel by the shirt sleeve and pulling him into the café.

The café was more crowded than Israel expected. The half dozen wooden tables were nearly all taken up by patrons. Macho Man was seated in the back, next to a table with four blonde women likely in their twenties, who were drinking coffee and speaking in German. A man with graying brown hair stood by their table checking his phone. He appeared to be their tour guide.

As Israel crossed the length of the café, a hush fell over it. Israel smiled, tipping his bag hat to the guests.

Could the women be models, thought Israel. *Acquaintances of a particular individual?*

"The Americans must try your *chouriço*!" exclaimed Martelo to the waitstaff as he strolled toward the table at the back, breaking the silent spell.

"Portuguese Americans," corrected Israel.

"Yes, yes," said Martelo, waving Israel's comments away. "I've told them all about it!"

Israel took a seat across the table from Macho Man and the Germans.

"What are the odds that they are here for a photo shoot?" whispered Israel, leaning into Judah, who was seated next to him.

Judah glanced at the Germans, then looked at Martim and Martelo as they seated themselves at the table across from them. "Hard to say," he said, his face turning pink. "Do you think you need to wear that … hat?"

"Oh, come now," said Israel, raising his voice. "I most certainly do."

"What's that?" asked Martelo.

"Nothing," said Judah, hurriedly. "I could use a coffee. Have you ordered yet?"

"We should order *mazagrã*," said Martelo.

"Do you like iced coffee?" asked Martim.

"Really any sort of coffee will do," said Judah.

"But *mazagrã* is better," said Martelo, motioning for a waiter. "*Mazagrã*, please, for the table."

"A traditional drink, I suppose?" asked Israel.

"And don't forget the rum!" shouted Martelo.

"It's from Algeria," said Martim. "But we've adopted it as our own."

"It helps take off the edge," said Martelo.

"You might be surprised to learn that despite being almost entirely Iberian, the Portuguese have been influenced by many peoples," said Martim. "We were great sailors, like yourself."

"Like me, you mean," said Judah. "Israel had his challenges crossing the Atlantic."

"Challenges!" cried Israel, attracting the attention of the Germans. "Come now. Gross exaggeration!"

"Hardly saw you standing on your own two feet."

"I prefer a supine posture when sailing."

"Or prostrate. Over the toilet."

"You really struggle distinguishing fact from fiction."

"*Mazagrã*," interrupted a waiter, holding up a tray with five iced-coffees.

"Yes, what took you so long?" asked Martelo.

Judah glanced at the wall clock over the café counter.

"Hardly been more than a minute or two," said Judah.

"Seemed like an eternity!" exclaimed Martelo.

The waiter handed out the drinks.

"It's difficult to say where we come from," said Martim, sipping his *mazagrã*. "It's said that our country is among the least diverse in the world. But I say, who are we, really?"

"Portuguese?" ventured Judah.

"But are we really?" asked Martim. "With the Jews, the Moors, the Vikings, the Celts, the Phoenicians all romping through our land, we are more mutt than purebred, if you ask me."

"Like this drink," said Martelo, downing half of the spiked iced coffee in one go.

Israel lifted his bag and took a gulp of the *mazagrã*. "I'm dying of thirst," he said, wiping his lips and then taking another swig of it.

"Excuse me," said a woman, turning in her chair to face Martim. "If you don't mind me asking, we were all wondering about the bag."

"What is that, now?" he asked.

The woman pointed to the bag on Israel's head.

"Do you mean *o chapéu de Mambrino*?" asked Israel, lowering the bag on his head.

"I'm sorry .... The what?" she asked.

"Allow me to explain," said Israel.

"Oh boy," muttered Judah, sinking in his seat.

"You see, we are sailors."

The woman glanced at her friends. They all bore a resemblance to each other, being tall and thin with shoulder-length blonde hair pulled into a ponytail or bun.

"Where's your sailor's hat?" she asked.

"So, we're not the dixie cup hat-wearing sailors of the U.S. Navy," said Israel. "We're members of the Transporti Maritime Line cargo vessel and are presently fulfilling courier duties on behalf of our first officer."

She stared at Israel, blankly. Judah sank lower in his seat.

"As part of our official offshore duties, we came upon these fine gentlemen, who explained to us the tradition of the hat of Mambrino. You see, we are not just ordinary merchant marines but are of Portuguese descent. For us ..."

Israel paused and shook his head. The rum, brandy, and wine were beginning to get the better of him. He thought he saw the floor sway from side to side.

"For us," he continued, "connecting with the ways of our ancestors is of paramount importance. This hat is part of an ancient tradition!"

"So, the bag, er, hat you are wearing is part of an ancient Portuguese tradition?" she asked.

At this point a guitar strummed over the café's loudspeakers to a one-two-three, one-two-three waltz. It was soon accompanied by an accordion, a harmonica and a Portuguese guitar.

"The *chamarrita*!" exclaimed Martelo, jumping to his feet.

Macho Man stood up and yanked Israel to his feet.

"Time to dance," he said.

"You speak!" said Israel, surprised.

"It's a simple tune," said Martim. "There's room near the counter, over there, to dance."

The Germans began filming and snapping photos of Israel on their phones. Judah disappeared under the table.

"If you insist," said Israel, making his way toward the counter.

"Feel the rhythm of the *chamarrita*," said Martim, raising his drink. "Imagine dancing with a fine maiden."

"This is the rite of passage to the Portuguese brotherhood!" cried Martelo.

"Is that so?" asked Israel, tottering toward the counter and then pirouetting to the uproarious approval of the patrons.

"Dance!" shouted Martelo.

A hand reached for a mazagran glass from below.

"Dance!" bellowed Martim.

"Dance I will!" yelled Israel, imagining M&M in his arms as he spun and spun, muttering "mm-BAP-BAP, mm-BAP-BAP" while he made his way across the floor.

"It is most customary to remove your shirt as you dance," said Martelo.

"Do we need to see him without his shirt?" asked Martim.

"I vote for his shirt remaining in place," said a voice.

Martelo stood up and walked toward Israel. As he approached, he began mimicking Israel's prancing. "You must take off your shirt," said the tipsy Martelo. "Out of respect for our ancient traditions!"

Israel, having become extremely dizzy from his spinning, had a hard time hearing or comprehending what anyone said. Trying to stay in rhythm, he spun toward the table where Martim and Macho Man were guffawing.

"Off with it!" yelled Martelo, reaching for Israel's shirt but clumsily pulling down his pants instead.

The Germans screamed in horror and Benedita, who had her arms crossed and was glaring at Martim, stomped her foot in disgust. Israel's pants slipped to his ankles, revealing bright blue boxers that had the words "nice cheeks" embossed on the bottom.

"Enough of this!" she cried.

Martim and Macho Man howled and clapped their hands.

Israel, his balance now severely compromised, attempted to continue his dance with Martelo inches away but tripped and fell into him instead. The two crashed into Martim and Macho Man, causing the drinks and silverware to fly into the air as the table collapsed on its side, exposing Judah from his hiding place. The Germans leapt to their feet in fright. Their tour guide reached for his pockets and pulled out a wad of euros, which he tossed on their table.

"Get out!" shouted the furious Benedita, hurling a dish rag at Israel. "Pull up your pants and get out. The lot of you!"

Judah took a sip of his *mazagrã* from his cross-legged position on the floor and stared at one of the German women, who had a shell-shocked expression. "The boxers," he said shaking his head from side to side. "They were a white elephant gift from earlier in the year. Surprised he actually wore them."

CHAPTER TWELVE

Israel and Judah Deliver the Goods and Call Their Mother

The ship's yellow deck cranes had been erected, although no stores or supplies had been loaded yet. João held a cigarette in his right hand and was still wearing his kitchen apron over his jacket and cargo pants.

As soon as Israel and Judah started up the boarding ramp, he shouted, "What in the world is on your head!?"

"O *chapéu de Mambrino!*" cried Israel.

"What now? Take that ridiculous thing off!" exclaimed João. "We wear standard uniforms here!"

Israel lifted the feed bag off his head, causing his short hair to stick up from the static.

"As you command, my lahwd," slurred Israel.

"What took you so long? It's nearly two o'clock!" said João.

"We stopped for breakfast," said Israel.

"And lunch," added Judah.

"I believe it may have cost us more than expected," said Israel, scratching his head. "We treated three others."

"You kept a low profile, I hope?" asked João.

"Hardly made a profile …" Israel trailed off, confused.

"There was a wonderful restaurant outside São Brás. *Cozinha tradicional*," said Judah.

"We had drinks with food."

"You mean food with drinks?" asked João.

"There was a reason why I had drinks …," said Judah. "But it's a little blurry."

"The fried mackerel was delightful," added Israel, who appeared to be swaying.

João stared at Judah and Israel for a moment. "Are you drunk?" he asked at last, incredulously.

"Drunk?" cried Israel.

"What would make you think that?" exclaimed Judah, who hiccupped.

"You're both holding half-consumed bottles of cherry-flavored liqueur. Ginja de Óbidos," said João.

"What? Oh, these," said Israel, waving the bottle in the air. "We were just sampling some of the local digestifs. *Drunk* is a bit of a strong word. We practice moderation."

"That's right," said Judah, leaning heavily on Israel's shoulder for support. "We know how to hold our liquor."

The bottle slipped from Judah's hand, rolled the few feet down the gangway and smashed on the ground.

"Argh!" cried Judah. "This dock is unsteady!"

João placed his hand over his mouth and stared at the sisal sacks next to Israel.

"The dock isn't moving. And be careful," hissed João, having removed his hand from his mouth. "We don't need to attract attention. Hurry and bring those sacks with you to the galley. Can you handle that, or do I need to do it myself?"

"Oh, yes, we can handle that," said Israel, leaning over to grab a sack and causing Judah to slip and topple over.

"I'm fine!" shouted Judah, rising to his feet, "Nothing to see here. Just a slight bruise to my hip."

"*Oh, meu Deus!*" cried João. "You're lucky you didn't land down there in the glass, you idiot! Give me the sacks. I'll take them to the galley. Just try not to fall in the water."

Israel and Judah followed João up the gangway.

"I didn't know donkey milk was so valuable," said Israel. "I mean, it's certainly a delicacy, but ..."

"I wasn't expecting donkey milk," interrupted Judah. "I had to wash it down with a bottle of Arinto dos Açores, the digestif, and oh, there may have been two or three other things ..."

"You didn't open the envelope, did you?" asked João over his shoulder.

"Of course, I did," said Israel. "It would be irresponsible to deliver a letter without understanding its contents."

"But I told you explicitly not to open the letter!" exclaimed João.

"I assumed it was more a figure of speech, like don't ask how the sausage is made," said Israel. "Whenever someone says that, I become extremely curious about the sausage making."

"But you gave him the check, right?" asked João.

"Oh yes," said Israel, "all six million euros."

João stopped abruptly on the gangway and turned to face Israel. "Shut up, will you?" he said, shrilly. "We'll talk more about the milk later. Like I said, it's of the gourmet variety. Do not speak of this to *anyone* unless I say otherwise. Is this clear?"

"Very clear," said Israel. "We will not speak of the six-million-euro transaction for donkey milk to anyone unless otherwise directed."

"Shut it!" cried João. "No more speaking! Not a word until we get into the galley!"

"Yeah, shut up, Israel!" shouted Judah, who then hiccupped. "It's João's business if he wants to spend six million euros on ass milk. Six million euros may be a lot to us, but we haven't made rank yet as licensed seamen. Six million euros is nothing for João. Especially for ass."

When they arrived in the galley, João carefully placed the sacks in the refrigerated room next to the eggs, butter and milk. Israel and Judah sat down on stools beside the countertop.

"I want to level with you two," said João, emerging from the refrigerated room with a sack of potatoes. "We have a chain of command on this ship. It is part of maritime law and tradition. When I tell you to do something, you do it, no arguments."

"Yes, sir," said Israel.

"Roger that," said Judah.

"I don't need you trying to interpret things. Just do as I say," said João, spilling the potatoes on the countertop. "Like right now, I order you to peel these potatoes. Got it?"

"Yes sir," said Israel.

"Ten-four," said Judah.

"Good. So, for the rest of this afternoon, you just sit here and peel potatoes. You can leave at five o'clock, once the dinner crowd arrives. I can handle the cooking on my end for today."

João turned and walked back into the refrigerated room.

"We'll make bangers and mash this evening," he shouted. "Not *cozinha tradicional*, but it's a simple crowd pleaser."

João stepped out of the room with a package of butter and a gallon of milk.

"All you need to do is peel."

João stopped in his tracks and dropped the butter on the countertop. Israel and Judah were face down, snoring.

"Insufferable, insubordinate ingrates!" yelled João.

Later that evening, Israel and Judah were sitting on their couch with their feet up on the coffee table. Judah popped an aspirin in his mouth and took a sip from a glass of water.

"Mother!" bellowed Israel. "Let me put you on speaker-phone."

"Israel? Judah?" said Ida.

"Hi, Mom. Yes, it's us," said Judah.

"It's so wonderful to hear your voices," she said. "What time is it in Portugal? Where are you exactly?"

"It's eight o'clock in the evening in Ponta Delgada. We're in the Azores," replied Israel.

"We haven't heard from you since Baltimore, other than one text message," said Ida. "Are you having a good time? I want to hear all about it."

"Can't complain. We're sailors on a working ship, but we have our sea legs under us now," said Israel.

"At least I do," said Judah. "I was expecting a bit more of a traditional cruise experience, but we've adjusted."

"Oh really? What do they have you doing?" asked Ida.

"You know, engaging in the culinary arts. Supporting local farmers, that sort of thing," said Israel.

"I see. And you're able to get by without knowing Portuguese?" she asked.

"Oh, there are universal ways to communicate," said Israel. "This is actually an Italian ship, but our supervisor's Portuguese."

"And how's the Azores?" asked Ida.

"Wonderful," said Israel.

"Very green," added Judah. "Lots of donkeys."

"I feel much more grounded," said Israel. "There's a part of me that feels awakened."

"That's nice," said Ida. "I mean, you have a home here, and I'd say you were fairly grounded to it before you left. In fact, you were underground. But I'm glad this trip is opening up a new world to you."

"How's Dad?" asked Judah.

"Oh well, your father's stressed," said Ida. "He's been working nearly nonstop since you left. He's managing over thirty clients facing various felonies. It's too much. He refers to it as assembly-line justice. The legal system is a mess. But there's one case in particular that's keeping him up at night. It's a local case involving a mentally ill man. Your father thinks the man was being used as a pawn by the mob."

"That's interesting," said Judah.

"Some people are so susceptible to getting sucked into a life of crime," said Israel. "They can't see that they're being taken advantage of. I mean, it's sad, really. The naivety. They ask for a simple loan from a guy named Al, and the next month, they're involved in a machine gun shootout with assailants dressed in police uniforms on Valentine's Day."

"I'm not sure about all that, but yes, it is a stressful case," said Ida.

"And you're doing well, Mother?" asked Judah.

"Oh, just swell. Your father's driving me up the wall, your grandmother is nagging me nonstop and the house is falling apart. But I'm hanging in there," said Ida, who paused before speaking in a softer voice. "It's a lot quieter with you two gone, though."

"Don't worry about us," said Israel. "We'll have plenty more opportunities to speak, once we dock in Lisbon."

"Worrying is, by definition, motherhood," said Ida. "But I'd appreciate that. I miss you."

CHAPTER THIRTEEN

Israel and Judah Arrive in Madeira

João sat on a stool in the galley with his arms crossed, staring at Israel and Judah. The ship had just arrived at the Caniçal Commercial Port in Madeira after sailing for nearly two days, and the crew was preparing to offload cargo.

"To reiterate," said João, "as you know, we have orders from First Officer Montilla to deliver the envelope I have in my hands in exchange for precious goods. I don't want any funny business this time around. Is that understood?"

"You can count on us," said Israel.

"We'll be as efficient as possible," added Judah.

"Good. And that means no wine or anything like that during the errand," said João. "We're a … uh … a drug-free operation."

"Understood," said Israel.

"As you command," added Judah.

"And this envelope, Israel, is not to be opened under any circumstances. Understood?" said João.

"No need to," said Israel.

"Good," said João, nodding his head contentedly.

"I already opened it," said Israel.

"What?" cried João, placing his hands on his head.

"It was on the countertop when we came in," said Israel. "You must have left to use the restroom when we arrived."

"*Ay!*" exclaimed João.

"You can be assured that your eight million euros will be held in our strictest confidence," added Judah. "It took us fifteen minutes to add up all the bank notes."

"I must say," continued Israel, "this milk is extremely overpriced. I knew the Japanese had expensive tastes in fish, for example, but wow! Eight million euros. Eight million euros for milk. Who would have known?"

João was perspiring. Beads of sweat were forming on his forehead. "Keep your voices down," he hissed.

Israel looked around the galley. "There's no one here but us," he said.

"That's not the point," said João in a hushed voice. "You never know who might walk by. This is a discreet operation. Not everyone on the ship has been, uh, read in."

"Read in?" asked Israel, now keenly interested in the subject.

"Yes, right, read in," repeated João. "This is a sensitive project, as you can tell by the sum of money."

"Eight million euros," added Judah.

"Hush it!" cried João, sweat trickling down his chin. "This is a sensitive operation that only certain members of leadership are aware of. You, by default, because you report to me, have been read into this program."

"I don't remember reading about this in our onboarding forms," said Israel.

"It was in the fine print," said João hurriedly. "The key is that this is a special program that requires the utmost discretion."

"So, we're like secret agents?" asked Judah.

"Yes, like … uh, no!" said João. "There is nothing secret about this. It is just a sensitive, *perfectly* legal business transaction. Did I say perfectly legal? Because of the value of the goods you are picking up, we don't want to draw attention. Criminals are everywhere nowadays. Can you imagine being robbed? The horror!"

"That would be horrible," agreed Israel.

"Eight million euros is a lot of money to lose," said Judah.

"Right, and I don't want you to be put in harm's way," said João. "We have a strict security plan. If you refer to, uh, section sixteen, part three, uh, let me see, paragraph two, you'll find details about how we handle sensitive business transactions."

"We should check that out," said Israel.

"No need to do that today," said João. "It's in there. Somewhere. Anyway, just focus on the trip at hand."

"Right," said Israel. "So, what's the trip at hand, sir?"

"Salt," said João. "Sea salt from the Canary Islands. You will pick it up from a house in Funchal and bring it back to the ship. Easy."

"What's so special about this salt?" asked Judah. "Seems above the average asking price."

"You will load a van full of salt crates," said João. "This isn't ordinary salt, of course. It's considered white gold. Producing this type of salt is very manually intensive, with people working in reservoirs under extreme conditions. The salt has the most mineralized crystals in the world. It produces flavors unlike anything you can imagine and dissolves rapidly in water. It's a delicacy, sought by chefs at Michelin star restaurants across the continent."

"Can we try it?" asked Judah. "I mean, take just a little for the galley?"

"No!" shouted João. "Under no circumstances are you to open the salt crates." He wiped his brow with a dish towel. "There are less addictive … I mean, less expensive but high-quality varieties of salt we can pick up in Madeira, if you like," he said in a softer voice. "I like the idea of enhancing the ingredients we have onboard the ship."

"Will we be taking the van from the port to the house?" asked Judah.

"No, you will take a taxi halfway up the mountain in Funchal toward Monte Palace." João pulled out an index card with an address on it. "You will give this to the driver, and he will take you directly there. It's straightforward. I can't imagine any complications."

Israel and Judah stepped onto a long quay and stood beside the Transporti Maritime ship, which was the only container ship at the port. The sun was bright and the weather cool but pleasant, with only a slight northeasterly breeze.

Israel could make out the little fishing village across the water that gave the port its name. The village was along the foothills of the green-carpeted mountains, comprising homes that burst with orange and white colors that spilled down to the azure sea below. The island was enchanting, and Israel was eager to see more.

Judah stood beside him, adjusting a map on his phone.

"Funchal's only thirty minutes away by taxi," said Judah. "We should check out Monte Palace and the tropical garden. The house with the salt is right nearby. Who knows when we'll come back to Madeira?"

"Good point," said Israel.

"Madeira is famous for its port wine and something called *poncha*," said Judah. "João told us not to drink wine, but he mentioned nothing else."

"That's because he wants us to experience the local culture," said Israel. "It's like if you were visiting Chicago for the first time, I would tell you to avoid eating a hot dog with sauerkraut. That's not how it's done in the city. You need to eat a hot dog with yellow mustard, neon-green relish, chopped onions, pickled sport peppers and a pickle. It's common sense to follow local customs."

"I agree. When in Rome …"

"When in Rome?" asked someone from behind.

Israel and Judah turned around to see First Officer Montilla with a clipboard in hand.

"Where are you two headed?" he asked.

"Oh, we were just saying we should try the local food of Madeira," said Judah. "You know, when in Rome, do as the Romans do."

"I see," said First Officer Montilla. "Good, you do that. We will depart early tomorrow morning, so now's the time to see the island."

"Right, that's our plan. We plan to see some attractions and pick up a few things," said Israel, winking.

First Officer Montilla narrowed his eyes. Israel wasn't sure, but he didn't seem to pick up on his signal.

"Just stay out of trouble," said First Officer Montilla at last. "We have a tight schedule."

"You got it, sir," said Israel. "We wouldn't dream of causing trouble and tarnishing the reputation of the Transporti Maritime Line."

The taxi took Israel and Judah from the far eastern Caniçal Commercial Port southwest along the coast, through mountain tunnels and on bridges overlooking chasms and the glittering Atlantic Ocean. They passed banana plantations, rows of date palms and curlicue agave hanging along the side of the roads.

As they approached Funchal, they entered a natural amphitheater with slopes stretching from the bay and rising steeply to over three thousand feet to surround the city. At the Funchal port, they could make out two cruise ships, one larger than the other, that allowed passengers to amble from the quay to Avenida Sá Carneiro, which led to the city center.

"There, that's what we want to take!" said Judah, pointing to a cable car gliding up the mountain.

"No problem," said the taxi driver in perfect English. "I will take you to Almirante Reis. You can buy tickets and take it up to the gardens. You're on vacation?"

"Yes, sort of," said Judah.

"We're sailors," said Israel. "We work for the Transporti Maritime Line and are on shore leave for the day."

The driver glanced at Israel in his rearview mirror. He was a slight, middle-aged man with a stubble beard and wire-framed glasses.

"We get many yachts in the harbor, but I am not familiar with this Transporti Line," he said.

"The Transporti *Maritime* Line," corrected Israel. "It's a commercial container ship. We've crossed the Atlantic from Baltimore and just came from Ponta Delgada."

"You are Americans?" asked the driver.

"Yes, we're from Chicago," said Israel. "But we plan to move to Portugal. We are Portuguese, you see."

The driver appeared confused. "You are Americans but have family in Portugal?" he asked.

"Our ancestors," said Israel. "From many years ago. We are sure."

"And you are visiting Madeira only for a day?" he asked.

"We are on our way to Lisbon," said Israel. "Once there, we will find work and apply for citizenship."

"And do you speak any Portuguese?" he asked.

"Some, here or there, more or less," said Israel. "We plan to study on the mainland."

"That's good," said the driver. "I've heard of some Americans moving to Portugal. There is a special visa one can apply for."

"By the way," said Judah, changing the subject. "What's the best way down from Monte Palace?"

"There are many options," said the driver. "You can take the cable car, of course, or a taxi or bus. Some people walk, but it is very steep, so I would not recommend it. There's also the Carreiros do Monte. Have you heard of this?"

"No, we haven't," said Judah.

"It's a kind of toboggan that will carry you halfway down the mountain," said the driver.

"Halfway down?" asked Judah.

"Yes, it takes you halfway down the mountain, and you can take a taxi to the city center from there," the driver continued. "It has become popular with tourists. In the past, it was a quick way to travel from Monte to Funchal. It covers more than two kilometers and has been used for over a hundred years."

Judah glanced at Israel. "Sounds perfect!" he exclaimed. "That should take us near the house."

"It sounds promising," agreed Israel. "And a way to get a feel for traditional customs."

The driver pulled up to the curb on Avenida do Mar, near the fitness park. He turned on his blinkers.

"The cable car is there," said the driver, pointing to a modern terminal with large glass windows. "It costs a few euros."

"Well, that was interesting," said Judah, about three hours later, sipping *poncha* from a margarita glass at a restaurant patio overlooking the cable car and the ocean below. "I wasn't expecting a Chinese garden and Buddhist statues in a Portuguese archipelago. They had lovely floral arrangements."

"It was unexpected," said Israel, taking a sip of *poncha* from his glass. "This is a refreshing beverage after a long walk."

"Indeed. I like it better than the ruby port we just had."

"The port was exquisite as well. It's important to try the local staples. Take a bite of my scabbard fish," said Israel, holding out his fork with a piece of fish on it.

"No, I'm full. They provided generous portions of *espetada*. My favorite was the grilled limpets appetizers. Never had that before."

"Your loss. Do you recall, by the way, when João wanted us back on board?"

"Did he specify a time?"

"I think not," said Israel, draining the remaining *poncha*. "Think we have time for another?"

"Of course!" said Judah encouragingly, waving down a waiter. "First Officer Montilla said the ship was leaving tomorrow, so we have the whole day free."

"That's true," said Israel. "It can't take too long to pick up salt."

"I was wondering … just going out on a limb here," said Judah. "Do you think there's anything odd about these trips João has us making?"

"In what way?"

"Well, the quantities of money we seem to be exchanging, first of all."

"I wouldn't dwell on it."

"We'll have two more *ponchas*," said Judah to the server.

"We're dealing with millions of dollars in cargo. Who knows what the individual freight containers are worth? Could be twenty million dollars of dried camel milk in one of them, headed to Dubai. I wouldn't be surprised."

"That's true," said Judah. "I'll try not to think about it too much. It's not my business, and I'd rather keep it that way. Sometimes it's better *not* to know what is going on."

"Couldn't agree more. What's important is that we soak in the local culture and start thinking about the work we'll be doing once we get to Lisbon. Or at least the work you'll be doing. I've brought copies of my resume with me and expect to have discussions with the leading tech companies in the city … after we get acclimated, of course. Wouldn't want to rush into it."

"Rushing into things is usually not a good idea."

"Right, not a good idea to be hasty."

"Exactly, like deciding to move to another country on short notice."

"Right."

"But I'm enjoying this, nonetheless."

"Wait, I wasn't hasty in deciding to come to Portugal," exclaimed Israel.

"Just a tad."

"I thought about it for at least four or five days."

"Case closed."

"Your *poncha*, gentlemen," said the server, interrupting their conversation.

"Thank you, kind sir," said Israel.

"*Obrigado*," said Judah to the server, before turning to Israel. "Anyway, I have no regrets. Onward and upward!"

"Good. Well, like I said, I gave this trip careful consideration," said Israel, looking momentarily at the ocean. "And perhaps the better expression, right now, once we finish our drinks, is onward and downward. For the Canarian salt!"

"Cheers!" said Judah, tapping his glass against Israel's glass. "For the good of the salt!"

The line for the Carreiros do Monte was long, and Israel and Judah were feeling unsteady on their feet. Israel had underestimated the potency of the *ponchas* and felt the world swaying more than he would have liked.

"Why don't we sit down for a moment," he suggested.

Israel and Judah plopped down on the street behind a group of seven other tourists waiting to ride the toboggans, which were of wicker construction and resembled patio furniture on skis. The parties in front of them were laughing as they watched two men, dressed in white button-down shirts, white slacks, brown rubber-soled boots and straw boater hats, push tourists downhill in the toboggans as they ran behind.

"They're going to crash!" cried a young woman.

"They're going so fast!" exclaimed another.

One of the *carreiros* emerged from under the green awning of a shed at the launch point and sneezed, causing his hat to fall to the ground. This caught Israel's attention, and the two locked eyes for a moment. The *carreiro* picked up his hat and moved in their direction, but this seemed to anger one of the other *carreiros*, who grabbed his arm and began scolding him.

"There seem to be strict protocols here about who takes passengers down the mountain," said Israel. "Got to wait your turn, so it appears."

Israel turned his attention to a middle-aged couple, both wearing T-shirts, khaki shorts, fanny packs and crew socks with loafers. They appeared to have come straight from the cruise ship in Funchal and were settling nervously into their toboggan.

"Simon, tell them to go slow," Israel heard the woman say.

"Don't be daft, Agnes. They can hear you just fine," said the man. "You understand English, right?"

There was a brief conversation between the *carreiro* and the couple before he pushed the toboggan down the hill to a high-pitched scream.

"Come, you're next," said one of the *carreiros* to Israel and Judah a few minutes later.

The brothers stood up and stumbled toward the toboggan.

"I wonder if this all got started after someone's coach accidentally slid down the road," asked Judah.

"It's an environmentally sound mode of travel," said Israel. "Remarkable craftsmanship."

"Are you ready?" asked one of the *carreiros*.

"I believe we ..."

The two *carreiros* began pushing the toboggan before Israel could finish his sentence. Israel turned to look at them and noticed that there was a commotion in the queuing area. A *carreiro* had shoved one of his coworkers away and was pushing an empty toboggan by himself down the road.

"Huh, some of the *carreiros* must be anxious to get home," said Israel.

"What was that?" asked Judah.

The toboggan was picking up speed now. The *carreiros* were alternating between running behind it and standing on its wooden skis as it moved downhill. The sharp turns reminded Israel that he had just had a large lunch.

"I was saying," said Israel, glancing over his shoulder again, "some of the *carreiros* are in a hurry to get home."

"Why do you say that?" asked Judah.

"The gentleman behind us with the empty toboggan seemed anxious to leave," said Israel, pointing.

"He just lost his hat," exclaimed Judah.

"Ouch!" said Israel. "He just banged his shoulder against that building."

"He just hit a street sign!" cried Judah.

"He's losing his grip!" shouted Israel.

"Watch out for that garbage can!" shouted Judah.

The *carreiro*'s toboggan crashed into a thirty-two-gallon garbage can near an intersection, causing its contents to launch into the air, landing on the unfortunate man and spilling in the surrounding vicinity. The *carreiro* flew off the toboggan and landed on his back on the side of the road, while the garbage can and toboggan slid in tandem downhill.

"That's gotta hurt," said Judah, shaking his head, as their toboggan turned a corner, and the *carreiro* was out of sight.

"Does that happen often?" asked Judah of one of the *carreiros*.

"No, that never happens," the man replied, shaking his head. "Maybe it was his first day. I couldn't tell who it was."

"Bad luck, I guess," said Judah.

"Yes, bad luck," agreed both *carreiros*.

Soon they arrived at a neighborhood of Funchal called Livramento, which was lined with taxis and confused tourists trying to determine if the long, steep walk down to the city center was worth it or if instead they should pay the extortionate fees for a ride down the mountain. Most opted for the latter, but fortunately for Israel and Judah, their rendezvous point was close by.

"He said it was about three hundred yards southeast of the taxi queue in a white two-story house above a garage with a green-painted door," said Judah.

They walked past the taxi drivers, who called to them, offering a range of services, including a ride down the mountain, photographs and a personal tour of the island.

"They are remarkably enterprising individuals," said Israel.

"They are tenacious," agreed Judah, looking at the homes to his left and right. "Not sure if you noticed, but most of the homes here are white with orange roof tiles."

They came to an intersection where a road led downhill. From the intersection, they had a clear view of downtown Funchal and the ocean in the distance.

"I think we need to head this way," said Judah, following the road downhill. "The garages would seem to be at the lower level, at the rear of the homes."

They walked for a short distance down the side street, past gardens overflowing with rose bushes, hibiscus and palm trees. There were cars parked on the side of the road, making it difficult for vehicles to maneuver through the narrow streets. After about two hundred feet, the road bent sharply to the northwest, and they saw a white van parked next to an overhead power line and utility pole.

"There! That must be it," said Judah.

"I see a green-painted garage," said Israel.

The garage served as the structure for a fenced-in patio above. Beyond the patio, tucked back and up the hill, was a cream-colored home with large windows, green shutters and an orange-tiled roof. Judah pressed the button on a doorbell beside the garage door.

After a several-second delay, "*Sim?*" said a man gruffly over the intercom.

"Uh, so we are here to pick up the salt," said Judah.

"Yes, we are here on behalf of João Abreu and Dantel Montilla," said Israel. "From the Transporti Maritime Line."

There was another delay, and then the man said in English through the intercom, "Good. Please wait."

Ten minutes later, the garage door opened to reveal a young man wearing sunglasses, a navy-blue Arsenal soccer team cap, a black polo shirt and brown slacks.

"Are you Israel and Judah Cruz?" asked the young man.

"Yes, we are," said Israel. "What's your name?"

"My uncle asked me to take you to Caniçal," said the man, ignoring Israel's question and shutting the garage door. "I will drop you off near the port, but I will not go inside. There are two dollies in the van. You can stack the crates onto the dollies and walk the short distance to your ship."

"I suppose this simplifies dealing with port security," said Israel.

"Do you have the cash?" asked the young man, walking toward the van.

Israel patted the pockets of his cargo pants, pulled out the envelope bulging with cash and handed it to the man. The man hastily opened the envelope and began counting the euros.

"*Muito bem*, let's go," said the man at last.

"Expensive salt, huh?" asked Israel.

The man nodded and motioned for them to get inside the van.

"Before we reach Caniçal, we will stop in Santa Cruz so I can drop this envelope off," said the man. "If there is anything missing, I'm afraid you will not be getting back to your ship."

"I'm sure it's all there," said Israel.

"I should hope so," said the man. "If not, your feet … I'm not sure how to best express this in English. Let's say that it will be like your feet are moored to concrete. You will be going nowhere until this is resolved."

"I'm sure it will be fine," said Israel.

"Right, but if not," said the man, lowering the brim of his hat over his dark glasses, "you should plan for an extended stay, with your feet firmly planted at the bottom of the sea."

CHAPTER FOURTEEN

Israel and Judah Stop in Chicago and Hear a Story

"After all these days at sea, we seem to have come full circle," said Judah.

"It does appear that way," agreed Israel," studying the menu of the Chicago Café.

"Obviously, Madeira has a much better view than the Windy City," said Judah, staring out of the window at a row of palm trees and the ocean beyond. "I'm glad we had a chance to see Monte Palace earlier today."

"This reminds me of Marcela's Cafeteria," said Israel.

"Ah, I do miss the Jibarito Lechón sandwich," said Judah. "If only we had lived closer to the city."

"Dad was reluctant to take us to Humboldt Park," said Israel. "He worried about the proclivities of young men, such as us, to engage in criminal enterprises. Gangs you might say. But here we are, still insulated from the merest possibility of lawbreaking."

Judah turned his attention to the menu.

"Should we try the *bolo do coco*?" asked Judah. "It has *chouriço*."

"I've had my fill of *chouriço*, I must say," said Israel, placing his foot on one of the salt crates that they had placed under the table. "Perhaps something lighter."

"Sardines?"

"Excuse me," interrupted a portly man with a bushy, gray-speckled mustache.

He appeared to have come from the restroom, as his hands were still wet with traces of soap.

"I couldn't help but overhear you mention something about Marcela. Is that correct?" he asked.

"She was, if I could use a bit more colorful language, our muse," said Israel. "She captured our hearts."

"And our stomachs," added Judah.

The man's eyes bulged at these statements, and he glanced over at a table in the patio where a group of men were seated.

"Come with me," he said. "I must introduce you to my colleagues."

"Of course," said Israel. "We would be delighted to meet the locals."

Israel and Judah followed the man outside to the table where four other men were sipping *bica* and engaged in con versation.

"Friends, it's worse than I feared," he exclaimed, motioning toward Israel and Judah. "These men ..."

"Israel and Judah," said Judah. "We're brothers."

"Israel and Judah have similarly been enchanted by the devious mistress Marcela," he said.

"We have most certainly come under her spell," agreed Israel.

The men looked up at Israel and Judah. Their expressions were dark. One of the men pressed the butt of his cigarette into an ashtray and shook his head from side to side.

"Allow me to introduce ourselves," said the man with the mustache. "My name is Pedro da Costa Cabral. And here we have Vicente, Miguel, Francisco and João."

"We've met a number of Joãos," said Israel.

"A popular name," said João, pulling out another cigarette.

"Tell us about this Marcela," said Judah.

"Sit, sit," said Pedro, pulling up two chairs from a nearby table. "It's a sad story."

"Tragic," added Miguel.

"The talk of the town," said Vicente.

"You see, we are just returning from the funeral of our dear friend Crisóstomo Cardoso, who died the most wretched of deaths," said Pedro.

"And what would that be?" asked Judah.

"Death from a broken heart," said Pedro.

"Ah, I offer you my condolences," said Israel. "There is indeed no worse death."

"But you do not fully understand," said Pedro. "I'm surprised you haven't heard, but perhaps that's because you're not from around here."

"Heard what?" asked Judah.

"That Crisóstomo died from the scorn and rejection of none other than Marcela," said Pedro.

Israel glanced at Judah.

This is not where I envisioned this discussion going, he thought. *But what is worse than unrequited love?*

"And just how did you come to know Marcela?" asked João.

"We met her in the city," said Israel, disinclined to reveal their affection for an American café and prematurely end the conversation.

"In the city?" asked Miguel.

"An unusual place to find a shepherdess," said Vicente.

"Nevertheless, it's true," said Israel. "Please, tell us more."

"Marcela Coelho, daughter of Guilherme Coelho the Rich …"

"Did you say Coelho?" interrupted Israel.

"I did," said Pedro, who appeared irritated by his questioning.

"I apologize," said Israel, thinking of M&M's last name. "Go on."

"As I was saying, Marcela, the only daughter of Guilherme, grew up just outside this Caniçal parish," continued Pedro.

I see. No relation to M&M, Israel said to himself. *I think.*

"Her father is a wealthy man involved in commercial port operations, and they own an estate in the mountains overlooking the waters," said Pedro. "Guilherme has long been married to Lúcia, who is in her own right, a woman of great beauty. But as their daughter Marcela grew, it was clear that she was a unique gift to the world. A woman so alluring, none of the men in the parish could resist her, as I assume you understand fully well."

"She is most certainly irresistible," agreed Israel.

"Men from all over the parish sought her hand in marriage," said Pedro. "Or worse, some of the coarser sailors that came through these shores sought her company for a brief night or two. I find these men despicable."

Judah chuckled nervously. "Right, sailor. Blah!" said Judah.

"If anyone could win her over, Crisóstomo would have been the most likely," said João. "No disrespect meant to you, but she preferred the company of Portuguese men."

"We are of Portuguese descent," said Israel.

"It isn't the same," said João.

"Regardless of nationalities," said Pedro. "Crisóstomo was so handsome, it is said that international modeling agencies came to recruit him. He was also very clever, a wizard with numbers, although he sadly declined to fully maximize his potential because of his affection for Marcela."

"And yet Marcela spurned his advances?" asked Israel.

"Indeed. She spurned his advances, much like she rejected all the other men who approached her," said Pedro. "This you must understand."

"Of course," said Israel.

"But it wasn't only the rejection that broke Crisóstomo," said Pedro. "It was her decision to abandon the parish entirely. She was tired, I presume, of the attention she received. Or perhaps, out of some sort of cruel scheme, she left this parish with the intent to be at the remotest convent possible."

"She vowed a life of chastity as a shepherdess," said Miguel.

"And that was the cruelest decision of all," said Vicente. "Because none of us, Crisóstomo in particular, would ever get to see her again."

"Couldn't Crisóstomo visit her at the convent?" asked Judah.

"True, he could visit her," said Pedro. "But it is in a mountainous location in the island's interior, difficult to access. For all practical matters, she chose to escape all her suitors for good, preferring to stay in the company of other celibate women, like herself."

"Then how did this Crisóstomo die?" asked Israel.

"It was from a degenerative heart," said Pedro. "A natural progression of love sickness that can only be logically explained by Marcela, devil that she is."

"Wouldn't her commitment to celibacy and her devotion to her faith make her ..." Judah paused for dramatic effect "... righteous?"

"Come now!" shouted Pedro. "Who's side are you on?"

"Well …"

"Self-righteous you should say!" scolded Miguel.

"I'm just pointing …"

"Cruel," added Vicente.

"Unprincipled," said João.

"Ignore my brother," said Israel. "He's not enraptured by Marcela in the way that normal men are. So, you were saying that Crisóstomo died of heart disease. Has Marcela caused similar distress among others in the parish?"

"Very much so," said Pedro. "It's not only the many suitors that were heartbroken by her departure. Her parents too were crushed by her decision to leave. It is said that Guilherme pulled out his hair and mourned for weeks after she left home."

"Tragic," said Israel.

"And that is what has brought us here today," said Pedro. "We've come back from the funeral of Crisóstomo and are trying to make sense of this incomprehensible world. Was it folly to chase Marcela? Were we all consumed by madness? Did we have any choice over the matter? Could anything have been done to fix Crisóstomo's heart? These are all questions we keep asking ourselves."

"I feel the wounds of her rejection as well," said Miguel. "But being a simple man, I came to accept my fate."

"But Crisóstomo didn't accept his fate?" asked Judah.

"Perhaps," said Pedro. "Perhaps his lack of acceptance is what killed him in the end. Or maybe he was destined to die with a broken heart. Who is to say for sure?"

"I say it's foolish to chase a woman who has no intentions of ever reciprocating those feelings," said Judah.

"But who's to know what's truly inside her heart," said Israel.

"Exactly," said Pedro. "It's not so easy to move on when there might be the slightest possibility of love."

"And did Crisóstomo intend to follow her into the mountain wilderness?" asked Judah.

"He most certainly would have," said Pedro. "But she vanished into the night, like a ghost, and the shock killed him. God rest his soul."

"Then perhaps that is a warning for the rest of us," said Judah. "To tread carefully in the presence of Marcelas. She may be one of a kind, but there are others who provoke a similar effect on suitors. To love is to walk on the razor's edge, where an overzealous step can lead to an untimely end."

"Amen," said Miguel.

"Well said," replied Vicente.

"And now," said Judah, whose stomach grumbled audibly, "can we order those sandwiches?"

CHAPTER FIFTEEN

Israel and Judah Sail North toward Lisbon

"I'm not sure it was necessary for João to relieve us of our duties for the rest of the trip," said Israel from his bottom bunk bed in the ship's quarters.

"He seemed upset," said Judah from the bunk bed above. "I didn't think we were drawing a lot of attention."

"All I did was ask a police officer for directions," said Israel. "A perfectly reasonable thing to do when you are not familiar with a new town."

"He was kind enough to escort us to the ship," said Judah.

"Right. He even helped pull one of our dollies onboard," said Israel. "Honestly, I felt a bit of heat stroke coming on. It was a gracious gesture."

"I agree."

"João was bright red in the face."

"His eyes were bulging."

"He yelled at us in Portuguese after the police officer left," said Israel. "I'm afraid I didn't understand what he said. I haven't advanced beyond learning a handful of greetings."

"Me either," said Judah. "But if I were to guess, it likely involved colorful language."

"Certainly. He was spitting and pulling out his hair," said Israel.

"Speaking of João, I've been meaning to talk to you about something," said Judah.

"Yes, what is that, my dear brother?" asked Israel.

"It would seem to me we're associated with a criminal," said Judah.

"A criminal?" cried Israel. "What would make you say that?"

"Well, I suspected he might be a member of the underworld for some time now," said Judah. "But I figured we should just mind our own business because we didn't really have a lot of other options on this ship."

"Now, now," said Israel, "I agree João has us running odd jobs, but *criminal* … nah, that's an overstatement."

"You know, he had an unusually negative reaction to the police officer."

"He likely viewed it as an invasion of privacy."

"He's very secretive for a cook …"

"He only wants the finest ingredients."

"And the unusually large transfers of funds …"

"He's buying ingredients in bulk."

"For millions of euros."

Israel said nothing for a moment and stared at the underside of Judah's bunk bed. It was ten o'clock in the morning, and the ship had departed for Lisbon several hours earlier. He was getting hungry.

"Do we have any more of those sandwiches?" asked Israel.

"You mean the *bolo do caco*?" asked Judah.

"Yes, that."

"It's next to the sink," said Judah. "Anyway, are you listening to what I'm saying?"

"Yes, I hear you," said Israel, getting to his feet and walking over to the sink.

"I mean, if none of what I just said is evidence enough of the shady nature of our venerable steward, then what about the comment from our driver?" asked Judah.

"What are you referring to?" asked Israel, his mouth full of *bolo do caco*.

"The comment about finding ourselves firmly planted at the bottom of the sea if any cash was missing from the envelope," said Judah.

"Come now," said Israel, "just a figure of speech."

"Most people would call it a threat," said Judah.

"Details, details," cried Israel. "I find it really hard to believe that João is a criminal."

"Well, regardless, I'm just saying that we need to exercise caution. It's probably best to steer clear of João from now on."

"All right, I can go along with that," said Israel. "I mean, we're going to dock in Lisbon in a couple days, anyway."

"Right," said Judah. "So, let's try to keep a low profile until we get there. I mean, the goal was to get to mainland Portugal. I would hate to see our plans disrupted by a cook who's a crook."

Israel pulled his cell phone from the pocket of his pajama pants and began furiously typing with his thumbs. "I agree," he said, after a minute. "Keeping a low profile is a good idea."

Judah sat up in his bunk and stretched his arms to his sides, yawning. "Will you save some of that bread for me?" he exclaimed.

Israel had eaten two-thirds of the *bolo do caco*.

"What? Oh, sure," said Israel absentmindedly.

"What are you typing on your phone, anyway?" asked Judah.

"Just a little this and that."

"Don't tell me it's more of your godawful love poetry," said Judah, crossing his arms and sitting cross-legged. "You might get banned from the internet."

"Since when is there a central internet authority?" asked Israel.

"There is for bad haikus, I'm sure."

"I like to stay active on social media," said Israel. "It's an especially good way to log your travel diaries. I was just posting an update about our latest delivery."

"You posted an update about delivering salt?"

"Yes, I took some pictures of it and posted them to Instagram," said Israel. "I also posted photos of our driver."

"Why on earth would anyone care about that?"

"People find this kind of stuff fascinating," said Israel. "I received favorable comments about it already."

"I thought we just agreed to keep a low profile."

"Of course," said Israel. "This is just social media. It's not like I'm running around shouting about our work, trying to amplify it."

"Did you do the same thing with our milk delivery?"

"Yes, of course," said Israel. "The photo I have of you on the donkey was especially popular."

"Ugh," Judah shuddered. "You know, those deliveries were probably illegal."

"Let's not go there again," said Israel sternly. "The evidence is really flimsy."

Judah sighed and plopped down on his pillows. "For the first time in ages, I think I would enjoy a game of Assassin's Creed as a mindless distraction."

"I've given up my gaming pastime," said Israel. "There's nothing to worry about. Trust me. Everything's going according to plan."

CHAPTER SIXTEEN

Israel and Judah Are Snared

"There's been a change of plans!" shouted João as he pounded the door to Israel and Judah's cabin.

Israel yawned and stretched his arms from his bunk bed.

"Wake up you lazy, good for nothings!" cried João, on their door again.

"What's going on?" asked Judah, sitting up from his top bunk.

"This is an emergency!" cried João. "Red alert!"

"I'm not decent," said Israel calmly. "I need to put on pants."

"Pants," chuckled Judah. "The look on the faces of the German tourists were priceless."

"Red alert!" shouted João. "Open up this instant!"

Israel stood up and reached for the cotton flannel pajama pants on the floor near his bed.

"You have to understand, *senhor*," began Israel, hopping as he slipped one foot into the pants. "You have to understand that we were relieved from our duties. So, we can't be expected to be up at this hour."

"Just open the door, you stupid Americans!"

"We're Portuguese," said Judah, climbing down the bunk.

"That's right!" exclaimed Israel, proudly. "We've been accepted into the brotherhood."

Israel slipped his other foot in the pants and pulled them up.

"Could you make some instant coffee?" asked Israel. "It's barely 9:45 in the morning. An ungodly hour."

Judah yawned and shuffled over to the small kitchen. He pulled out two mugs from a drying rack near the sink and filled them with water.

Israel walked over to the bathroom and shut the door.

"I'll be out in a moment!" Israel yelled.

There was more banging on the door.

"I swear to God almighty!" shouted João. "This is serious. Open the door!"

"Is the boat sinking?" Israel called out.

A few seconds later, Israel flushed the toilet and went over to the bathroom sink to wash his hands.

"Open the door!"

Israel shook his hands to air dry them, then stepped out of the bathroom. Judah offered him a warm mug of instant coffee, which Israel gratefully took.

"This hits the spot," said Israel, inhaling the coffee aroma as he walked to the cabin door and opened it.

João was leaning into the doorway, staring at the floor, his hands gripping both sides of the frame. Sweat was dripping from the tip of his nose and his hair was protruding from his cap in multiple directions.

Israel looked at him and was convinced João was deranged. "João, I must say, this is a surprise."

João extended his hands toward Israel's neck. They were shaking, as if resisting lethal action.

"I said …" hissed João, "I said … this is an emergency!"

Israel took a sip of his coffee.

João took a deep breath, his hand still in the air. "Did you, Israel Cruz …"

"Go ahead, spit it out," said Israel.

"Did you post videos of the salt and dairy packages to the internet?" he asked.

"Yes."

João's eyes popped.

"I am doing a travelog," said Israel. "I'm sure we've discussed this before."

"We never discussed this," said João, his vibrating hands inching closer to Israel's neck.

"Honestly, *senhor*, you must get a grip," said Israel, patting one of his outstretched hands.

"The police are here, you idiots!" he shouted.

"What does that have to do with us?" asked Israel.

João groaned and dropped his hands to his sides, his body sagging from an invisible weight.

Judah walked over to the door and stood behind Israel. "What's gotten into him?" he asked.

"This has everything to do with you," João said, sinking to the floor. "Everything!"

"Our father is an esteemed member of the legal profession," said Israel. "We have great respect for law enforcement."

"You need to make a getaway," said João. "You can crawl down the mooring lines and sneak out of the port. Yes! Yes, you must do that!"

Israel glanced at Judah. "I think João's having a nervous breakdown," said Israel.

"Why do the police want us?" asked Judah.

"You damn well know why," said João, looking back and forth in the corridor. "And you'll take me down with you!"

"Nonsense," said Israel.

João grabbed Israel's ankle and attempted to pull him out of the cabin.

"That way!" he pointed toward the end of the hallway. "Take the stairs down one level, they will lead you to the mooring lines. If nothing else, you will give me some time. Go! Now!"

"Okay, we're going," said Judah, closing the cabin door shut and grabbing Israel by his pajama shirt sleeve. "*Vamos*."

Israel followed Judah down the corridor, coffee cup in hand, glancing once over his shoulder to see João sprinting in the opposite direction. Soon they had walked past second-class ratings, where the more junior members of the crew stayed, and approached the galley and the mess.

"It's really shocking how ignorant João is about immersive storytelling," said Israel, slightly out of breath.

"Uh huh."

"Travel documentaries are among the highest forms of artistic expression, capturing the events of real people."

"Did you bring your cell phone?"

"I never leave without it."

"Is it charged? We may need to make some calls."

"I've been thinking about Ken Burns, his approach to panning the camera," said Israel, placing his hands on his hips. "For example, my slow pan and close up of the salt crates were done to convey how artisan packaging can attract buyers interested in authentic commodities."

Israel heard some shouting from the mess hall. A moment later, three men and a woman burst out of the galley, spinning around in search of something. They were wearing gray windbreakers with navy-blue vests over the top embroidered with *Policia Judiciaria* on the back. One of the men had a pistol raised and pointed at him. Another had a bandage around his head, and Israel thought he looked familiar. The woman held up one of the sisal sacks that Israel and Judah had delivered to João.

"Americanos?" shouted one of the officers.

"I am Oceana da Conceição Metrass, detective, of the Judiciary Police," said the woman, pulling out her badge. "We believe you have been in possession of illicit contraband."

"Oh boy," muttered Judah, raising his hands in the air.

"My dear officers," said Israel calmly. "What you have in your hands is freeze-dried donkey milk. I can vouch for it, because we were the ones who delivered it!"

Judah groaned.

"Please understand that what you say can and will be used against you in a court of law," said Officer Mestrass. "Can you confirm that you are indeed Israel and Judah Cruz, citizens of the United States?"

"We are," said Israel. "Now about the court of law comment …"

"And that you, Israel Cruz, are the account owner of the Instagram handle, 'Seeking M&M?'"

"Yes," said Israel. "I have an active following."

"Thirty-six followers," said the man with the gun.

"And you have taken photos of this contraband as well as salt crates?"

"As I was explaining to my brother earlier, I've been working on a travelog. About that comment …"

"This travelog, as you describe it," interrupted Detective Metrass, "contains other videos, such as poetry to the celebrity M&M, as well as videos of you dancing at a café in the Azores."

"Ah, *o chapéu de Mambrino!*"

"What's that?" asked the officer with the raised gun.

"From the voyage of discovery," said Israel.

The officers stared at him with blank expressions.

"Never mind," said Detective Metrass. "You are under arrest for charges of narcotics trafficking. Where is your boss, João Abreu?"

Judah pointed in the direction from where they had come.

"Under arrest!" protested Israel, spilling some of his coffee. "This is shocking. Utterly shocking!"

"Is it, really?" asked Judah, sighing.

"Where's the evidence!" Israel cried.

"Very clever," scoffed the officer with the raised gun. "Trying to come across as innocent. Trying to act stupid."

"There is no reason to be insulting, *senhor*, especially to someone returning for the first time to his homeland," said Israel.

"This is a very serious offense," said Detective Metrass. "Officer Sequeira was making a logical observation, given the overwhelming facts at hand."

"So you're saying that we're criminals?" cried Israel.

"Seems like it," said Judah.

"Exactly," said Officer Sequeira.

"You've taken photos, videos, and provided written and oral testimony about your criminal behaviors and intentions," said Detective Metrass. "Because of this evidence, you are under arrest and will accompany us as we make inquiries with other members of the crew, including your boss."

"Viper," said Officer Sequeira. "Please handcuff them."

"I demand due process!" protested Israel.

Viper, the largest of the three men, with a neck as thick as a tree trunk, approached Israel and Judah.

"I assure you, all laws and regulations are being followed as part of this interdiction," said Detective Metrass.

"Hands behind your back," barked Viper.

"Is Viper your real name?" asked Judah as his hands were being cuffed behind his back.

"This is no time for small talk," said Viper.

"His name is Jorge Simões da Costa," said Detective Metrass, placing her hand on Officer Sequeira's gun to lower it. "He's from Rio and has experience with your type."

"I kick PCC gang members to the curb," he said, placing Israel's cup on the floor and then securing his wrists with the handcuffs. "Thieving smugglers. Don't you even think of playing games with me."

Detective Metrass lifted her walkie-talkie and held it to her ear. Static emanated from the microphone momentarily.

"The ship's in port," she said to someone on the other end of the line. "Two of the three suspects are in custody. You're cleared to go."

"Let's move, boys," she said, jogging past Israel and Judah and down the corridor in the direction of their cabin.

CHAPTER SEVENTEEN

A Fall from Grace

Israel and Judah sat on the floor near their cabin door and watched the Judiciary Police tear through their belongings. Clothes were tossed in the air, cabinets yanked open, suitcases turned upside down.

Detective Metrass was speaking into her walkie-talkie, a few feet away from them.

"Do we need to get the navy involved?" asked a man at the other end.

"I don't believe so, Sebastião," said Detective Metrass. "It's unlikely the captain or the crew are complicit, other than the cook and the two Americans. It was the first officer who reported the suspicious activity. That said, we will need to conduct a thorough sweep."

Judah elbowed Israel in the ribs.

"Officer Montilla ratted us out!" whispered Judah. "We've been snared!"

"What do you mean by ratted?" whispered Israel. "We're innocent."

"Sure, whatever," said Judah. "But they don't seem to think so!"

Israel thought about the First Officer. *Had a bad impression of him from the get-go.*

"This reminds me of the Russian cargo ship we intercepted last year," the voice of Sebastião came through on the walkie-talkie.

"The one that originated from Trinidad and Tobago?" asked Detective Metrass.

"Oh yes, that was a big one," said Officer Sequeira, walking over to Detective Metrass. "Over two tons of cocaine confiscated."

"It was a similar situation, where we had an informant onboard," said Sebastião. "But we had to get the navy involved because they were armed."

"We've established the proper precautions," said Detective Metrass. "I sent you the raid plan this morning. I can walk you through it, if you like."

"No, that won't be necessary," said Sebastião. "I've reviewed it already. Just exercise caution. You never know with these PCC gang members."

⁓

Thirty minutes later Israel and Judah were standing on the ship's truss gangway with four Judiciary Police officers. There was a cool breeze, and Israel could make out the port below with its rows of multi-colored containers and trucks. He spotted at least half a dozen police cars parked beside the ship with their LED strobe lights flashing.

"So, we've finally arrived in mainland Portugal," said Judah, staring at a navy-blue police van that had pulled up to the ramp.

"Wait here," said Viper, slapping Israel on the shoulder, as he followed Detective Metrass and the others down the ramp.

"We've been cuffed to the handrail," said Israel, indignantly.

"You know," said Judah after the police were out of earshot. "Detective Metrass is rather attractive, if you can ignore the arresting part."

"Not a fan," said Israel.

"She reminds me of some of the other models I've seen in photos of M&M. Not that I'm an expert," said Judah.

"M&M would never fraternize with vigilantes," said Israel.

"Yeah. We seem to have become entangled in something big," said Judah. "Who is this PCC they keep referring to?"

"I don't know," said Israel, squinting at the police van in the distance. "It appears that they are bringing backup."

Detective Metrass was in the center of the gangway with her partners, waving to the police who were exiting the van.

"What kinds of dogs are those?" asked Judah.

"Hard to tell," said Israel. "Black with curly fur I think."

"Anyway, if we happen to be given an extended, confined residence in Portugal, how should we explain this to Mom and Dad?" asked Judah.

"If by extended residence you mean prison, then I have to strongly disagree," said Israel. "There is no chance we get prison time for offenses we didn't commit."

"Well, I think we may have committed offenses," said Judah. "We were in too deep to disobey orders from João. We were used."

"I'm an excellent judge of character," said Israel. "João had his faults, but the first officer was the real scoundrel."

"Because he reported us to the authorities?"

"Exactly! Because he falsely reported us to the authorities."

Detective Metrass was leading the Judiciary Police and their dogs up the gangway.

"I find her smug, if you want to know the truth," said Israel, glaring at Detective Metrass.

"Just try to stay in her good graces," said Judah, staring at the police. "We don't need to dig a deeper hole than we're already in."

Detective Metrass was scribbling in her notebook as she led the police up the ramp. The police officers stopped when at the top of the gangway, where Israel and Judah were handcuffed.

"Why do you have poodles?" asked Israel.

Detective Metrass slapped her pen against her notepad and shot Israel a menacing look. "These are drug-sniffing Portuguese Water Dogs," said Detective Metrass. "For maritime operations."

"Zip it," hissed Judah.

"They're hypoallergenic," said Officer Sequeira.

"National treasures," added Viper, who had a dog on a leash.

"Wouldn't German Shepherds or Bloodhounds be more appropriate?" asked Israel.

Viper's dog sniffed Israel's foot, then stepping forward, lifted its left hind leg.

"They look like … Hold on!" cried Israel as he felt the warm liquid soak through his slipper.

"Now look at what you've done," said Viper. "You upset him!"

"Viper, unshackle these criminal masterminds," said Detective Metrass. "We need them to lead us to Senhor Abreu."

What do these people know about crime! thought Israel as he and Judah were rushed through a rust-colored, starboard-side corridor on the main deck. His right slipper squished with each step. *We live in the digital age, where packages are delivered with the swipe of a button. What could possibly be so suspicious about us?*

"These two Americans were hired under highly suspicious circumstances," said First Officer Montilla, emerging from a passageway into the main corridor.

Israel felt Viper's powerful grip on his shackled wrists as they stopped in front of First Officer Montilla.

"But they are petty criminals. It's the chief steward you need to question," said First Officer Montilla.

"How dare you call us petty!" protested Israel.

First Officer Montilla produced folded papers from the pocket of his cargo pants.

"Copies of the manifest, as instructed," he said, handing them to Detective Metrass. "The full paperwork is in the bridge. You can see the crew details on the second page."

Detective Metrass took the paperwork from Officer Montilla and flipped it to the second page.

"Has the master been informed?" she asked. "No."

"You don't suspect him of being involved?"

"I don't."

"How will he react to seeing the *Jornal de Notícias*?" asked Officer Sequeira. "They've been tipped off about the raid."

"He will be very unhappy with the journalists, the police, with me, but most of all, he will be furious at the Americans," said Officer Montilla, looking at Israel. "It's fortunate the police are here, otherwise they might be in for a long swim across the Atlantic."

"As the master of this ship, he's liable," said Detective Metrass. "Take us to the bridge."

The Judiciary Police surrounded the master and his chief officer on the ship's bridge. Israel and Judah were in the center of the circle, beside to the two men in question, and Detective Metrass. Several other Judiciary Police officers were searching the bridge with their drug sniffing dogs.

Israel's ears were ringing. There were curses and insults thrown in Italian, Portuguese, French, Spanish and English. Master Capurro's face was so red, Israel thought he might be able to cook an egg on it. The yelling was mainly in Italian, the master's native language, but there were other abuses, such as obscene hand gestures. Chief Officer Russo joined in the ruckus, yelling and stomping his feet. Between the two of them, who were inches from Israel's face, there was enough spittle to warrant a windshield wiper.

"You were aware of this?!" cried Master Capurro, pointing at First Officer Montilla. "We follow a strict compliance program on this ship. I have detailed logs and a comprehensive security plan."

"Be that as it may," said Detective Metrass. "We have evidence of illegal behavior."

"It's the good-for-nothing cook. Your *chief steward*," said First Officer Montilla, emphasizing the last words.

"João Abreu?" asked Chief Officer Russo.

"Yes. And these two Americans," said First Officer Montilla.

"Chief steward?" cried Master Capurro, spitting out the words. "I will strangle him, I swear!"

"No need for that," said Detective Metrass. "You have enough trouble at hand."

"He's a lousy chef," said Chief Officer Russo. "You should never have promoted him."

"He makes a decent *torta barozzi*," said Master Capurro defensively.

"He has it delivered in bulk," said Chief Officer Russo.

The master placed his hands on his hips and stared at the floor momentarily. "Does he really?" he asked.

"The only good thing he produces is food someone else prepared," said Chief Officer Russo.

The master scratched his head.

"Can I at least strangle these Americans?" he asked.

"Come now! We've been dutiful sailors," protested Israel.

"Master Capurro, you will stay on the bridge with one member of the Judiciary Police until we give the all-clear," said Detective Metrass. "There's a serious criminal at large."

"We just installed additional lighting to remove potential shadow spaces on the deck. I routinely check the overboard openings and all the possible exposed areas, like the propeller regions," said Master Capurro. "I can't believe this is happening on my watch."

Detective Metrass' walkie-talkie received an incoming call. "The suspect is in my line of sight," said a voice.

"Officer Sequeira, what do you see?" asked Detective Metrass.

"There's a man on the side of the ship, throwing things overboard," said Officer Sequeira.

"Oh, crap," said Detective Metrass. "Where is he?"

"He's, uh ..." Officer Sequeira paused. "What are those nautical terms again? Dang it. Back side?"

"Stern?"

"No, not that."

"Aft?"

"Not that either."

"Port side?"

"Yes, that's it," cried Officer Sequeira. "That sneaky little devil must have thought we wouldn't notice."

"Did you see what he was throwing overboard?"

"Some type of crate," said Officer Sequeira. "Looks like he was rushing it because the crates are floating out to sea."

Detective Metrass turned to Viper. "We need to intercept the cook. Now!"

First Officer Montilla grabbed her wrist. "I'll take you. You'll never find him without a guide."

"We're coming too!" exclaimed Master Capurro.

A minute later, Israel, Judah, the ship's crew leaders and the Judiciary Police were racing through the twisting corridors, down various flights of stairs, up one flight, down another two, and through a vast cargo bay, as they made their way to the port side of the ship. When they reached the port-side deck, the wind smacked them in the face as they stepped outside, searching frantically to stop João from destroying the evidence. They ran past an empty swimming pool, past exposed containers stacked one on top of another, until they saw a man in an orange jacket and pants hastily unfastening a free-fall lifeboat. Officer Sequeira was several feet away, with a walkie-talkie in hand.

"We're with the Judiciary Police!" shouted Detective Metrass. "Please stop what you are doing and put your hands up in the air!"

"That's what I told him," said Officer Sequeira, "but I didn't want to wrestle him to the ground, given my injuries."

The man looked at Detective Metrass, then looked at the lifeboat as if torn about what to do next.

"João, I order you to stopa now, before you hurta yourself!" shouted Chief Officer Russo.

"The game's up," shouted Viper.

Detective Metrass put her hands in the air to calm the situation. She took a step forward. João took a step back, leaning against the railing.

"It's okay, João," said Detective Metrass reassuringly. "There's no need to make this any worse. Just turn yourself in, and you can hire a lawyer."

"You don't know the half of it," said João, wringing his hands. "I can't turn myself in."

"We all make mistakes," said Detective Metrass. "There's a better way. Trust me."

João stared at Detective Metrass.

"Viper, Rui, please put your guns down," said Detective Metrass.

She took another step forward, her hands out, pleading with João to turn himself in.

"Please come with me," she said, reaching out her hand.

João lifted his right hand, holding it in the air momentarily before placing it over his nose. Then, leaning precariously against the railing next to the lifeboat, he launched himself backward over the side of the multistory cargo ship and into the chilly waters far below.

PART III

CHAPTER EIGHTEEN

Israel and Judah Are Interrogated

Israel and Judah were escorted down the gangway of the Transporti Maritime ship by Viper, Officer Sequeira and a pack of Portuguese Water Dogs, which Israel feared might pee on him again. There was a news crew at the dock with several cameramen filming their walk of shame toward a waiting squad car. Their wrists were handcuffed behind their backs, and they were still in their cotton flannel pajamas.

Master Capurro, also handcuffed and escorted by the Judiciary Police, was livid and kept elbowing Israel and Judah in the ribs whenever he was in striking distance. Chief Officer Russo, likewise arrested, muttered apparent insults in Italian.

Israel refused to believe the accusations of trafficking cocaine across international borders. When he tried to dispute the allegations, several members of the police suggested he hire a really competent lawyer, because the evidence was on board the ship and irrefutable. The police also had video footage of them transporting the contraband onto the ship, as well as various incriminating social media posts.

"You will spend time in jail here, that is certain," said one police officer.

"You will be deported," said another.

"You will spend time in jail here, then will be deported," said someone else.

This was not the sort of welcome Israel had envisioned upon arriving in mainland Portugal, his ancestral home. *How am I going to explain this to Mom and Dad? Everything seemed so right. I felt a connection to this country. I felt like I had a purpose for the first time in my life.*

Judah, to his credit, refrained from the cutting remarks he was so good at. No "I told you so!" No "Look what you got us into!" Instead, he kept his head held high as they descended the gangway and onto solid ground.

"At least we'll have accommodations for the first night or two," he said at one point, but this didn't cheer up Israel.

Detective Metrass had rushed off the ship, frantically speaking into her walkie-talkie for backup after João flung himself into the River Tagus. When Israel and Judah finally descended the gangway and stepped onto the quay, a squad car was waiting for them.

"Come with me," said Officer Sequeira, opening the rear door of the squad car and motioning for Israel and Judah to get in. "We'll be taking you to the station for questioning. You'll be given a letter of rights."

"I can assure you, we're innocent," said Israel, falling flat on his face on the rear seat cushion as he attempted to situate himself. The handcuffs seemed to affect his balance, and his feet protruded from the vehicle.

"The dog's got my slipper!" cried Israel.

Israel felt someone reach in and pull him out of the car.

"Let's try this again," said Officer Sequeira, guiding him into the squad car this time. "And I'm not falling for your sinister ploys. No one can be this incompetent while trafficking this much contraband."

"Our father's a lawyer," said Israel, even though he knew Estephan would be of no help. In fact, he suspected his father would fully support any criminal charges brought against him.

Officer Sequeira tossed Israel's slipper at his chest. "We'll have time for an interview at the station," said Officer Sequeira. "I'm just informing you of your situation."

"How kind of you," said Israel sarcastically. "You know, our intent was actually to move to Portugal. But seeing how you handle prospective immigrants, I can tell this was a big mistake!"

Judah plopped down beside Israel.

"I didn't even have time to have a proper cup of coffee this morning," cried Israel. "Don't you have a concept here about prohibiting cruel and unusual punishment? In America, we have the Eighth Amendment to the US Constitution!"

The door slammed shut, and Israel stared bleary-eyed through the windows at the officer and the dogs.

"You're not in Kansas anymore, sweetheart," he said, walking away.

"You're not crying, are you?" asked Judah a minute later.

"What? Me, crying? Never!" said Israel, rubbing a tear from his eye with his shoulder.

"You're right about the coffee," said Judah, pausing. "Look, Israel, let's try not to get too down on ourselves yet. We didn't know what was in those deliveries. And it's not like we had a choice. We did what we were told. It's what we signed up to do."

"Right."

Judah glanced at Israel and sighed. "I know how much this trip meant to you," he said. "Now's not the time to give up hope. We've actually already been to Portugal. We've visited the islands. We just need to clear our names, somehow, and move on with things. We've been snared by gangsters."

Israel bit his lip. His eyes stung, and he was surprised how much this incident affected him. It wasn't so much the arrest that bothered him. The bigger issue was the fact that he could be deported. That his destiny could be so quickly shredded like a piece of scrap paper. That his aspiration of fitting in, once and for all, was shriveling like a raisin in the sun. If not this, then what? He felt unmoored as never before, spinning in an intertropical convergence zone with no hope of escape.

What about M&M? It's over, isn't it? A breakup before we ever had time to meet. I didn't even mail her a letter.

A large man with a broad black mustache, dressed in full tactical gear, opened the driver's-side door and got in.

"Good morning, gentlemen," said the man. "I am Officer Brito. I'll be your chauffeur to the station, free of charge." He slammed the door shut.

"Let me correct myself. There may be a charge down the road," he added. "Given what I've just seen, I'd say it's rather likely."

"When will we be fully informed of our charges?" asked Judah. "We understand that drugs were found on board, but we were not aware of this. We would like to see a lawyer."

"You will be given a duty lawyer automatically," said Officer Brito. "Unless you prefer to use your own lawyer, but your lawyer must know Portuguese law. If not, I suggest you go with the one we provide."

"These allegations are baseless!" exclaimed Israel.

"Based on the brief discussion we had with your boss, they certainly do not appear to be baseless," said Officer Brito. "He leapt from the deck of the ship, at great personal risk to his life. He must have envisioned a less cruel fate in the cold waters of the river than in custody."

"Did he survive?" asked Israel.

"He's in critical condition, so I'm told," said Officer Brito.

"How long can we be expected to be detained before we go to trial, assuming that's the process here?" asked Judah.

"Fortunately, pretrial detention has improved, and most people are out of jail after eight months," said Officer Brito. "Only twenty percent of cases involving serious criminal matters—I suppose that includes international drug trafficking—involve pretrial prison sentences exceeding one year. At least you have a range to work with."

This just got worse, thought Israel.

"The other issue, and this is just bad timing," said Officer Brito, driving slowly out of the port, "is that this administration is really keen on showing it's tough on crime. You saw the cameramen. You are, I'm afraid, going to be made an example. Politicians are foremost concerned about their electoral prospects, and this is a good story. We've captured foreign drug traffickers. The foreign element plays really well with the public. You might expect to exceed the detention spectrum I mentioned earlier."

This just got way worse, Israel thought again.

"The good news," continued Officer Brito, "is that even though lengthy pretrial detentions are common, the maximum period for pretrial detentions authorized by law is two and a half years. I suppose you might adjust the range I mentioned earlier, extending it up to two and a half years. Fortunately, any time spent in pretrial detention will count toward your official sentence."

This got way, way worse.

"By the way, is this your first time in Lisbon?" asked Officer Brito.

Israel and Judah nodded.

"Great! Welcome to Lisbon. *Bem vindo!*"

Israel and Judah stared at Officer Sequeira across the table in the bare, soundproof room that seemed designed to maximize discomfort. He wore a navy-blue beret. Just underneath the hat, Israel could make out a bandage. Israel could have sworn he had seen him somewhere.

"Officer Sequeira, as I stated earlier, we are not familiar with their last names. All we know was that one man was called João, a boy by the name of Lourenço and three other gentlemen who went by Martim, Martelo and Macho Man," said Israel. "We were given instructions to meet them at the address I gave you in São Miguel. I have no recollection of the town. It was in a rustic area."

"And where did you pick up the cocaine?" asked Officer Sequeira. "Was it at the address, or was there a different rendezvous point?"

"We were dropped off at the address I gave you, and then we were met by the boy, who took us to a donkey farm," said Israel. "We must have ridden for a couple miles to get to the farm."

"Ridden?"

"Yes," said Judah. "We unfortunately had to ride some wild mustangs."

"Donkey, you mean, in your case," corrected Israel.

"That explains why I couldn't find it … coupled with the allergies …" muttered Officer Sequeira.

"I didn't catch that," said Israel.

"Nothing, nothing," said Officer Sequeira, swatting the air as if trying to rid himself of a housefly.

"Anyway, we did not know what we were picking up," said Israel. "We were misled by the first officer. We thought the delivery was related to gourmet dairy products."

"But you were aware of the contents of your envelope?"

"Yes, we opened the envelope and discovered that it was six million euros," said Israel. "It seemed excessive, but then again, we're not from here, and we didn't feel like it was our place to question the transaction."

"But you were suspicious?"

"I wouldn't say suspicious," said Israel.

"We were just doing what we were told," said Judah.

"Six million euros is a rather unusual sum of money for milk, is it not?" asked Officer Sequeira. "You didn't think that perhaps it might be worth contacting the police?"

"We would say that donkeys are a rather unusual purveyor of milk," said Judah. "So no, the thought of contacting the police didn't cross our minds."

"And what about the Transporti Maritime ship? Did you follow the proper procedures? Did you record the deliveries in the logbooks? Did you follow the ship's security plan? Did you follow ISPS codes and the guidelines set forth with port operations?" asked Officer Sequeira.

"My job was peeling potatoes," said Israel. "Well … and making these deliveries."

"Israel only peeled potatoes for a few days before he was reassigned to delivery duties," said Judah. "Trust me, you're better off avoiding his brunch menu."

"João has a sensitive palate," said Israel.

"So, you had no compunction delivering questionable goods to suspicious people in remote environs for astronomical amounts of money?" asked Officer Sequeira. "You never asked yourself, 'Wow, this is odd. Should I report it to the authorities?'"

"Never," said Israel.

"Can't say we did," said Judah.

"I see. This all sounds highly implausible, I will just add," said Officer Sequeira, leaning back in his chair, clasping his hands in his lap. "Now, let's continue with your account. Where did you pick up the second delivery of cocaine while in Madeira?"

"We picked up the crates of salt …" began Israel.

"Salt mixed with cocaine and spiked with fentanyl," corrected Officer Sequeira.

"If you say so," said Israel. "We picked up the crates at the address we gave you in Livramento."

"And while you were on your way to the rendezvous site, were you under the influence of narcotics? Cocaine perhaps?"

Israel looked quizzically at Officer Sequeira. "We are not drug users," he said. "Now, we might enjoy a beverage from time to time. You know, when in Rome ..."

"You did not ride a toboggan down the streets of Funchal in an erratic fashion, causing bodily harm to the local inhabitants of the island?" asked Officer Sequeira.

"We had a lovely ride down the mountain, if I recall correctly," said Judah. "We were pushed by two *carreiros* in an orderly fashion."

"You did not—to confirm—intentionally cause personal injury to law-abiding citizens for sport while riding a sled fashioned out of a wicker basket?" asked Officer Sequeira.

"Doesn't ring a bell," said Judah.

"That may have resulted in spinal bruises, traumatic brain injuries, things of that nature?" continued Officer Sequeira.

"Not sure where you are going with this," said Judah.

"You did not have any objection to carrying over eight million euros in cash as part of this so-called delivery?" pivoted Officer Sequeira.

"No objection," said Israel.

"Just doing what we were told," said Judah.

"You did not take any of the eight million euros? Who would notice a few hundred thousand missing?" asked Officer Sequeira.

"The full sum of money was delivered, as instructed," said Israel. "Not a penny, or a euro, was removed for personal use."

"And you did all this at the explicit instruction of your boss, João Abreu?" asked Officer Sequeira.

"Correct," said Israel.

"As instructed," said Judah.

"I'm going to play this recording for you," said Officer Sequeira, reaching for his mobile phone. "I want you to tell me what you think of this conversation."

He swiped his phone and a voice rang out.

"Hello?"

"João?"

"Yes, it's me."

"Give me a second. I'm going to dial in …"

"Okay."

"You're in a suitable location?"

"Yes, yes. At my cabin. It's just me."

"Make sure you use burner phones."

"I'm fine. I'm in the middle of the Atlantic."

"There's a saying: 'Be cunning like a fox to recognize the traps. Be fierce like a lion to chase away the wolves.' Or, some might say, the pigs."

"Understood."

"This is a significant delivery. My boss tells me you are the cousin of …"

"Yes, of course. This is a family business."

"I heard the deposit went through successfully."

"That was my understanding, too."

"The mules, you can trust them? The second delivery is larger than the first."

"They are fools. Crazy, idiot fools. But we can trust them, believe me. They do as I say. I am their boss."

"Just monitor them. If anything goes wrong …"

"Nothing will go wrong."

"But if it does, you know how serious this is."

"When are you going to wire my percentage of the fee?"

"Once the goods are delivered in Lisbon, and we have confirmation that everything is as it should be."

"The white stuff is that good?"

"Better than good. It's mixed with fentanyl."

"They will keep coming back for more, that's for sure."

"That's for sure."

Officer Sequeira paused the recording as the door to the interrogation room swung open and Detective Metrass stepped into the room. She was prim and smartly dressed in her navy-blue police uniform. Her hair was pulled back in a bun, and she appeared superior and accusatory at the same time.

Israel glanced at his pajamas and felt the blood rush to his face. Here he was, a shabbily attired villain in a developing story, yet he wasn't aware of the villainous scheme that he had become part of, and for which he was going to be locked up in jail.

"At one point, are we going to be given our clothes and other belongings?" asked Israel. "I don't feel appropriately dressed here."

"We will provide a standard-issue uniform," said Officer Sequeira.

"I don't suppose you're referring to civilian garments here?" asked Judah.

Officer Sequeira grinned. "Prison attire," he added.

"That's what I was afraid you'd say," said Judah.

"Back to the recording," said Officer Sequeira. "What have you to say about it?"

Detective Metrass walked over to Officer Sequeira and placed her notebook on the table.

"We were used," said Judah. "You can hear it for yourself."

"What I hear is you being called fools, but you're innocent, no," said Officer Sequeira.

"I'll take it from here, Salvador," said Detective Metrass. "I'd like to corroborate the testimony, starting from the beginning. We have plenty of time. And I'm sure these gentlemen have nothing to hide."

Officer Sequeira stood up to leave and laughed as he squeezed past the desk and walked to the door.

"Our prisons are filled with inmates with nothing to hide," he said. "And what these two gentlemen appeared to hide in the galley's refrigerator is now plainly visible in our storage compartments at the police station. Best of luck to you two."

CHAPTER NINETEEN

Israel and Judah Experience Novel Accommodations

The sound of the harmonica reverberated through the corridors of the prison. The tune was slow, with each note carefully stressed by the musician to overcome the tendency of the instrument to slur things together. There was a pronounced wah-wah vibrato. A melancholy voice rang out.

> Nobody knows the trouble I've seen.
> Nobody knows my sorrows.
> Sometimes I'm up, sometimes I'm down.
> Sometimes I'm almost to the ground.
> Oh, yes, lawd!

"What a story! I'm floored."

The harmonica player stopped. "You got the lines mixed up," said Judah, who was sitting cross-legged on the floor in the corner of the prison cell. He had been given a harmonica by Viper as a "house-warming gift."

"Did I?" asked Israel, standing against the prison bars, grasping them in his hands.

"Improvisation is fine," replied Judah.

"Okay, let's try again," said Israel, staring forlornly into the corridor.

"Maybe we should get some rest," said Judah, placing the harmonica in his lap. "You were tossing and turning all last night."

"Was I?"

"The prison cots are more comfortable than I imagined. I would have probably slept just fine had you not been such a hot mess."

Israel continued to stare through the prison bars. Judah fiddled with his harmonica.

"Think we should call Mom and Dad?" asked Judah after some time.

Israel turned his head slowly toward Judah and said, "Uh, not yet?" His eyes were glazed over.

"Yeah, it's probably best to wait," said Judah. "With Dad being all stressed, no need to add to his troubles. Plus, what can they realistically do?"

"Oh, the troubles I've seen!" sing-songed Israel.

"The thing that gets me," said Judah, "… okay, so we were apparently mixed up with this trafficking business. But were we the criminals or the victims? It seems to me that we were the latter."

Israel pressed his face against the prison bars. The cold metal numbed his cheeks. He wanted to feel numb. Their predicament was unbearable, otherwise.

"We need to get our lawyer to come to our defense better. Senhor Fonte. Can't say that he's been useful so far. What do you think?" asked Judah.

Israel said nothing.

"I can't think of anything he's done that's helped advance our cause," Judah continued. "He made some vague remark about contacting the embassy that wasn't especially helpful. Who knows how long we'll be here? The more I think about it, the more I'm convinced we were used as mules. Two mules and a snare."

Israel wondered if he could somehow squeeze through the bars.

"As far as prisons are concerned, it could be worse, though. At least they let us share a cell."

There was a rattling of keys in the corridor, and Israel heard someone making their way down the hall.

"I once did a *Harry Potter and the Prisoner of Azkaban*–themed cosplay with Benny and Cassandra," said Judah. "Now Azkaban was a truly terrible place. Dementors sucked any positive thought out of the prisoners' minds, causing them to go mad."

"Dementors …" mumbled Israel.

"Azkaban was soul crushing."

"Israel and Judah Cruz," announced a man outside their cell.

Israel looked up and saw a prison guard standing before him in the corridor. Judah stuffed the harmonica in his pajama pants pocket. The prison had allowed them to wear their own clothes.

"You've been permitted notepads and pens," said the guard, tossing them into the cell through the bars.

Israel stared at the two notebooks on the floor. The guard began to walk away, then stopped, and turned around.

"You are a man with a sorrowful face," said the guard, looking at Israel. "Get yourself together. This is time for reflection."

"Senhor, we have been incarcerated for ages," said Israel.

"It's been one night."

"My soul is crushed!"

"Then use the pen to heal yourself," said the guard. "It's been said that you are a poet."

"Has it really?" asked Israel, his spirits rising.

"The Judiciary Police is well aware of your social media," he said. "Write a letter to a loved one. A girlfriend, perhaps?"

"A letter to a loved one?" repeated Israel.

"There you go," said the guard encouragingly. "Anything, really, to stop that awful singing."

<hr>

Israel was a man possessed. Two hours passed but it seemed like a blur. Judah, uninterested in writing, had fallen back asleep, shortly after the guard had stopped by. Israel, meanwhile, had filled six pages of notebook paper with poems and essays and had crumpled and tossed a dozen sheets of paper around the cell.

"To dream the impossible dream," muttered Israel, as he scribbled, "that is my quest. My most beauteous damsel, my muse, my reason for being."

Israel tapped his temple with his pen. The concentration required for long-form prose was causing him to sweat.

"Oh thou, wherever thou art!" cried Israel.

Judah groaned and rolled over in his cot.

"Wherever you are," Israel said in a lower voice, "I write to you in captivity. I find myself behind the bars of the bleakest dungeon. They seek to deprive me of my one true love. But hear me loud and clear! They cannot hold me back. Even though I am in pain, I find glory in prison, knowing there is nothing that can keep us apart. I came to this land, riding a stallion named love. Even in the darkest night, your visage is clear and bright in my mind's eye. You are my north star, my lighthouse as I approach from rough waters. You are the reflection of the divine. You are the essence of virtue. And here I declare, knowing that while we've been separated, going forward, as fate has foretold, we are to be together, betrothed, my dearest, most lovely, Maria Maia Coelho."

Israel stretched his legs across the floor and leaned back against the bars of the cell. He placed his notebook and pen on his lap.

"This is my masterwork," he said, wiping away a bead of sweat from his forehead. "To have time for this kind of reflection is indeed a gift."

Israel looked at Judah, who was curled up in a ball pressing a pillow over his ear.

"My dearest, youngest brother," said Israel out loud to himself. "So lacking in learning, so devoid of worldly experiences … Ah! What I would give for an older sibling such as myself. One who has matriculated from the rigors of a two-year degree. One who has read Aristotle, Plato and other philosophers such as Dr. Phil. One who could guide me through periods of melancholy. But alas! This is not my fate. Instead, I must avail myself of trial and error. I must blaze my own trail, through thickets of thorns, until I find that one ruby rose who is mine alone for the taking."

Israel turned and stared into the corridor through the bars of his cell. The guard that had stopped by earlier was making his rounds again. Israel picked up his notebook and pen and began scribbling on the top of the page.

"My name, that will come later," said Israel. "But your address, that I will never forget. It is imprinted in my mind, like your most glorious face."

Israel heard the guard knocking on the cells as he approached. He shouted something in Portuguese that Israel did not understand.

"This letter, my fairest of fair, will change the trajectories of many hearts," he said. "Your heart, most surely, but that too of your adoring fans and also of your present and future families."

Israel kissed his letter and with great care tore off the perforated sheet.

"Count time!" said the guard, approaching.

"*Senhor*," said Israel to the guard, "I have taken your advice and written a letter of momentous importance."

The guard stopped in front of the cell and scanned the floor.

"I implore you to mail this letter to my beloved," said Israel, folding the paper in thirds.

"I see you have made good use of time," he said.

"Given the extreme length of time we have spent in this institution, it is only reasonable that some communication with the outside world be permitted," said Israel.

"And where will you have it delivered?" asked the guard, reaching in between the bars to take the letter from Israel.

"To Cascais. You can find the address at the top of the page," said Israel.

"Why does Maria Maia Coelho sound familiar?" asked the guard. "Wait, I see, this is to M&M?"

"It is indeed."

"The supermodel?"

"None other."

"Do you know her?" asked the guard. "I mean, on a personal level?"

"Our hearts are intertwined."

"You are the reflection of the divine?"

Israel gave the guard the side-eye.

"I'm just reading what you wrote. Anyway, I need you and your brother to follow me," said the guard, pulling out his keys and unlocking the cell door.

"You'll deliver the letter, right?" asked Israel.

"I don't believe it will be a problem," said the guard. "But I'll need the detective to authorize it."

"Don't tell me we are going in for more interrogation with those defamatory police officers?" asked Israel.

"What's going on?" asked Judah, getting up from his cot and rubbing his eyes.

"Detective Metrass has asked for you two to come in for additional questioning," said the guard.

"This is an abuse of power!" protested Israel. "How many times must we be subject to these indignities?"

"You're facing felony charges for international narcotics trafficking, money laundering and possession of illicit contraband with the intent to distribute," said the guard. "I'd try to keep your composure in front of her, or else she might transfer you to the maximum-security wing."

"Israel, get a hold of yourself," scolded Judah.

"If you really piss her off, she might even call your mother," said the guard.

"Oh God, not that!" cried Israel.

Fifteen minutes later, Israel and Judah were seated in the G Unit of the prison, in a therapeutic treatment room with Detective Metrass and the guard. The detective was seated beside a medical examination table and was reviewing a dossier.

"As I mentioned previously," said Detective Metrass, flipping through several pages in the dossier, "you're permitted to have a lawyer, but it will cause delays, due to scheduling challenges."

"You mean we'll be stuck in jail longer?" asked Judah.

"You increase the likelihood of prolonged pre-trial detention," she said.

The door swung open, and a nurse entered the room, walking backwards while pulling a man in a wheelchair.

"João Abreu? Is that you?" exclaimed Judah.

João was wearing a light-orange prison uniform and had orthopedic casts on both legs and his right arm.

"João, do you remember meeting Detective Metrass?" asked the nurse, a woman who appeared to be in her early forties. She spun the wheelchair around, so he faced the detective.

"I've not had the pleasure of meeting her before," said João. "You do not see many women detectives in Portugal."

"How are you feeling?" asked Detective Metrass.

João stared at Detective Metrass as if not fully comprehending the question.

"Uh, João, you leapt off a multistory cargo ship the other day because of her," said Judah.

João looked at Judah and blinked three times. When he turned his attention to Israel, his body began to shake.

"He's having another one of his fits," said the nurse.

"I have his medication," said Detective Metrass, reaching into a drawer in the examination table. "I was told to bring this in case he started a seizure."

"Move me closer to that man, so I can get a good look," said João, raising his one functional arm in the air.

"He looks like he wants to strangle him," said the guard.

"I don't want to strangle him," said João.

"Oh, that's a relief," said the guard. "I was hoping to avoid having to restrain you any further."

"I want to KILL him!" he shouted.

At that moment Officer Sequeira entered the room.

"I can relate," he said, patting João on the shoulder. "We've all suffered because of them."

Israel stared at Officer Sequeira's bandage on his head. "I saw you in Madeira!" he exclaimed. "You were riding one of those wicker baskets down the mountain."

"Playing dumb. How clever!" said Officer Sequeira.

"Eh, what?"

"Can we please focus?" asked Detective Metrass. "We need to ask you a few questions about the events surrounding your accident."

João was attempting to wheel himself toward Israel with his one good hand.

"Can I get some help here?" asked the nurse, struggling to hold the wheelchair in place.

"João, we need to ask you some questions about your employer," said Detective Metrass.

The guard and the nurse were both gripping the wheelchair's handles.

"He seems very determined," said the guard.

"We need clarifications around Master Franco Capurro," she added.

João stopped struggling to move the wheelchair and focused on the detective.

"He is not my employer," said João.

"I thought you worked for Master Capurro as his chief steward," said Detective Metrass.

"Capurro? No, no, no. He is just an errand boy," said João. "I report to the owner of the Transporti Maritime Line. *Senhor* Sérgio Ricardo de Carvalho."

"Carvalho?" asked Judah. "Isn't that the son-in-law of Domenico de Stefano, who we met in Highwood?"

"Go on," encouraged Detective Metrass.

"Well, we discussed our travel plans with Domenico de Stefano back in the States," said Judah.

"The Transporti Maritime Line is involved with both legal and ... not-so-legal activities, as perhaps you have deduced," said João. "The master and his crew were oblivious to this. *Senhor* Carvalho had me running a trafficking operation, using mules, for many years now. These mules were usually of the desperate variety. Poor people from Brazil. Mentally challenged people from the States."

"Mentally challenged!" yelled Israel.

"Yes, imbeciles! Buffoons! Half-witted, good-for-nothings ... ayeee!"

The insults and stress caused João to go into convulsions again.

"So, these men were not aware of the drug trafficking operations?" asked Detective Metrass.

"We should nevvvv-eeeer have hirrrr-eeeed them!" said João, his teeth chattering. "Ussssse-lessss foooollllssss!"

CHAPTER TWENTY

Israel and Judah Evaluate Customer Service

The interview with Detective Metrass had to be cut short when João's eyes began twitching uncontrollably. Israel and Judah were promptly escorted back to their cell, where they attempted to pass the time by playing tic-tac-toe on sheets of scrap paper. It was extremely boring, so Israel was excited to hear that familiar jangling sound of keys as the guard made his way to their cell again, about a half hour later.

"Israel and Judah Cruz!" bellowed the guard.

"Yes, yes. We've done introductions more than a dozen times by now," said Israel.

"Standard protocol," said the guard defensively, unlocking their cell. "I need you to come with me."

"*Senhor*, do you know why we haven't been issued orange jump suits, like the other prisoners?" asked Judah.

"There are different policies depending on the type of prisoner," said the guard, leading them down a sterile corridor that comprised various cell blocks and concrete walls.

"Maybe they want us to get comfortable, for an extended stay?" mused Judah.

"It's possible. Times are changing," said the guard. "In the past, for detainees, this prison meant suffering. It was designed to break people. Today, the government has a more nuanced view of the welfare of its residents."

The guard led them into an expansive office, not far from their cell. A portly man dressed in a navy-blue suit and red tie was seated behind an antique cherry-wood desk, sipping an espresso.

"Take a seat," he said cheerfully, pointing to the wooden bench in front of the desk.

Israel and Judah sat down on the bench as the prison guard shut the office door and then stood in the corner of the room with his hands on his belt.

"How have you enjoyed your stay?" he asked. "Were you lacking anything?"

Our freedom! yelled Israel to himself.

Judah shook his head.

"Do you happen to know if my letter was mailed?" asked Israel.

"The letter?" asked the man in the suit.

"*Senhor*, the one addressed to the supermodel," said the guard.

"Ahh, that letter!" exclaimed the man in the suit. "About riding a stallion named love?"

"Yes, that's it," said Israel. "You know, that was intended to be private."

"You have lofty ambitions."

"I have a vision."

"Well, I'm happy to inform you that it has been mailed. I saw to it myself," said the man in the suit.

"Wonderful!"

"Good. I'm glad we sorted that out," said the man. "Now about the accommodations, any feedback for us? Were the beddings of suitable material?"

"They were suitable," said Judah. "Given the circumstances."

"Excellent. You see, this is a historical building and may appear more severe than it is," said the man in the suit. "We've been renovating various wings to bring them up to more modern standards. The architectural history is really quite fascinating. We've had Americans come to do studies on the building. Did you know it was modeled after the Prison Leuven in Brussels, Belgium?"

Israel and Judah glanced at each other, not sure what to say.

"It has a unique radial structure." He paused and took a sip of his coffee. "Anyway, I digress. I didn't bring you here to discuss the design of this carceral establishment. Let me introduce myself. My name is Paulo Rudolfo Rui Passos Vargas. I am the warden of this institution and am responsible for the well-being of our residents."

"Nice … to meet … you?" squeaked Judah.

"I've been fully briefed about your situation," said Paulo, frowning slightly. "Very serious crimes. International drug trafficking."

Israel rolled his eyes. *Where is he going with this? What happened to the presumption of innocence?*

"The lengths you will go …" Paulo paused, placing his hand on his chin. "Let me rephrase. The lengths traffickers will go to send their illicit wares across international borders never ceases to amaze me. Donkey milk?"

"We weren't aware that donkey milk was a thing people consumed," said Judah.

"Oh, yes," said Paulo, exhaling. "Brings back memories. My grandmother, God rest her soul, used to serve me a tall glass of donkey milk whenever we came over to visit. Sometimes, I'd have it with little cakes or cookies. It's such a delicacy."

"Rrriiight … of course, a … delicacy …" said Judah, his words trailing off.

"Especially the Azorean variety," continued the warden. "It's the volcanic soil. Anyway, getting back to your present situation."

"Yes, our present situation," said Judah, encouragingly.

"Presently, you are being released," he said, taking another sip of coffee.

Israel slipped from the edge of his seat and fell to the floor. "Did you say … released?"

"Now, get ahold of yourself," admonished Paulo. "Yes, you are going to be released. This is a highly unusual move, I will add. But there are conditions."

Israel pulled himself back onto the bench.

"And what conditions might those be, kind sir?" asked Israel.

"You still may be charged with a crime. It's not for me to say," said Paulo. "What I can say is that you will be released but must wear an electronic tag for monitoring. You may not leave the country, and should you attempt to do so, you will be arrested. You are still in a pretrial period as the investigators gather additional evidence. Should the police decide to clear you of any charges, then you will be free to move about as you please."

"We can't thank you enough," said Judah.

"We are indebted to you," added Israel.

"Don't thank me," said Paulo. "Thank the Judiciary Police. If it were up to me, I'd keep you here at our fine institution. We have everything a criminal detainee could need. But alas, at least for now, that will not be the case for you. Of course, once—or should I say *if*—you are charged and sentenced for a crime, then we will welcome you back with open arms."

"Right," said Judah.

"*Senhor* Teixeira will escort you to one of our technicians, who will fit you with a tag. Then you will be free to go," said Paulo.

"Thank you very much, honorable Warden Vargas," said Israel.

"As I said, don't thank me," said Paulo, reaching for papers in his desk drawer. "Before you go, if you wouldn't mind filling out these surveys, I'd appreciate it. We're a customer service organization and value the opinions of our guests. The customer experience is of paramount importance."

CHAPTER TWENTY-ONE

Israel and Judah Meet Another Cruz

"Form an orderly queue!" shouted a correctional officer.

Israel stepped behind Judah, but there were nearly two dozen inmates in the narrow reception area jostling for space in the out-processing line.

"What are you in for?" asked a man in an orange jump suit who had his hands cuffed behind his back.

"Oh, you know, the normal stuff," said Israel. "But we're being released today."

"The x-ray machine is broken!" exclaimed a correctional officer. "Everyone will receive a pat down."

"I am J. J. Cruz," said the man in the jump suit. "The system's rigged against people like us, you know what I mean?"

"Did you say Cruz? You're a Cruz?" asked Israel, suddenly interested.

"I am. My family has a history with this institution. We can't get a break," he said.

"You don't say?"

"My grandfather was arrested by Salazar for failure to align with the national interests," said J. J.

"That sounds vague," said Judah.

"Yes. Very vague," agreed J. J. "My father was arrested years later for similar crimes, but we all know it was because he was the son of my grandfather, who defied the Salazar regime."

"What do they have you in for today?" asked Israel.

"You can guess, I'm sure," said J. J.

"Dear god!" cried Israel. "The injustice!"

"Form two lines!" bellowed a correctional officer. "Nice try! You're not all leaving the prison today!"

J. J.'s eyes darted toward the correctional officer.

"Did you know that we too are Cruzes? What are the odds?" asked Israel.

"Well, Cruz is a common name …" began J. J.

"There must be some mistake. You surely cannot be incarcerated for the perceived crimes of your father!" said Israel.

"That's what I said!" agreed J. J.

"I wonder if we were jailed because of the Cruz connection?" Israel mused.

"You cannot trust the state."

"Maybe we can explain your situation to the warden?" said Israel.

J. J. rubbed his chin against his shoulder. "I have an idea," he said in a hushed voice. "I'll stick with you in this line."

"Okay, good plan," said Israel.

"But how will that help you?" asked Judah.

"You said you are being released, no?"

"We are."

"Then I'll say I'm your brother. I'm with you."

"But won't they know that you're in for different charges?" asked Judah.

"Nah, look at them," said J. J. pointing to the two correctional officers. "They're overwhelmed. People are out sick, and the machines are down. It's chaos."

"They do look overwhelmed," admitted Judah.

"Do you have the discharge papers?" asked J. J.

"These?" Judah held up a manila envelope.

"Yeah those! Quick, show me what's inside."

Judah carefully lifted the envelope's flap and pulled out a ream of documents.

"Keep the line moving!" shouted a correctional officer.

They shuffled forward. There were three prisoners ahead of them in the out-processing line.

"Let me get a closer look," hissed J. J., his eyes darting from side to side.

"The government seems to be really bureaucratic here," said Judah. "There's got to be over a hundred pages."

"This is good," said J. J. "There're too many words. It'll confuse them."

There was a sudden commotion as the prisoner at the head of the out-processing line was roughly escorted to the other line.

"Don't waste our time!" yelled the correctional officer, who gave the protesting prisoner a kick in the rear end before turning and walking back to the out-processing line.

"Geez, they mean business around here," said Judah.

"This is a sinister place!" exclaimed Israel.

"I'm not sure about this plan, J. J.," said Judah. "No offense, but I don't want to get caught aiding and abetting a prisoner. I've had enough of this place."

"Don't worry, we'll be fine," said J. J. "I'll say we're all Cruzes, so there's plausible deniability."

Two more correctional officers entered the reception area. One of the men, wearing a black beret and short-sleeved duty uniform was walking a dog on a leash.

"Oh god, it's one of those devilish poodles!" hissed Israel.

"It's a Portuguese Water Dog," corrected J. J.

"For those being admitted to this property, you will be thoroughly searched!" shouted the guard with the dog.

"Next!" shouted the correctional officer, as the prisoner at the head of the out-processing line was escorted out of the prison for release.

"Hey, listen carefully," said J. J., pressing his body against Israel. "I need you to reach into my trousers."

"Excuse me!" cried Israel.

"I have two packs of beef jerky in my left pocket," said J. J. "Take them, but make sure not to attract attention. Hurry!"

"Oh, I see," said Israel, glancing at the guards.

He reached into J. J.'s pocket and pulled out two beef sticks in red wrappers.

"A gift from a friend in the UK," said J. J. "Anyway, keep them hidden. When it's our turn for release processing, you unwrap them and chuck them across the room, where the other prisoners are standing. Got it?"

"Is that your grand plan?" hissed Judah.

"Actually, keep it a little more subtle," said J. J. "slide them or something. When the guards aren't looking."

"You're in the wrong line!" shouted the correctional officer to the individual in front of them. "For god's sake, no more games! Next!"

Israel, Judah and J. J. walked up to the correctional officer, who stood behind a counter and was speaking to someone on a handheld phone.

"He's not happy," said Judah under his breath.

The officer hung up the phone and pounded his fist on the granite countertop. "The customer is always right, says the warden ... bla, bla, bla!" exclaimed the officer. "All I want is backup. You're all criminals, for cryin' out loud!"

"We're Cruzes, senhor," said J. J. "Hand him the paperwork."

Judah passed the manila envelope over to the officer.

"One of these days I'm going to give that Vargas a piece of my mind," said the officer, pulling out the paperwork from the envelope. "The way they treat people around here, I tell you!"

The officer scanned the first page of the document.

"Have you considered retirement, *Senhor* Torres?" asked J. J., glancing at his name tag. "Early retirement, I should say."

"Every day," said Officer Torres, looking up at J. J. He appeared to be in his late fifties or early sixties. He was mostly bald, with thinning gray hair on the sides.

"The administrivia around here is enough to drive one mad."

Officer Torres flipped through a few more pages. Israel felt a sharp elbow to his side. He glanced over his shoulder and saw the guard with the dog walking along the in-processing line, toward the prison's entranceway.

Israel unwrapped the beef sticks from under the counter-top overhang, then with one quick flick of his wrists, he tossed them across the room, where they landed on the floor next to one of the prisoners in the other line.

"Oi!" shouted someone.

The dog yelped. Israel shoved the wrappers in J. J.'s pocket.

"What's going on now?" said Officer Torres, placing the paperwork on the countertop.

The dog had spun around on the officer's leash and was straining to get to the beef sticks.

"What's got into him?" asked Officer Torres.

"Illegal contraband, perhaps?" suggested J. J.

"There's always something," said Officer Torres, flipping through a few more pages.

The dog whined as it attempted to break free from its restraint.

"There's something on the floor!" shouted the guard with the leash.

"Make sure to inspect it, before the dog gets to it!" shouted Officer Torres. "I can't tell you how many times I've seen these dogs eat the evidence."

"He ate it!" shouted the guard.

Officer Torres placed his fist on his forehead and shook his head.

"It looked like beef jerky!" yelled the guard. "Someone must have dropped it."

Officer Torres exhaled and placed both hands on the countertop. "Okay, boys, take your paperwork and come around the counter," he said. "Senhor Teixeira will escort you out of the premises."

CHAPTER TWENTY-TWO

Judah and Israel Join a Traveling Party

Israel and Judah stepped out into the bright early-afternoon light on Rua Marquês de Fronteira. The clouds that had swept into Lisbon the day before had been nudged away by a southerly breeze, and the city was bathed in color again. Teixeira, a diminutive young man with a thin mustache, stood by their side.

"Your brother was in a hurry to leave," said Teixeira, as they watched J. J. sprint down the road and into a side alley.

"He served his time," said Israel.

"It was time well spent …" added Judah. "With us."

"Well, he'll miss out on my technology overview," said Teixeira.

"He clearly had other things on his mind," said Judah.

"Your ankle bracelets have been programmed," said Teixeira. "These are the latest devices that we ended up buying after attending a trade show late last year. State-of-the-art."

"Very nice," said Israel, wishing the man would make his way back into the facility.

"They are fully submersible and can withstand extremely high water pressure," he continued. "Of course, GPS tracking is enabled for the most accurate assessment of your location. German engineered ...”

"Incredibly insightful,” said Israel. "Now, what are the odds that our belongings, which were on the ship, will be sent to this fine institution? As you can see, my brother and I are still in our pajamas.”

"Good question,” said Teixeira.

"Yes?”

"Fair inquiry.”

"Yes ... yes?”

"It’s something we’ve looked into.”

"Okay ...”

"... I’m sure arrangements have been or could be made ...”

"Go on ...”

"I have no idea.”

Israel groaned.

"Not even the slightest hunch?”

"Nope.”

"Not even an inkling about who we might follow up with?”

"Really can’t say,” said Teixeira, glancing at his watch. "Oh my, I am dreadfully late for my next appointment.”

"Well, good riddance.” Judah coughed. "I mean, good afternoon. I’m sure your next detainees are looking forward to receiving such state-of-the-art technology.”

Teixeira pulled out his phone and began typing. "What was that?” he asked. "Anyway, I’m sorry. I have to run. My mother has been having issues with hangnails, and I told her I would take her to the physician. Family! What’s more important than family? Nice meeting you two. And best of luck, wherever you go.”

Teixeira turned to leave, then stopped in his tracks. "And wherever you go, we’ll be watching,” he said, cheerily. "*Até logo!*”

Israel and Judah watched Teixeira scurry away.

"*Até logo!*" parodied Israel under his breath at a loss for a better comeback.

"I thought you handled that well," said Judah.

"A karate kick came to mind," said Israel.

"Very reasonable," said Judah. "It's just that we've barely been out of prison for five minutes, so I appreciate your restraint. I hope to never set foot in there again."

Israel and Judah stared out into the busy street. A Hop-On Hop-Off bus passed by. A young blonde girl stuck out her tongue at them from its passenger-side window.

"Well, where to? You are finally home, and I assume, you know your way around," said Judah.

"How about a café? I'm dying for a proper cup of coffee," said Israel.

"Ditto. Lead the way," said Judah.

"Right," said Israel, pulling out his cell phone. "Thank goodness, they at least returned our wallets, passports and phones."

A black Volkswagen minivan with a green roof and a lighted taxi sign on top pulled to the curb a few feet away from Israel and Judah. The driver rolled down the front passenger-side window. "*Olá!* Awaken Cafe Hostel?" the wiry man in the passenger seat asked.

"Did you say café?" asked Israel.

"Yeah, that's what he said," replied Judah.

"Do you know where it is?" asked the man in a RP English accent.

"No, but we were looking for one," said Israel. "We're desperate for it."

The man leaned back in his seat and turned his head toward the rear of the car. Israel could hear a discussion taking place, although he couldn't make out the specifics. A moment later, he popped his head out the window.

"Okay, come with us," he said. "It's somewhere close by."

Israel turned to Judah and shrugged.

A moment later, they were seated in the minivan. Israel sat in one of the second-row captain's chair seats, behind the man he had spoken to moments earlier. To his left was a woman around his age in high-waisted shorts with sandals. Israel thought she had perhaps come from the beach. Her long legs and face were a distinctly toffee color, and she had a slight but bony nose.

Judah was seated behind Israel on the third-row bench in the back, next to a woman in a strapless beach dress and sandals. She sat cross-legged, and her white dress accentuated her smooth, mahogany skin.

"Are you coming from a pajama party?" asked the man in the passenger seat, inspecting Israel and Judah.

Israel glanced at his pants. *I really wish I had taken a shower.* "Not exactly," he said.

"I'm João," said the man. "João Rocha. But I'm not Portuguese, exactly. My parents are from Angola and moved to the UK when I was three. Some people think I'm from Rio, which I take as a complement. Carnival in Rio is to die for!" João stroked his throat, the fake gems on his rings sparkling in the sunlight.

"I'm Israel, and that's my brother Judah," said Israel.

João looked Israel and Judah up and down.

"Such biblical names. I hope you won't cast judgment on a wayward character like me," said João. "Anyway, this is Maggie." He pointed to the woman sitting next to Israel. "And this is Sahara."

Maggie waved. She seemed to find Israel's appearance amusing.

"You're at least the fourth João we've met on this trip," said Judah.

"Oh, how wonderful." João clapped. "It's a very common name in Portugal. Please tell us more about these Joãos and your choice of attire."

"It's a long story …" started Israel.

"We spent the night in jail," said Judah. "We may as well spill the beans. We were just released. That's why we're wearing pajamas. We didn't have time to gather our belongings. Ironically, it was all on account of a João."

"Wrongly accused, of course," added Israel. "Embroiled in nefarious transnational affairs because of the aforementioned João Abreu."

João's eyes lit up. He placed the tips of his fingers in his mouth, as if trying to contain his excitement.

"How absolutely, positively dreadful," he said, leaning farther over the console separating the two front seats. "How incredibly alluring and fascinating. Two hardened criminals in our midst. Were you handcuffed?"

"We were," said Judah.

"And taken to an all-male facility, I presume?"

"As far as we could tell."

"Blindfolded, perhaps?"

"Not that I recall."

João sighed. "Now you have no choice but to come with us," he said. "Tell us all. Please tell us!"

Fifteen minutes later, the taxi pulled up to an H&M at the Colombo Centre, about four miles northwest of the prison.

"And you did not know the deliveries contained cocaine?" asked João for the third time, opening the passenger-side door of the minivan and stepping outside.

"I had my suspicions about the deliveries, but we absolutely knew nothing about the drugs," said Judah.

"You see," said Israel, ducking his head as he followed Maggie out of the minivan, "we were hired as sailors, and this was part of our duties at ports of call. How could we have known what was inside those boxes and crates?"

"Right," said Judah, following Sahara out of the minivan. "We learned that the drugs were mixed with perfectly legal goods. Clever bastards, if you'll excuse my French, ladies."

"The reality is that we were set up," said Israel. "Only criminals would be so coldhearted as to take advantage of honest sailors. Despite my frustration with the Portuguese judicial system, I have to admit that it's refreshing to see how earnest they are in pursuit of the law. You might say they are vigilant to a fault in pursuing justice. But at least I have confidence now, based on the evidence at hand, that the Portuguese police have only our best interests in mind!"

João put on a wide-brimmed straw sun hat, hooked his arm around Israel's and headed for the mall.

"Okay, so let's focus on fashion," said João. "While I love your flannel PJs and it's adorable that you are wearing a matching set, we need to bring out your personalities. To start, we need more color. Maybe some mixed prints and definitely some accessories."

"We should start by ditching the Velcro sandals and socks," said Sahara.

Israel looked at his feet. "But the arch support these …" he protested.

"We can't possibly walk into a hostel in pajamas," interjected João. "It just wouldn't do."

"I totally agree," said Sahara, "cute as it is to see two brothers in matching outfits."

Israel glanced at Judah and thought he saw him blush.

"Oh, right. I meant to ask about that," said Judah, trying to change the subject. "We got a little carried away with our story. What are you doing in Portugal?"

"We're backpacking through Europe," said Maggie. "It's our gap year."

"Gap year for Maggie and Sahara," corrected João. "I've already completed my certificate as a stylist."

"And you're taking the year off, too?" asked Judah.

João looked over his shoulder at Judah. "Yes and no, sweetheart," he said. "I'm taking a sabbatical. It's part of my quest for self-discovery."

"He had a falling out with the manager of his salon," whispered Sahara to Judah. "Stylistic differences."

"So, you weren't looking for a cafe? You were looking for a hostel?" asked Judah.

"What was that?" asked João.

"When we first met, we thought you were looking for coffee," said Judah.

"Ah!" said João. "No, we were looking to stay at the Awaken Cafe Hostel. It's pet friendly."

Israel looked blankly at João.

"Didn't you notice Samson?" asked João, stopping in his tracks and unzipping his oversized man purse.

Israel and Judah gathered around João and peered into the handbag. There was a teacup size, chocolate-colored, long-haired chihuahua curled up in a ball inside.

"Is it a rat of some sort?" asked Israel.

Judah elbowed him in the side.

"Ow!"

"It's a hamster," said Judah. "I'm sorry, my brother can be a little … *je ne sais quoi*."

"Oh, I see now," said Israel,. "A ferret."

"The more I'm looking at it, I think you may be right," said Judah. "Or perhaps a mink."

João rubbed Samson's back. The dog made a squeaking noise, its eyes fluttering momentarily before they closed.

"It's a chihuahua," said João, smiling.

"There's actually some debate about his origins," said Maggie. "I remember seeing his proof of pedigree paperwork suggesting a cross between a chihuahua and a hairy-legged vampire bat."

"Awww …," cooed Israel, placing his head close to the handbag.

At that moment, the handbag vibrated, and there was a violent snarling sound, followed by a gnashing of teeth. Israel's head was pulled into the handbag by his hair, and the strap yanked him to the side.

"Samson!" shouted João, staggering sideways. "Bad boy! *Bad* boy!"

The handbag shook some more, then abruptly stopped.

"I'm okay," said Israel unsteadily, pulling his head out of João's handbag and placing his arm around Judah's neck. There was a tuft of hair missing.

"Samson!" cried João again. "*Not* nice!"

Maggie covered her mouth, her eyes wide at the spectacle.

"Just a flesh wound, as they say," said Israel.

"I don't see any blood," said Judah. "You're fine."

"I'm *so* sorry," said João. "I don't know what got into him. He must be a little on edge, given how much we've been on the road."

"Perfectly understandable," said Israel, his hair sticking out in several directions.

"Let's take you to the salon first, then we'll go shopping," said João. "Samson, you naughty devil!"

Israel stepped out of the dressing room at H&M with a pleasant but subtle aroma of sandalwood and rosemary. His hair was heavily moussed into a curly quaff, covering the small bald spot on the side of his head, and his previous stubble had been manicured, giving him a rugged but groomed look. Judah stood outside the dressing room wearing a navy-blue wool blazer over a black T-shirt, charcoal skinny jeans and black loafers. He was holding several pairs of pants, assorted shirts, shoes and various accessories that partially obstructed his vision.

"I'm not sure this is my style," said Israel, who was wearing a rainbow-colored knitted vest over a white button-down shirt, tan khakis and brown leather loafers.

"You look fabulous," said João, removing his sunglasses to better analyze Israel's appearance. "The more important question is how do you feel?"

Israel turned and studied himself briefly in the full-length mirror outside the dressing room. "I do feel a little more sophisticated," he conceded. "You know how it is, being away for weeks at sea."

"I can only imagine."

"Not much time to focus on high-society things … fashion, so on and so forth …"

Maggie and Sahara walked over to João. They were holding a small bag apiece.

"What a transformation!" exclaimed Sahara.

"Very English," said Maggie. "Give him a tie, and he'll be ready for term."

"I think they look Portuguese," said Sahara. "Did you say your parents were Portuguese?" she asked, turning to Judah.

"It's a little complicated …" began Judah.

"We came here to trace our Portuguese lineage," said Israel.

"Which goes back a couple weeks," said Judah under his breath.

"And how has that worked out for you?" asked Maggie.

"Well, we've met various members of Portuguese society," said Israel.

"You look Portuguese," said João. "Definitely can pass for Portuguese better than we can."

"In the UK, we're all considered black, even though I have a white Polish father. My mother's from Ghana. Maggie's half-Indian, half-Welsh, and probably something else," said Sahara.

"My mum has family from Scotland, too," said Maggie.

"We've been at the beach the past two weeks, so we're probably looking especially black now," said Sahara.

"The sun suits you," said Judah, who tensed up after he spoke. "Uh, I mean, you look lovely …" He buried his face in his clothes.

"Aw, isn't he sweet!" cried João. "Anyway, I think we are all set. You are coming with us to the hostel, right?"

"Why yes, of course," said Israel. "We need to find accommodations." He thought about the haikus he had sent to M&M. "And perhaps we can make a quick stop to pick up stationery," he said.

"How adorable," said João. "Personalizing your correspondence with your parents."

"Right. And how long were you planning on staying in Lisbon?" asked Israel.

"We don't have definitive plans," said Maggie. "We've just begun our trip. We flew into the Canary Islands, where we spent a couple weeks island hopping before arriving in Portugal just a couple days ago. We were planning on making our way north. Maybe to Finland or Poland. We discussed taking an odd job here or there, but it's not urgent. With all the Brexit craziness, we may not have an opportunity to move about like this in the future."

Samson popped his head out of João's handbag and began pawing his hand.

"Oh, that's our cue," said João. "Samson needs to attend to his business. Are we ready to check out?"

"Are you sure this looks okay?" asked Israel, pulling at his vest.

"Certain of it," said João. "And those jeans really bring out your butt."

CHAPTER TWENTY-THREE

Judah Falls in Love

Chalk it up to Sahara's choice of attire during a stroll along the beach in Cascais on Thursday, nearly a week after Israel and Judah had joined the travelling party. Her black skinny jeans, sandals and oversize long-sleeve sweater that revealed her bare left shoulder … It wasn't the amount of skin that was showing. Israel and Judah had seen more during their first encounter. It was the way she dressed. Her sense of style. Her dark-brown eyes. Her beautiful, abundant hair that created a halo that even Israel could not ignore. It was hair that broadcasted itself as angelic, saintly, beatific.

It was clear to Israel that Judah had lost his mind. *Really, get a grip*, he thought. *Why am I always the rational one? When's the last time I talked such nonsense?*

Israel couldn't deny, however, that his brother was smit ten. He had seen this once before with Judah's past love, Penelope Rodríguez, a charismatic member of the high school cheerleading squad who had bright eyes and a big smile that made up for her short, stocky frame. She too had an interest in cosplay, which in and of itself would have vaulted her to the top of Judah's love list. And she was a woman. It was difficult to find members of the opposite sex in Highland Park who enjoyed cosplay, so Judah immediately took an interest in her. The relationship, sadly for Judah, had only lasted a few weeks during his junior year. She was drawn to a more interesting and accomplished member of the soccer team, who had the potential to play in Division 1, and Judah was cast aside in pursuit of the better option.

Judah had eventually recovered, acting out different romantic scenarios when role-playing with his friends to fill the void in his life. It was awkward—for Israel, at least—to see his brother doting on a partially bearded Kanao while acting as Tanjiro from *Demon Slayer*, but who was he to judge?

Sahara's admission that she, too, enjoyed cosplay from time to time had sealed the deal, and Israel watched with some amusement as Judah went out of his way to demonstrate his gallantry. A rush to open the door here. An innocuous bouquet there. God forbid, a puddle on the sidewalk! Judah was there to guide her around it.

To Israel's surprise, this behavior did not turn Sahara off. She did not flee to the other side of town or smack him in the face with her purse. In fact, she seemed to encourage it, touching him gently on the shoulder or sitting next to him on a loveseat late in the evening to discuss things.

Judah seemed to pay special attention to his appearance, seeking João's advice for applying the right ratio of mousse to his curly hair or tips for managing cuticles. João was thrilled to be of support, serving as a not-so-subtle matchmaker and image consultant. The trip to Cascais the day before had cemented Judah's love and, to his delight, their status as a couple.

This left Israel and Maggie in the somewhat uncomfortable position of needing to spend lots more time together but not sharing the same passions as their traveling companions. Maggie did her best to remain cordial and talk to Israel from time to time when they were alone. Israel, however, did not demonstrate the best conversational skills during these more intimate moments. He was not ready to lose sight of his true love, his original calling to Portugal: M&M.

Israel had been working on drafting poetic letters to M&M on stationery. He was convinced that additional physical letters would bring out his true, beguiling character and wanted to get them just right. He had written more than a dozen letters, many of which were crumpled and scattered about his bed. He wanted to write something more involved than his prison letter this time. He experimented with villanelles, sonnets, anagrammatic poems, ballades, but nothing seemed to hit the mark.

Maggie had come across these letters the night before they went to Cascais and asked Israel who they were for.

"I have been keeping this to myself, and I apologize," said Israel. "I don't mean to give a false impression about my intentions."

Maggie stood in Israel and Judah's bedroom in her nightgown, holding a piece of stationery in her hands. She raised her eyebrow at this comment. "I didn't mean to pry," she said. "João had mentioned that there was extra stationery in the room. I had thought of sending a letter to my mum and dad for a more personal touch."

"No need to apologize," said Israel, magnanimously. "You are more than welcome to have some. I have plenty to go around."

"Are these letters to your girlfriend?" she asked.

"Well, yes and no," said Israel. "That might require a little more explanation. The love is … how should I put it?"

"Unrequited?"

"Right."

"Do you think the letters will make a difference?"

"Why, yes," said Israel, reclining against the wall beside his bed. "I should think so."

"I hope it works out."

"That's very nice of you. I have high hopes."

"Is she a beautiful woman?"

"The most beautiful in the world."

"Is she a kind woman?"

"The kindest known to womankind."

"Is she in a relationship?"

Israel was silent for a moment. "I can't say for sure. I think not."

"Wouldn't it just be easier to meet her in person? Ask her to dinner?"

"I would very much like that, but alas, she is a busy woman. She travels frequently. I'm afraid long-distance correspondence is the best option presently."

Maggie walked over to Israel and handed him the stationery she had in her hand.

"It is a nice poem," she said. "I would be flattered to receive something like this."

On Friday afternoon, João burst into the hostel lounge where everyone was lazing about. Maggie was immersed in *Madame Bovary* and had her legs crossed on an armchair in the corner of the room. Israel was scribbling lines of verse on sheets of stationery in a nearby armchair, trying to master anapestic tetrameter, like in Moore's poem *'Twas the Night Before Christmas*. He was unsuccessful. Judah was lying on a loveseat in the middle of the room, his head on Sahara's lap, his feet dangling over the armrest.

"Ladies, gentlemen, lovers, and seekers!" announced João, as he skipped up to Sahara and Judah. "I have news to share!"

"What tidings bringest thou?" asked Israel.

Sahara laughed. "Please, spit it out, João," she said.

"As it happens," he began, "I was having brunch with Roberto."

"Oh, how was your date?" asked Maggie, shutting her book.

"I don't think we're right for each other." João frowned. "Last night was something special, but no, it's impossible. Did you know he is already seeing two others?"

"You're kidding," exclaimed Maggie.

"I'm so sorry," said Sahara.

"Nothing to worry about, sweethearts," said João merrily. "Anyway, I bumped into another young buck after our brunch. Rómulo Santos. We got to speaking, and I came to discover that he works as an artisan at none other than Sant'Anna!"

Israel glanced at Maggie. He wasn't sure what João was talking about.

"Fábrica Sant'Anna," said João helpfully.

"That doesn't ring a bell," said Judah.

"Fábrica Sant'Anna is a ceramic and tile factory. The oldest in Lisbon. It has been around since 1741. Everything is handmade."

"That's great," said Judah, "but how does it relate to us?"

"That's what I'm getting to," said João. "They have openings for interns. They don't pay much, but they do pay nonetheless, and Rómulo can help make all the arrangements. Isn't this fabulous? We can work at a historic Portuguese tile factory and earn a little extra cash in the process."

The idea of earning extra cash while working in a historic Portuguese factory piqued Israel's interest. He sat up straight in his chair.

"Is this just about Rómulo?" asked Sahara.

"Of course it is, honey," said João. "But it also sounds like great fun, don't you think?"

Sahara rolled her eyes and leaned her head back against the cushion on the loveseat.

"You know, we could use a little extra spending money," said Israel.

"That's true," said Judah. "My Pancake House savings can only take us so far."

"I suppose it could be fun," said Sahara, sighing, "as long as it's just for a short while."

"I agree," said Maggie. "I assume it's just part time."

"No worries. And Maggie, you'll love this," said João. "This is right up your alley."

Israel turned to Maggie. "Are you an artist?" he asked.

"Not just any old doodler, she's an amazing painter and sculptor. She's been accepted into the University of the Arts London. Her work has been displayed at galleries in London, Paris and Berlin," said João. "I'm probably missing other cities."

"New York and Chicago, too," said Maggie. "I think Tokyo, as well. Anyway, It's something I've loved since I was young," she added. "Every time I apply paint on a canvas, I feel like a child, and it's one of the greatest feelings in the world."

"So, take your talents and apply them to Portuguese tiles. You'll be a sensation," said João.

"That's really impressive, Maggie," said Israel. "I've never met a professional artist before."

"It's nothing," said Maggie. "It's not likely I'll make a career of it. I haven't actually decided on my course of study. I was thinking about something a little more practical, like computer science or engineering. My father wouldn't know what to make of a starving artist for a daughter."

"Her father's put a lot of pressure on her to pursue a more traditional degree, even though I think it's rubbish," said Sahara. "She's as smart as they come, though."

"Look who's talking, Ms. Cambridge," exclaimed Maggie.

Judah sat upright on the couch and rubbed his head.

"They're posh," said João seriously.

"Isn't that like the best school in the world?" asked Judah.

"Pretty much," said João. "Unless you're specializing in art, then the University of the Arts London checks that box."

"Wow, I feel unworthy," said Judah, blinking. "I already felt unqualified to be around you two, but now—wow!"

"Oh, stop it," said Sahara, grabbing Judah by the shoulder and pulling him down into her lap. "No, you're not unworthy. You just need to figure things out."

"Yeah, I suppose we do need to figure things out," said Judah.

Israel glanced at his stationery. His cursive was unintelligible. *This isn't working!* he said to himself, shaking his head and crumpling the stationery in his hand. "Anyone interested in getting lunch?" he asked, standing up.

"Did I mention that I have *pasteis de nata*?" asked João, holding up a paper bag. "Anyone up for ..."

Israel and Judah were at his side before he could finish his sentence.

⁓⁓⁓

Later that evening, Israel and Judah were in their bedroom getting ready to head out for dinner. João had made a reservation at A Severa.

"You have to experience authentic fado while in Portugal," he exclaimed.

Judah was wearing an undershirt tucked into his khakis and was holding a button-down dress shirt in each hand.

"Sahara thinks pink brings out my eyes, but I'm not sure," he said, inspecting himself in the small beveled-glass mirror above the dresser.

"Mom's been texting us this past week," said Israel, pulling out his phone. "We should check in."

"Do you think a blazer is necessary? I also have a cardigan ..."

Israel dialed his phone. "Calling Mom."

"What? Wait, do you think that's a good idea? Can't we delay for a bit more?"

"Israel, is that you?" asked a voice over the phone. "What was that about delaying?"

"Hi, Mom, yes, it's Judah and me," said Israel. "We're in Lisbon preparing to head out for dinner. How are you?"

"I'm glad you called," said Ida. "I've been calling you but haven't heard anything in a couple weeks. Judah's phone goes straight to voicemail."

"Ah, yes, his phone was damaged on the ship," said Israel. "We'll take it in at some point."

"I'm just happy to hear your voice. I wanted to make sure you were okay, but by the sound of it, I gather you are," she asked.

"We're great," said Israel. "We met a few backpackers from the UK. Everything's fine. Uneventful."

"Yeah, it's honestly been a little boring," added Judah, settling on the pink button-down shirt. "Just doing the typical touristy stuff."

"Boring? Really?" asked Ida. "I wouldn't have expected that. I suppose your cruise ended well?"

"We had a ..." Israel coughed. "... slight delay during customs, but otherwise, things are going swimmingly."

"Very swimmingly for certain individuals," muttered Judah.

"What was that?" asked Ida. "Can you speak up? I can't hear you that well."

"Everything's great. No need for any monitoring ... I mean, worrying," said Israel hurriedly. "How's Dad?"

"Did I mention that he's working like crazy?" Ida said.

"I recall you saying something along those lines," Israel said.

"As it turns out, he stumbled into a major case involving the Chicago Outfit," said Ida. "One of his defendants was being used as a mule."

Israel had a coughing fit.

"Are you okay?" asked Ida. "You didn't come down with some sort of tropical disease or anything of that sort?"

Israel inhaled deeply and regained his composure. "Went down the wrong pipe," he said meekly. "Nothing to worry about."

"This is a Mediterranean climate, Mom," added Judah. "There aren't tropical diseases here."

"It's a sad case. The boy is clearly not right in the head," said Ida. "The mob was taking advantage of him, having him travel all over the place with narcotics. He finally got caught, and the minute he did, the mafia abandoned him, which is how he ended up needing representation from the public defender's office. It's reprehensible what these criminals will do to people. Especially people as naïve and mentally impaired as Patrick. They caught him at O'Hare with cocaine stashed in the soles of his shoes. He was on his way to Lisbon, coincidentally. That made me think of you. When they opened his luggage, they found six other pairs of shoes with the contraband. The police ended up confiscating over three pounds of cocaine."

Israel and Judah glanced at each other.

"He's going to end up in jail for a long time, I fear," said Ida. "He was set up. I hope your father can make a vigorous defense, but he's worried he doesn't have the time or resources to prove that he was actually a victim of the mob. The boy was coerced."

"That's a highly unusual story," said Israel. "Who would have thought that you could inadvertently get caught up in an international drug trafficking racket?"

"An *extremely* strange story," said Judah, pulling the collar on his shirt. "Gosh, this feels tight. As I was saying, please wish Father all the best. We need to be going soon. We just wanted to say hi."

"All I need is a few minutes of your time to know you're okay," Ida said. "Let's plan to talk next week. Or anytime you feel like calling."

"Of course, Mother," Israel said. "And no need to worry about us. We're street smart. We've got a sixth sense for spotting trouble."

"Where could you possibly have developed street smarts?" asked Ida, who paused, then shouted, "Estephan, are you out of the bathroom yet? Your sons are on the line!" She sighed then, after a moment, said, "Your father's been having indigestion. What am I to do with him? I'll tell him you called. He's been asking about you. Have a lovely evening tonight. Send pictures. Hugs and kisses!"

CHAPTER TWENTY-FOUR

Israel Speaks with a Recovering Addict

Israel had risen early the next day and had decided to take a stroll. It had been some time since he was alone. *To walk in this manner is to think like the great philosophers.*

In his hand he sipped instant coffee from a small plastic cup, which he had made at the hostel. He was ambling southeast along the cobblestone streets of Rua do Arsenal, past graffiti- tagged storefronts, when a man emerged from the recess in a building and hailed him. He wore a blue and white-striped polo and jeans and was deeply tanned.

"I'm afraid I don't speak Portuguese well," said Israel.

"How far is the truck?" asked the man, switching from Portuguese to English.

"The truck?"

"How far?"

Israel looked up and down the narrow road. He noticed the tram line and tracks, and rows of bollards, but no trucks. "Senhor, if I can be candid, this isn't very good," said Israel, pointing to his cup.

"It's no matter," said the man. "I'm used to it."

"There are many better options," Israel said.

"Where'd you get it?"

"From my hostel."

"From your hostel?"

"Yes, they make this available. You see, I'm a little short on cash."

The man rubbed his chin and studied Israel's cup of coffee. He appeared confused. "They hand out methadone at your hostel?" he asked at last.

"Methawhat?" asked Israel.

"For addicts."

"Drug addicts?"

"Yes. Heroin."

"Heroin!"

"Yes, and other opioids."

"Now, look, I don't do drugs. I try to stay away from the whole business."

"Then what are you drinking?"

"Instant coffee."

"In a plastic cup?"

"Yes."

"Why would you do that?"

"That's what we have in the hostel."

"There are so many better options. Portugal is famous for its coffee!"

"Yes, I know. Perhaps I should buy a cup of coffee."

"You know that caffeine is a drug."

"Well, sure …"

"So don't be one to judge. The government provides methadone clinics to the public. It has proven to reduce harm."

"Is that so?"

"I have not used a needle in over two years."

"That is progress!"

"I thought that you had come from a methadone mobile clinic close by."

"I'm afraid not."

"Well, in that case, let me show you where to find coffee. My name is Jorge," said the man, extending his hand.

"Israel," he said, shaking Jorge's hand.

"What are you doing here? Backpacking?"

"Trying to reconnect with my ancestors. It has been an interesting journey so far."

"An uncommon name for the Portuguese," said Jorge, leading Israel down the road. "Where are you from? South Africa? England?"

"Chicago. In the United States."

"I've never left Portugal. I've hardly gone outside Lisbon."

"There's a whole world out there."

"For me, Lisbon has been my world."

"Did you ever want to get out of the city?"

Jorge reached for Israel's shoulder and squeezed it. "It is a sad story. I don't want to impose."

"You must go on, *Senhor*," said Israel, curious to learn of the man's misfortune.

"So be it," said Jorge, leading Israel down the road and a roundabout. "Many years ago, when I was much younger, around your age, I was in love with Claudia Alves, the most beautiful woman in all of Lisbon."

"Was she a fashion model?" asked Israel.

"No, fashion models were not common then," said Jorge. "But she could have easily graced the covers of any fashion magazine you might see today. She had eyes like emeralds and luscious brown hair that flowed across her shoulders like the tailfeathers of a bird of paradise. Her skin was pure alabaster, and her lips were plump slices of strawberry. She was the crown jewel of Graça, a neighborhood of Lisbon, and she was, remarkably, betrothed to me."

"You were engaged?"

"We were indeed engaged, and I was the happiest man in the world. She made my heart swell and my ambitions grow. Shortly after our engagement, I enrolled in a vocational school to study pharmaceuticals. I had come from modest means, but I was determined to move up in society. I was committed to giving Claudia the best life possible."

"There must be some twist to this story?" asked Israel.

"As I alluded to up front, this is a sad story," said Jorge. "Just as I was about to begin my studies, my father came down with a mysterious ailment causing him to have seizures. Being the youngest of three children, and the only one not to have children yet to raise, I decided to postpone my studies to look after my father. Claudia was supportive, of course, and acquitted herself well as a nurse. But as the months went by, his condition deteriorated, and I found myself more and more consumed with his health at the expense of spending time with Claudia. My mother was overwhelmed with his daily needs, and I was afraid she would have a nervous breakdown. Soon, a year had passed, my father's condition had yet to improve, and Claudia and I were no closer to matrimony than the day I proposed.

"Idle time is the devil's playground, and my increased estrangement from Claudia created an opportunity for other suitors. I'm ashamed to think that I neglected her during this time. She was always ready to help, but as time went by, I shunned it.

"'Could this be me?' I asked myself. 'Could this be what I become as I age?'"

"I was terrified at the thought of becoming an invalid. I was terrified that Claudia would see me in him. I was terrified that she would reject me. And because of this fear, I allowed Bruno Metrass to enter the scene. I created the conditions for a self-fulfilling prophecy."

"Did you say Metrass?" asked Israel.

"During my extended absence, Bruno, a rising star in the Judiciary Police, began to court Claudia. I was not aware of this at the time, and I can only presume that she rejected his overtures in the beginning. But my absence from Claudia had taken its toll, and after fourteen months of neglect, Claudia returned my engagement ring.

"'This is not meant to be, Jorge,' she told me one evening. 'I have agreed to marry Bruno. We are to be wed in three weeks' time.'

"And so, she married Bruno. As fate would have it, one week after her wedding ceremony, my father died. Two months later, my mother succumbed to a broken heart. They were buried, side-by-side, in a small graveyard overlooking the city."

"An unbearable tragedy!" exclaimed Israel.

"It was unbearable, yes, which is what led me into a different kind of pharmaceutical," Jorge explained. "Alcohol was not strong enough to drown my sorrows, so I began to experiment with harder drugs. Years went by, Bruno and Claudia were happily married with children, and yet I was stuck in a spiral of depression. I began to live on the streets and was in and out of prison and drug treatment centers. My whole life pivoted on this one event. It shouldn't have. My siblings couldn't understand what I had become. I became comfortable with commiserating with the most wretched people. I sought them out.

"Meanwhile, Bruno had risen, after many years, to Deputy Director of the Judiciary Police. He had become, once again, my arch nemesis. A crusader against addicts and traffickers. He was my personal persecutor, and I found myself always on the run. A vagabond, unmoored from respectable society. A loser. A failure."

"You are too hard on yourself," said Israel, grasping his hand. "You are a tragic figure, yes, but all is not lost."

Jorge stopped and pointed at a small café with outdoor seating. "They have good coffee there. And if you are hungry for breakfast, you can walk over to the Time Out Market. It is popular with tourists."

"But what about today? What is it that you do?" asked Israel.

"Today, I'm in recovery. I've met a kind woman. We live together as partners, both recovering from a difficult past."

"And do you love her?" Israel asked.

"It's affection of a different nature," Jorge said. "Not the passionate love of my youth. But a respectful sort of camaraderie that develops with age."

"Are you happy?"

"I'm at peace," he said Jorge. "So many years have been wasted, but I don't attempt to run against the tide, anymore. The wheel of time keeps turning, and with it, I go."

CHAPTER TWENTY-FIVE

Israel Sees the Most Beauteous

Israel had to admit that the couple of euros spent on a *galão*, a Portuguese version of the latte, was preferable to the instant coffee he had made earlier. So much so that he ordered it again and again.

Soon, an hour had passed in the café, and he was brimming with ideas.

"I mailed one letter, but without a return receipt I have no idea if it was received by my beloved," he muttered to himself at a small table in the corner of the café. "But sitting here, a lover pining away, I feel overwhelmed with the conviction that, like troubadours of old, my sonorous odes will claim the heart of the one and only."

Jorge's story had struck a chord with him, and he felt waves of emotion wash over him. He had asked him to join him at the café, but Jorge had kindly refused.

"So much has transpired over the past few weeks," Israel continued speaking to himself. "A connection to my heritage, an awakening of passion, an inspiration for action. What I have learned, as evidenced by the tragic tale of *Senhor* Jorge, is that our hearts should never be suppressed. I must let the world know of my adoration!"

A waitress passed by, and Israel pointed to his mug.

"*Mais uma, por favor*," Israel said, the Portuguese flowing from his tongue. "I am nearly fluent. The language of my lover was but a dormant flame that needed kindling."

"Are you an actor?" asked a gray-haired woman who was seated at a table nearby.

Israel nearly jumped out of his seat. The coffee had made him jittery.

"An actor, did you say?" Israel asked.

"Are you reciting lines from a play?" she asked. "I'm not familiar with it."

"You should try to enunciate," said a man across the table from her, without glancing up from his newspaper.

Israel blinked. He had not noticed the other patrons of the café.

"All the world's a stage …" began Israel, although he couldn't remember the rest of the lines.

"Go on," encouraged the woman.

"It's a simple story," said Israel. "About a man on a quest to find his true love."

"A universal theme," said the man.

"Perhaps it's the *Romance of the Rose*?" asked the woman.

"It's similar, but different," said Israel automatically, although he wasn't sure why. He wasn't familiar with the *Romance of the Rose*. "This is a modern tale of an extraordinarily handsome man, who is travelling with his brother."

"The brother, I assume, is there for comic relief?" the man asked, flipping a page of his newspaper.

"Of course, the most comical of characters. Short, squat, intellectually inferior."

"And who is the hero's object of affection?" the woman asked.

"Ahh! This is none other than the princess of Portugal, the most beautiful damsel in the world. But enemies, including the Portuguese government, stand in their way."

"What do they do to them?" asked the woman.

"Terrible things," Israel lamented. "Jealous government officials capture them and throw them into the deepest dungeon. The hero is shackled and chained to the wall. He can withstand the pain and the darkness, but the cries from his brother drive him mad. In a fit of rage, he manages to break free from his bondage, and together with his brother they fight their way out of the dungeon. Soon they are riding royal stallions across the plain where they come upon a tower where his beloved is kept. 'Maria Maia, Maria Maia, let down your hair!' he says."

"This sounds like *Rapunzel*," said the man.

Israel thought about this for a moment. He had seen *Tangled*. "There are some parallels," Israel admitted. "Although in this case, Maria Maia's hair is brown."

"Does the hero encounter a witch? In *Rapunzel*, the hero is blinded after coming across her," said the man.

"That is where the similarities end," Israel said. "But he does encounter bandits, who attempt to kidnap his beloved."

"Unsuccessfully I assume?" asked the woman.

"Our hero's goal cannot be thwarted," Israel pronounced proudly. "Although the bandits greatly outnumber them, they are no match for the ferocity of our hero."

"And in conclusion, the audience sees them riding away into the sunset, I presume?" asked the man.

"Exactly. This play is both logical and a crowd-pleaser," Israel said.

"I can see why," said the man. "A bit formulaic, though."

"I think it's lovely," said the woman. "And where are you performing?"

"Performing?"

"What theater?" she asked.

"I am performing at the ..." Israel paused for dramatic effect. "... at the Public Theater."

"How wonderful," said the woman.

The waitress walked over to Israel's table and handed him another *galão*.

"If we had more time in Lisbon, we would love to explore the theater district," she said, standing up. "But we are leaving for Porto this afternoon. Best of luck with your dramatic endeavors."

"*Adieu*," said the man, rising and placing a handful of coins on the table.

"*Adeus*," Israel said.

Israel left the café an hour later, his heart swelling with possible amorous scenarios. *Sure, there had been some travails, but I am now finally able to reach out and grab the destiny I so richly deserve. This land has called me home.*

He wandered around central Lisbon and soon found himself under rainbow-colored umbrellas that hung over Rua Cor de Rosa, otherwise known as Pink Street, because the pavement had been painted pink. A crowd had formed outside a restaurant, and there were cameramen and photographers, as if the entire scene was being staged.

Curios, Israel edged forward. He could not tell what exactly the crowd was buzzing about, but when a soccer ball flew up in the air, the crowd erupted.

"It's him!"

"Patrício!"

"A legend!"

Israel tapped a man on the shoulder.

"What's all the fuss?"

"The fuss?" repeated the man, incredulous. "It's João Patrício!"

"Another João?"

"He's a football icon. Don't you know?"

"I've never been that into soccer," said Israel, immediately regretting the obvious misstep.

"Psh!" exclaimed the man in disgust. "Then you're in the wrong country."

"Is he doing a photoshoot, or something," asked Israel, quickly changing the subject.

The man ignored him and pushed his way further into the mass of people congregated in the center of the street. Israel turned to leave, but when he heard the crowd erupt in cheers again, he spun around. About fifty feet away was a man standing on an outdoor table in the middle of the street.

"We love you Patrício!"

"You're so beautiful!"

João blew a kiss to the crowd, then bowed. In his right hand, he held a letter.

"Is it time?" someone asked.

"Will he do it?" asked another.

"What in the world is going on?" Israel asked out loud.

Israel found something about João Patrício off-putting. Perhaps it was his chiseled jawline or his curly blonde locks of hair. He found his smile vexing, although he couldn't say why. He disliked his designer jeans and his shirt, which seemed to reveal more chest than necessary.

Despite these misgivings, he was more curious than before to see what was going to happen. João Patrício kept waving and blowing kisses to the crowd. Out of the corner of Israel's eye, he saw two women in trench coats and sunglasses squeeze through the crowd. He thought they looked familiar.

A moment later, the crowd exploded in excitement. João Patrício held his arms out as if ready to embrace someone.

"Oh my god! It's her!"

"They're both here!"

The crowd was beginning to swell. Israel squeezed his way forward.

"Ladies and gentlemen!" shouted João Patrício.

Israel pushed his way toward the front of the crowd.

"Ladies and gentlemen!" João Patrício said again, and this time, a hush fell over the assembled people.

Israel was now standing behind a row of cameramen, who were kneeling as they filmed the soccer player. Israel could not see the woman the crowd had gushed about. He thought she might be behind the two bodyguards, who were standing in the center of the street, not far from João Patrício.

"Today, I have something to say," he began.

"Please tell us!" someone cried.

"Hear me loud and clear!" shouted João Patrício as he read from the letter. "Nothing can hold me back! My true love, I know there is nothing that can keep us apart."

Israel frowned. A woman to his left appeared to faint.

"I came to this land, riding a stallion named love," he continued.

"Now hold on a second," Israel said under his breath.

"Even in the darkest night your visage is clear and bright in my mind's eye," said João Patrício. "You are my north star, my lighthouse as I approach from rough waters. You are the reflection of the divine. You are the essence of virtue. And here I declare, knowing that while we've been separated, going forward, as fate has foretold, we are to be together, betrothed, my dearest, most lovely, Maria Maia Coelho."

João Patrício tossed the letter into the crowd and then bent to one knee. He pulled out an engagement ring, which even from a distance sparkled in the dappled sunlight.

Israel felt lightheaded. *This cannot be!* he thought. *This cannot possibly be my beloved. The most beauteous?*

A woman stepped forward, taking off her trench coat and sunglasses. Israel felt a lump form in his throat. His eyes began to water.

"Oh my god!" he cried, pushing his way past the cameramen and approaching her. "It's you! It's really you!"

"Hey!" shouted someone in the crowd. "Get out of there!"

"Maria Maia!" shouted Israel. "My beloved."

"Er … who's this?" asked João Patrício, still on one knee, with the engagement ring in the palm of his hand.

"I've been searching for you," Israel said. "This whole time, I've been searching for you."

He couldn't believe what he was seeing. M&M was there, steps away from him, in a simple red summer dress. Her hair was pulled up in a bun. *The most beauteous,* he thought. *Are my eyes deceiving me?*

M&M looked at Israel, and for the first time there was an unspoken connection. A man. A woman. An admirer. A supermodel. He felt time slowing down. *This moment. This moment is my everything.*

M&M's expression darkened. She shook her head from side to side, then turned to João Patrício. "I have absolutely no idea who this nutjob is," she said

"Get him out of here!" someone shouted from the crowd.

Israel took a step forward. "But it's me?" squeaked Israel, feeling lightheaded.

"Loser!" shouted someone.

"Jerk!" shouted another person.

Israel felt something squishy pelt him on the side of the head. A sandwich landed near his shoe.

M&M turned her back to him and placed her arms over her chest. She mouthed something to João Patrício, then rushed toward him. A bodyguard approached Israel.

"I do!" she cried. "I very much do!"

CHAPTER TWENTY-SIX

Israel Blacks Out and Then Has a Dream

Israel ran. He ran from Rua Cor de Rosa like a wounded bear, shoving people out of his way as he sped toward the river.

A woman shouted at him. He thought he heard her call his name, but it wasn't coming from M&M, and nothing else mattered. He was numb with shock.

"He used my words!" he cried. "He used *my* words!"

He ran away from the pink street and up the cobblestone alleyway to Rua do Alecrim. He ran through the roundabout, nearly hitting one of the touristy tuk-tuks, and across the busy road where city buses queued. In Jardim de Roque Gameiro, he ran through litter from an overflowing receptacle and then clipped the back of a parked electric scooter, nearly tripping in the process. He ran past couples sitting on park benches until he finally reached the seawall overlooking the River Tagus.

He stumbled, nearly falling headfirst into the water, but gripped the seawall just in time to balance himself. He grasped the cold concrete, his eyes wide with dismay.

"He stole her from me!" he shouted. "The bastard stole her with my words!"

Israel panted and stared at the dark blue water below. "She was so beautiful," Israel lamented. "A vision."

He exhaled and ran his fingers through his hair. The water seemed inviting. It was getting hot, oppressive, and he thought for the briefest moment that he could end it all there.

You're in the wrong country, rang the rebuke of the man in the crowd. *You're a nutjob,* rang the more painful rebuke from M&M. *What am I doing here? Why am I here?*

"My hopes, my dreams!" he cried. "These are all profane to me! All nonsense!"

He saw a fisherman in a rowboat, and the image of the River Styx came to mind. Israel shook his head from side to side.

"How did he get my letter?" he asked.

It was obvious. M&M was a celebrity. She consorted with other celebrities. Famous people received fan mail. Hundreds of letters perhaps, and Israel was just one of the many attention seekers looking for affirmation that they weren't as insignificant as they feared.

"I'm a nobody," he bemoaned. "An afterthought."

He kicked a nearby loose stone. "Was I even a thought?" he asked. "Did she have any idea who I was?"

He stood up straight and began walking along the river. *These mosaic cobblestones, these* calçada portuguesa, *have such purpose, such intentional design. What is my purpose? What am I to do now?*

Israel rubbed his eyes. "Stupid allergies," he mumbled.

Everywhere around him there appeared to be lovers. A man and a woman held hands as they walked by. A young boy was having a picnic with a young girl. A pigeon cooed and chased another pigeon across the cobblestones.

Israel felt heavy. The effects of the caffeine had worn off and he was exhausted.

"There's such a weight on my shoulders," he said to no one in particular.

He tottered, feeling lightheaded. A boy zoomed by on a bike, and he staggered to the side.

"I need to rest," he said. "I need time to recover from this."

A fishmonger was selling the catch of the day in a pushcart.

"*Sardinhas*!" he exclaimed. "*Peixe-Espada-Preto*!"

Israel glanced at the scabbard fish with glassy eyes and razor-sharp teeth. "It's heinous!" he yelled.

Israel saw the world spinning around him. "I'm that fish!" he shouted. "A repulsive, reject of the sea!"

"Are you all right?" someone asked him.

Israel swayed, the world spun, then everything went black.

Israel stood at the edge of a livestock pond. A gentle breeze blew across the surrounding field and rustled the hair on the back of his neck.

"You're not an ass," said someone nearby.

Israel turned his head and saw a herd of donkeys approaching. There were seven or eight of them, and the leader was several paces ahead. It grunted.

"I feel like one," said Israel. "I feel like I'm the biggest ass in the world."

The donkey shook its head from side to side as it walked. "You're really not an ass," it repeated. "Look at the pond."

Israel looked down at his reflection in the pond. A sandy-brown mule stared back at him. He blinked. The mule blinked.

"Oh. I see," said Israel.

"You're not part of this herd," said the donkey. "You're a mule."

"Right."

"But you're also not an ass."

"Got it. You mentioned that already."

"What I mean," said the donkey, "is that you're not a dumbass. You fell in love. It happens."

"But it hurts. I feel foolish."

A white stallion approached the watering hole. "Hormones," said the stallion. "The mares go mad when they see me."

"I wish I could say the same," said Israel.

"You're not a horse," said the stallion. "You're a hybrid."

"What does that have to do with love?" asked the donkey.

The donkey herd was now drinking from the pond.

"Nothing … and everything," said the stallion.

"That makes no sense," said the donkey.

"His beloved is Portuguese. It's hard to connect with someone who's from a different culture, who speaks a different language."

"But not impossible," said the donkey.

"No, not impossible," said the stallion. "But us Andalusians prefer other Andalusians. Can you imagine me courting a Shetland Pony?"

"It would be odd," admitted the donkey.

"It's better to stop pretending, because otherwise you will never be accepted for who you are," said the stallion.

"But who I am is undesirable," said Israel.

"Undesirable to whom?" asked the stallion.

"Undesirable to my M&M," said Israel.

"Nonsense," said the stallion.

"Nonsense," agreed the donkey.

"If you're undesirable to your M&M, then you have the wrong love object!" said the stallion.

"You're not an ass," said the donkey.

CHAPTER TWENTY-SEVEN

Israel Has a Revelation

Israel heard noises, people speaking. He felt something wet on his cheek and groaned.

"I'm not an ass," he mumbled. "I'm not an ass."

"He's coming to!"

"He's waking up!"

"He'll need to pay for this!"

He opened his eyes and for a moment everything was blurry.

Israel's vision came into focus, and he saw a woman kneeling over him, waving a fan over his face. She had hazel eyes that were wide with concern.

"An angel?" said Israel under his breath.

"What was that?" someone asked.

"Is that you M&M?"

The woman backed away. "Israel, it's me, Maggie."

"Maggie?" he asked.

"Are you okay?" she asked. "You took a nasty fall. We weren't far away."

"Of course, you're not M&M," said Isarel, regaining his bearings.

He looked to his side and noticed that he was lying on a pile of fish. Samson, the chihuahua, was licking his forehead.

"We received a call from the detective," said Judah.

Israel looked up and saw his brother, Sahara, João, the fishmonger and Detective Metrass standing over him.

"What's she doing here!" cried Israel, pointing at the detective. "And, I thought your phone was broken?"

"Had that fixed," said Judah. "The detective called me about fifteen minutes ago. We were in the area. What happened to you?"

"I don't know …" he began.

"Let me explain," said Detective Metrass. "Let me explain the letter."

Israel felt a surge of heat course through him.

"As you can tell, the Judiciary Police delivered the letter to Maria Maia," said Detective Metrass. "It's not our business to prosecute delusions so long as it's not a crime."

"Let's be kind," said Maggie.

"I mean no offense," said the detective. "I really don't. I say this not as a member of law enforcement, but as a friend of Maria Maia."

"A friend?" asked Israel.

"You know her?" added Judah.

"I've known her for years," said Detective Metrass. "We used to work together."

"You used to work with M&M?" asked Israel.

"I knew you looked familiar!" said Judah. "You were a model too, weren't you?"

"Oh my god, I recognize you as well," said João. "You were in the RTP television series *Bem-Vindos a Beirais*!"

"I was," admitted Detective Metrass. "When I was a teenager, I worked for Fabian de la Fontaine at Ford Models. I was featured in commercials, magazines and even had a role or two on television."

"Could I get your autograph?" asked Judah, pulling out a pen and pocket notepad.

"This isn't the time for that!" scolded Sahara.

"It was at Ford Models that I met Maria Maia, who you refer to as M&M," said Detective Metrass. "But modeling wasn't for me. The industry is, and I say this with all due respect for Maria Maia … the industry is exploitive. I grew to detest it."

"Perfectly understandable," said João. "I've dabbled in modeling from time to time as well."

"It was too much for me, so I decided to attend university, where I studied law," she continued. "My father, you see, was a senior official at the Judiciary Police, which was how I ended up as a detective. Your case, Israel and Judah, was of particular interest to me because of the connection to Maria Maia. At first, I thought you were creeps, if I can be honest."

"No offense taken," said Judah.

"Well, maybe just a smidgen," said Israel, sitting up.

"You have a sardine attached to your head," said Maggie, gingerly picking it off and tossing it away. Samson ran after it.

"After a while, I realized that you were being used as mules by international drug traffickers," said Detective Metrass. "This made me much more concerned for her safety. We needed to protect her. I was terrified that your obsession with her would attract the mafia. That she would end up embroiled with gangsters."

"I don't suppose you were concerned about us?" asked Israel.

There was an awkward silence.

"Well, I've been extremely concerned about your well-being!" said Maggie, hotly.

"I'm very sorry about what happened just now," said Detective Metrass. "I was accompanying Maria Maia to Rua

Cor de Rosa. João Patrício had been planning the secret engagement for weeks and had asked me to bring her there on the pretense of meeting for breakfast. What I was not aware of was that he had your letter in his possession … that he would read it line for line. I had inspected the letter before it was mailed, as our protocol in the Judiciary Police demands, and was shocked to hear him use your words."

"So was I," said Israel.

"That's awful!" exclaimed Maggie.

"A low blow," added Judah.

Israel flicked off the tail of a scabbard fish that was on his shoulder.

"Would you like me to speak with Maria Maia?" asked Detective Metrass. "Your letter had such an impact on her."

Israel stared at the detective. *This is an opportunity to right a wrong*, he thought. *How ironic. My captor is now my liberator.*

"I must have hit my head hard, because in just a matter of minutes, my whole world view has changed," said Israel. "I feel reborn."

"What do you mean?" asked Detective Metrass.

Israel glanced at Maggie. *What did I really see in M&M? It's not like she's the only beautiful woman in the world. And how do we define beauty, anyway? She never even spoke with me!*

"It wasn't the letter that won her heart," said Israel. "Although, you have to admit, I do have a way with words."

"You're a blabbermouth," said Judah.

"M&M was already in love with *Senhor* Patrício," said Israel, ignoring Judah. "It was obvious by her reaction to the proposal."

"That's true," agreed Detective Metrass.

"I assume he didn't need to read a love letter for her to agree to marry him," said Israel. "The recitation of my letter was for dramatic effect. He's a stallion."

"A what?" asked Detective Metrass.

"I was shocked, to be clear," said Israel, rubbing his head. "Could it be considered plagiarism? I suppose so. Although it wasn't copyrighted. I didn't have that opportunity while in prison."

"You spent one night in jail," said Detective Metrass.

"Nevertheless, my dark shadow of ignorance has been replaced with a remarkable lucidity," said Israel. "The absurdities, the illusions, they are gone. I know now that M&M is not and was never meant to be with me. Although I find this clarity more than a bit painful—seriously, my head hurts—I feel liberated at the same time."

"Glad we cleared this up," said Judah. "Can we go to the beach now?"

"Judah! Your brother's been injured!" admonished Sahara.

"His heart's been broken," added João.

"I actually think a stroll along the beach would be nice," said Israel, standing up.

"Perhaps after a shower?" suggested Maggie.

"And after you pay me for the damages caused by this crazy man!" said the fishmonger.

"I bid you adieu, Detective Metrass," said Israel magnanimously. "There are no hard feelings. They are pliable and able to bend with the wheel of time. Let's pay this honorable vendor his dues."

Israel looked at his companions. They stared back.

"Okay, let me see what I have in my wallet," said Israel hurriedly.

He pulled out a handful of euro banknotes and handed them to the fishmonger.

"Oh, and one last question, Detective Metrass, if you don't mind?" asked Israel.

"Yes."

"Would your parents happen to be Bruno and Claudia Metrass?"

CHAPTER TWENTY-EIGHT

Israel and Maggie Get Separated from the Tour Group

On Saturday afternoon, Judah led Israel, Sahara, Maggie and João to Praça do Comércio for a tour of Lisbon.

"This will be a nice change of pace," Judah said. "A little sightseeing."

"I've never been on a segway," said Sahara.

"They're ridiculous-looking contraptions," protested Israel.

"Since when do you care about public perceptions?" asked Judah. "It's hilly around here."

"I prefer more traditional forms of transportation, such as horseback riding," said Israel. Judah shuddered.

"We're tourists," said Sahara. "There's no reason to pretend otherwise."

"Don't these segways remind you of the police back home?" said Israel. "Patrolling the streets of Chicago?"

"I saw a couple officers zooming through the Dunkin' drive-through lane once," said Judah. "Incredible balancing act with the coffee and munchkins."

"I prefer to think of you as outlaws on segways," said João.

"It must have been frightening to be in prison," said Maggie.

Israel thought about this for a moment. "For me, no," said Israel. "I barely noticed it. But Judah on the other hand …"

"Er, what?"

"I had to console him," said Israel. "Had me sing to him."

"Aww, that's so sweet," said Sahara.

"He was petrified," Israel added.

"I think that's our tour guide, Carlos," said Judah. "I recognize him from the photos online."

"Looks like there are a few segway tours gathering near the statue," said João.

"This is a surprisingly popular activity," said Israel.

"The tours sell out quickly," said Judah.

Carlos waved them down. "Judah Cruz?" he shouted, approaching them. "Yes, party of six," said Judah.

Carlos appeared confused.

"Five people, one chihuahua," said João, extracting Samson from his purse.

"Ah, yes. the dog," said Carlos. "Normally it's against company policy, but we made an exception. Is this your first time in Portugal?"

"For them, yes," said João. "I have some family here. I used to come to Lisbon from time to time as a kid."

"Welcome, welcome!" said Carlos. "How have your accommodations been?"

João, Sahara and Maggie looked at Israel and Judah.

"A little austere," said Israel. "At least, on our first night in Lisbon."

"Austere?"

"Anyway, are we waiting for anyone else?" asked Judah.

"No, we have everyone here now," said Carlos, who pointed to another couple. "We also have Erik and Alva, from Sweden."

They waved from their segways.

"Have you ridden a segway before?" asked Carlos.

"This is new to us all," said Sahara.

"No problem. Let me show you how this works," said Carlos, glancing at Israel. "Would you come with me, please?"

"Me?" asked Israel.

"Yes, let me show you how, and the others can follow along," he said.

Israel walked toward a segway near the statue. A bicycle helmet hung from its handlebars.

"The segway's been turned on and is ready to go," said Carlos. "If you don't mind, please put on the helmet, then step onto the segway."

"Does this activity require any skill at all?" asked Israel, grabbing the helmet. "It seems like we're automating everything nowadays."

"There is skill required," said Carlos. "It can take some getting used to."

Israel grasped the segway's handlebars and stepped on the platform. He began to spin in place.

"Hold on. Let me show you how to use it," said Carlos.

Israel spun faster. "I think I'm getting the hang of this," said Israel, leaning in, which caused the segway to lurch forward and nearly collide with the Swedish couple. He spun down the plaza for about fifty feet, before finally adjusting his pressure on the handlebars and standing upright. The segway came to a stop.

"That's one way to ride," said Carlos, chuckling nervously. "You can come back now."

Israel spun back to the group.

"I feel like I might tip over," said Sahara, attempting to maintain her balance on the segway.

Israel staggered off his segway.

"The segway will automatically balance, so no need to worry," said Carlos. "You steer by moving the handlebars sideways. But don't overdo it, otherwise you'll, um, spin."

"Are we going to stop at any of the shops along the way?" asked Erik.

"We'll visit a chocolate factory on Rua das Flores," said Carlos. "If you see an interesting shop and would like to briefly stop by, let me know. In the highly unlikely event we get separated, we meet back here in two hours. Okay? Ready?"

"Ready," said Judah.

"Can't wait," said João.

"Follow me!"

Carlos led the group in single file across the plaza and onto Avenida Ribeira das Naus. The road was congested, and they had to weave around pedestrian and vehicle traffic the farther west they went. Israel lagged near the back of the line, ahead of Maggie who was taking videos from her phone.

"I think this darned thing is malfunctioning," said Israel, leaning in. "It won't accelerate anymore."

"What's that?" asked Maggie.

Israel bent over and stomped on the segway's powerbase.

"There's got to be something wrong with the wiring," he muttered, banging the steel frame with his fist.

The segway spun like a dreidel around a yellow Fiat 500 and into the oncoming lane. A taxi slammed on its brakes and blared its horn.

Israel looked up at the driver, who shouted at him through the driver's side window.

"It's not me, it's the segway!" retorted Israel, navigating it onto the sidewalk. "Now where did they go?"

A few seconds later his segway came sputtering to a halt. Israel kicked the wheels and attempted to lean forward and back, but it would not budge.

"What's going on, Israel?" asked Maggie, pulling up to his side.

"My segway's broken."

"Did they go around the corner?"

"Must have. How about we walk for a bit and see if we can catch up with them?"

"Sure. It's a beautiful day."

They parked their segways next to a group of electric scooters and followed the general flow of foot traffic down the cobblestone sidewalk.

"London has a reputation for gloom," said Maggie. "It's often overcast."

"Chicago has a reputation for wind," said Israel. "Although, there's some debate about the origin of the nickname."

"I'm happy to be in sunny Portugal," said Maggie. "Or you might say, I'm sunny in happy Portugal."

"There really is something enchanting about this county," said Israel.

"It's the people," said Maggie.

They exchanged a brief glance.

"So …" Israel cleared his throat and placed his hands in his trouser pockets. He suddenly felt self-conscious.

"Right."

"It really is sunny here."

"It is."

"That big, bright ball in the sky."

"Uh huh."

"Yellow."

"An apt descriptor."

Israel began whistling "Don't Worry, Be Happy."

"How about a gelato?" said Maggie a minute later, grabbing his shirt sleeve and pulling him toward a *gelataria* by the river.

"What is the difference between ice cream and gelato?" asked Israel.

"Don't know," said Maggie. "But I'm a fan of both."

They entered a historic brown building with decorative half timbering on the exterior. Inside, the design was more modern, and it appeared to be more of a mixed-use establishment that included gelato and a restaurant.

"They sure know how to maximize this space," said Israel, picking up a menu from the bar near the gelato display case.

"So many choices," said Maggie.

"I wouldn't be opposed to a cold *cerveja*," said Israel, proud of his linguistic abilities.

"I'll take *framboesa*," said Maggie to the server. "Raspberry."

Israel placed the menu on the countertop and looked at the gelatos on display. "I've never seen such a bright blue color," said Israel.

"One raspberry and one blue caramel coming up," said the server.

"Wait!" said Israel, glancing at Maggie. "But sure, why not?"

"Looks good!" she said. "Let's grab a seat outside."

They made their way to the patio, where they sat down at a vacant table overlooking the Tagus River. A sailboat drifted past.

Maggie pulled out a pair of square-framed sunglasses and put them on.

"I've been working on a vlog," said Maggie. "To document our travels. João's extremely photogenic. I think he believes he's part of the Fab Five."

"Unbelievable!" said Israel. "I was working on one as well."

"Oh yes, I know all about it!" said Maggie.

"Judah, huh?"

"He became quite animated describing the downstream effects of the videos."

A server brought over their cups of gelato and placed them on the table.

"I think it's rather charming, though," said Maggie. "I watched most of your videos."

"Did you really?" mumbled Israel with a mouthful of gelato.

"They were heartfelt," said Maggie.

Israel felt his cheeks flushing. He pulled out a small tube of suntan lotion from his trouser pocket and dabbed his face. The subsequent white streaks, combined with the reddening cheeks and the blue lips gave him the appearance of using greasepaint. Maggie smiled.

"Israel Cruz, I really must say that you are unlike anyone I've ever met!" she exclaimed.

"I'm afraid that's how I ended up on this trip," said Israel. "I've got such an unusual heritage."

"Well, regardless of how you came here, I'm glad that you are here," said Maggie.

She licked her index finger and gently rubbed the lotion on his face so it blended in.

"Maggie, do you still plan to spend the next few months traveling throughout Europe?" asked Israel.

"There, that looks better now," said Maggie, studying Israel's face.

"Thanks."

"I'm not sure what our plans are," said Maggie. "They seem to change from day to day."

"It's interesting how traveling forces you to get out of your comfort zone," said Israel. "To rely on strangers. To meet new people, because everything is unfamiliar and new."

"Growing up in London, you can meet people from all over the world," said Maggie. "But at the same time, England is a small country, almost like a giant suburb, and it can be insular at times. That's why we planned this trip. We needed to get out."

"I suppose that's what I'd been missing with my studies," said Israel. "Geography isn't meant to be learned from a textbook. It's meant to be lived. To be experienced outside."

"From a cargo ship no less!"

Israel looked out at the river. "There really is a whole world to discover," he said. "There's a part of me that can see myself doing this forever."

"Why stop here?" asked Maggie.

Israel took another bite of his gelato, letting the rich cream melt in his mouth and swirl around his tongue before swallowing.

"Right, why stop here?" he stated, and then, glancing at Maggie, he wondered if he had the wrong idea. It was just the two of them. "How about a walk down along the river?"

CHAPTER TWENTY-NINE

Israel Discovers There Are More Interesting
Things Than Painted Tiles

"Are you familiar with *azulejos*?" asked Rómulo outside the Sant'Anna factory. "They can be found all over the city."

Israel shook his head. It was Monday morning, and he was standing next to Maggie and João. Judah and Sahara were taking selfies next to the factory entrance.

"This is as Portuguese as it gets," said João, turning to Israel. "Talk about connecting with your roots."

"João, after much consideration, I've accepted that I'm not Portuguese," said Israel.

"Oh really?"

"I'm a mule."

"Come again?"

"I've come to accept that certain identities are harder to explain than others," said Israel. "For me, I'm a mix of things."

João patted Israel on the shoulder. "Join the club, honey."

"Let me show you around the factory," said Rómulo, interrupting the conversation. He wore a white apron over his light-blue shirt and jeans. "You'll be working in the gift shop and sales department, so you'll need to know how the tiles are made. We get many special orders from the States and the UK."

"Everything is painted by hand," said João. "How many artisans are there, Rómulo?"

"There's about one hundred of us," he said. "Come, let me show you around."

They followed Rómulo through a green-painted door and into the gift shop. The walls were adorned with a tessellation of multicolored sample tiles, fountains and planters. Tables were filled with figurines, bowls, cups and plates. Elaborately decorated chandeliers hung from the ceiling. Israel stared at Maggie and could see her fascination with the artistry. She rubbed her index finger across a faience platter shaped like a lily pad and painted with a white base overlaid with blue cannas. She marveled at an owl-shaped figurine, no larger than her palm, painted in purples and yellows. She kneeled down and studied a large pot decorated with elaborate geometric shapes painted in various hues of blue.

"We do more than just tiles at the factory," said Rómulo, looking at Maggie.

Israel continued staring at Maggie. She wore a white V-neck, knee-length summer dress with a pink-floral pattern and sandals. Her black hair was pulled into a braided ponytail, revealing her shoulders and neck. *She has this muted, understated quality about her*, he admitted. *Like these azulejos. They're brimming with color and personality, but they can be easily overlooked if you're not paying attention.*

"It's pure magic, Rómulo," said Maggie. "The details …"

"When visitors schedule tours, you will take them to this showroom," said Rómulo. "Many will be interested in bringing a piece of Portugal home with them."

There was something about that comment—"bringing a piece of Portugal home with them"—that struck Israel. He wasn't sure if it was the atmosphere, being surrounded by so much creativity and beauty, but Israel felt a lump in his throat and a lightness in his feet. *I came here for M&M, the greatest souvenir of all. Will I leave with it?*

Maggie glanced at Israel, waking him from his reverie. Israel rubbed the side of his head, smiling awkwardly.

"Are these tiles all made from clay?" Maggie asked, turning to Rómulo.

"Yes, the tiles are made from clay. We have special molds for unique designs," said Rómulo, holding up two tiles with different floral patterns. "Once the tiles are pressed and baked, there is strict quality control. We can tell the strength of a tile by tapping on it. Did you hear the clinking sounds when you walked in?"

"I did, yes, now that you mention it," said Maggie.

"That sound can be heard all day," said Rómulo. "Once the tiles pass quality control, they are sent for painting. I specialize in painting. Let me show you the workshop."

Rómulo led them out of the gift shop to an adjoining building where there were half a dozen eight-foot-long rectangular folding tables set up as a square. On top of two of the tables were piles of unpainted tiles, each stacked a foot or more high. Rómulo walked over to a shelf on the far side of the room and pulled out a box containing an assortment of paints and brushes.

"The tiles on the table have a raw glaze," he said, placing the box on the table closest to the group. "Do you want to try your hand at painting? It is good to understand the basics of craftsmanship."

Sahara walked over to the table and picked up a tile from the top of a pile and studied each side of it. "These tiles … they appear delicate in my hand, but I suppose they can withstand the elements, given how prevalent they are in the city."

"They are extremely resilient," said Rómulo. "They are fired in a kiln that can reach over five hundred degrees Celsius. They can tolerate sun, rain and fire. When they are added to external and internal edifices, they become part of the architecture. They are used to tell stories. Take some time to walk through the Sintra National Palace and the Porto Cathedral, and you will experience a storytelling tradition that dates back centuries."

Rómulo pulled five tiles and paint supplies from the box and placed them side by side near the edge of the table. They had different pre-traced motifs. Two tiles had simple floral patterns, two had a ship design and one had a deer motif.

"Tiles like these are used in workshops. Please choose a tile and take a seat," said Rómulo, pointing to the plastic folding chairs. "We will use just the cobalt blue ink."

Rómulo pulled a small blue plastic bottle and a ceramic bowl from the box, walked over to a sink near one of the kiln racks and filled it with water. He then opened the blue bottle and poured ink into the bowl.

"This ink is highly concentrated, so it needs to be diluted," said Rómulo. "Too much water, and the blue will be too light. Too little water, and the ink will be black. Some people compare this balancing process to love. There are unhealthy obsessions, where, like too much ink, the heart is blackened with a self-centered objectification of another person. This isn't love but selfishness."

Israel winced at this statement.

"There are also unhealthy forms of love where there is too little passion, like too little ink, and this also is a type of selfishness. This creates misery and suffering. I've seen much of this in my life, I must admit. A father who takes no interest in his son ..." He trailed off, staring for a moment at the bowl of ink in his hand. "To achieve the right balance," he continued, stirring the ink in the water with a paintbrush, "is both difficult and effortless at the same time. Or so I've been told. When someone is truly in love, there is no exploitation of the object. It is a form of love that asks for nothing in return. It is a divine sort of love. This is represented in the azulejos. The blue symbolizes a heavenly sort of love. The white background symbolizes purity."

João was leaning on the table with his elbows, his chin held in his hands, staring at Rómulo. "I may be developing an unhealthy obsession," he cried, gaping at Rómulo.

"When you spend hours in this factory, painstakingly working on your craft, there is a lot of time to think," Rómulo said seriously, walking back to the table and placing the bowl and paint next to João. "It's the power of story, though, that I find most compelling with these tiles. But I digress. Please, choose, and we can get started."

"Bravo, Rómulo. So beautifully stated," said Sahara, leaning over the table, taking two of the floral-patterned tiles and handing one to Judah. "We can paint these."

"You're a poet, Rómulo," said Judah.

"I'll take the doe tile, in honor of our young buck minstrel," said João.

Maggie took the remaining two tiles and handed one to Israel. "It's a Portuguese galleon," she said, examining the stenciling. "Look at the details with the three masts, the flag, the beakhead, the port nearby."

"Yes, and the ship is moored," said Israel.

"Rómulo, can we apply the paint?" asked Maggie.

"Yes, please go ahead," he said. "This is just for practice, so you get a feel for how things are done at Sant'Anna. I'll fire these tonight so you can take them home."

"Maggie is a great artist as well," said João. "Did I mention that already?"

"You did, at least three or four times," laughed Rómulo. "I have much to learn from Maggie."

"Can we add more water if we want to lighten it?" asked Maggie a few minutes later, once she had completed outlining the galleon with paint.

"Please, go ahead," said Rómulo, handing Maggie an empty bowl from the supply box.

Israel followed Maggie's lead, outlining the galleon with paint. On the far left-hand side of the tile, he noticed there was a white space with enough room to add a custom design. He stared at it for some time, not noticing Maggie when she returned to the table next to him with a lighter color of blue paint in a bowl.

I've been practicing this for weeks, he thought to himself. *Now is the time when it most counts. Every word I say matters.*

He studied the tile, his mind adrift with images of men and women at sea, searching for land, searching for the promise of a better life, searching for a strong anchorage to keep them from being tossed by rogue waves. He thought of his quest for M&M. He thought of his desire to find community. He thought about his need to figure out what, exactly, he had in mind for his life.

Then he dipped his paintbrush into the bowl, and, with great precision, on the left-hand side of the tile, he wrote the most important words he had ever written in his life.

CHAPTER THIRTY

Israel Makes a Sale and Starts a Candid Conversation

It was late Friday afternoon, and Israel had just made his first sale of the week to the Navárezes, an elderly Puerto Rican couple from New Jersey on holiday in Portugal. Maggie, Sahara, Judah and João had fared significantly better over the course of the week, but Israel was pleased with his sale.

"What's this, son?" asked Mr. Navárez.

Israel stared at him wide eyed for a moment, paralyzed with fright. *What the heck is this thing called again?* he asked himself, trying desperately to recall the name of the ceramic vessel.

"It's a cruet, of course," said Mrs. Navárez. "Look how smooth and delicate the neck is … the intricately painted flowers. Absolutely splendid."

"Of course, a cruet," parroted Mr. Navárez, shaking his head. "Really, honey, I don't know how you know this."

"I ask myself the same thing when you talk about the Yankees," she retorted.

"Where are you from, son?" asked Mr. Navárez.

"I'm from Chicago, sir," said Israel. "I'm on … I suppose you would say a gap year from college."

"College, huh? We've encouraged all our children and grandchildren to focus on their education," said Mr. Navárez. "I can't overstate how important your education is. You don't have to go to college, but you need to develop some sort of employable skill. Our youngest son was trained as a plumber. He makes more than his brother and sister, both of whom are lawyers. Can you believe it?"

"He started his own business," added Mrs. Navárez, smiling. "He was always the entrepreneurial one. He used to charge the neighbors a quarter for each dandelion he pulled from their lawn when he was in middle school. He did quite well."

"What are you studying?" asked Mr. Navárez.

"I'm majoring in geography," said Israel. "I've always been interested in the way people interact with physical spaces. I also took coursework in remote sensing and geographic information systems."

"That's wonderful," said Mrs. Navárez. "I'm not sure what remote sensing or those geo systems entail, but it sounds like a great career field."

"Cruz is a Latin name," said Mr. Navárez, looking at his name tag. "Where's your family from?"

"Yes, sir, my father's Puerto Rican," said Israel as Maggie walked up to his side. It was the first time in weeks that he had said this out loud.

"I could tell," Mr. Navárez said. "Israel Cruz ... a Puerto Rican name, for sure. Where does your family live? In Humboldt Park? I have a cousin out there."

"No, I grew up on the Chicago North Shore. In a Jewish neighborhood. My mother's an Ashkenazi Jew ... Well, it's actually a little unclear if she's Sephardic or Ashkenazi, but she's Jewish."

"You don't see a lot of that," said Mr. Navárez.

"What about the Rosenthals?" Mrs. Nevárez pitched in.

"The Rosenthals?" Mr. Navárez scratched his chin.

"Isaac and Gabriela?"

"Oh yes, from the Heights?"

"Right. Their kids speak better Spanish than ours do," said Mrs. Navárez.

"They speak Hebrew, too, I believe."

"And what brings you to Portugal?" asked Mrs. Navárez.

"It's a long story," said Israel. "You might call it a voyage of self-discovery."

"How lovely," said Mrs. Navárez. "It's important, especially at your age, to have these types of experiences. It's much more difficult as you get older and have additional responsibilities." She looked at the cruet. "How much does this cost?"

"One hundred and twenty euros," said Israel, glancing at the tag on the bottom of the cruet.

"It is such a beautiful piece of artwork. What do you think, honey?" she asked, turning to her husband.

"Why not? At our age, who knows when we'll come back? This will be our little piece of the Old World," said Mr. Navárez.

Ten minutes later, Israel was holding the 120 euros in his hand, still in disbelief.

Maggie was leaning against the cash register, smiling. "I knew you could do it," she said. "You just needed to connect with a customer."

"It's not as hard as I thought it was," said Israel. "I suppose I picked up a few things watching you speak with people. You make everyone feel comfortable."

Maggie stood up straight and grasped Israel's hand. He wished this moment could last a lifetime.

"Maggie, there are a few things I wanted to speak to you about," Israel whispered, feeling slightly clammy. "As you know, I decided M&M isn't for me."

"Yes. She is engaged, after all."

"I know. But I think I developed, perhaps, just a slightly, teensy-weensy, unhealthy interest in her."

"Like an obsession?"

"Well, I wouldn't go that far …."

Maggie narrowed her eyes.

"Okay, yes, I was obsessed. I don't know what got into me. I guess …" Israel stared at his feet momentarily. "I guess I was lonely."

Maggie stared at him.

"I was caught up in a fiction. She was pixels to me. At least, up until the incident. She was an object to me. Something I wanted. An infatuation. It's very embarrassing. I'm sorry to say all this out loud."

Maggie said nothing.

"I didn't realize how caught up I was in this fiction until recently. The knock on my head seemed to clear up my brain cells. I decided, for reasons that are too complicated to explain, that I was Portuguese, like M&M. I look Portuguese. I have a Portuguese-sounding last name. And the fiction was easier for me to understand than the truth. The problem is that the truth can be a lot messier than reality. For example, Judah and I are both Puerto Rican and Jewish. I don't know anyone else who is Puerto Rican and Jewish, other than perhaps Juan Epstein from *Welcome Back, Kotter*, who is also a fictional character. Even my mother's Jewish origins are confusing. Is she Sephardic or Ashkenazi? Where did they immigrate from? We don't know for sure. It wouldn't be such a big deal for most people."

Israel looked at Maggie. She reminded him of the Bollywood actress Shraddha Kapoor but with hazel eyes that vacillated between green and brown depending on the lighting, hinting at more complex origins.

"I mean, you're mixed, too. So is Sahara. Lots of people are. The problem is that I grew up in a community that was

Jewish, among people who tended not to intermarry, and I just didn't fit in. It was hard to explain who I was, and people are always asking me that question. People always want to know where I'm from because they can't place me. Am I Italian? Am I Arabic? Am I Assyrian? Who the heck knows? So, I became Portuguese to clear things up. It's easier to be one thing. It's easier to explain. To be candid, race and ethnicity aren't as black-and-white as they might seem. They're variable. Cultures have been evolving for millennia. Certain groups of people have emerged, then disappeared or become assimilated into new groups of people. Lots of people identify with one group of people over another. I have a cousin from Humboldt Park who is dark-skinned. He's mixed like me, but he identifies as black. Black Puerto Rican actually, but still, he doesn't identify with his white half because he doesn't look white, and in the States, most people wouldn't perceive him to be white. The more I spend time in Portugal and come to better appreciate the people here, the more I realize I don't fit in here either. It's not that the Portuguese are unwelcoming … Well, the immigration officials weren't the friendliest, given our circumstances with the international drug smuggling syndicate."

Israel coughed and shifted his feet awkwardly.

"Anyway, the people in Portugal have been welcoming, and this is a lovely place to live. I've come across a bunch of Americans who are retiring here. But I don't speak Portuguese. I don't have a deep understanding of Portuguese culture. I'm not, for obvious reasons, Portuguese, so while I could become a Portuguese national if I moved here, I don't think that would resolve the underlying uncertainty about who I am."

"Do you speak Spanish or Hebrew?" asked Maggie, picking up a small vase and staring at it.

"No. Not really."

"Have you considered studying the languages to form a better connection with your heritage?"

"I think it is something I'd like to do."

"I've often felt the same way as you," said Maggie, placing the vase on the table near the cash register. "It's completely understandable. I think it took a great deal of courage for you to travel the way you did as part of a quest for self-discovery."

Israel looked up at Maggie, beaming. "Really?"

"Really."

Israel heard João speaking at the far end of the room. He seemed to be approaching.

"Maggie?"

"Yes, Israel."

"There's something else I wanted to say."

"Go on."

"I hope you won't think differently of me for asking."

"I can't guarantee that I won't but go on and ask. It will be an act of self-discovery."

"Right," said Israel, pulling his shirt collar and clearing his throat. "It might be easier if I show you something first."

Israel kneeled and reached for a small backpack that he had placed next to the cash register. As he was rummaging through the backpack, he heard a scream.

"Oh my God!"

Israel pushed the backpack against the cash register and stood up. Maggie had her hands raised in the air. Israel stared at her, then, slowly turned toward the commotion. He saw João, Judah and Sahara with their hands in the air as they were being marched through the storeroom by three masked men at gunpoint.

CHAPTER THIRTY-ONE

Israel Channels Alexios, and Judah Channels Aquaman

For Israel, one of the benefits of spending an extended period at sea was developing coping mechanisms for motion sickness. That wasn't to say that Israel didn't develop motion sickness anymore. It was just that, under circumstances such as those he found himself in on Friday afternoon, in the back of a hot and crowded van swaying wildly from side to side as it raced along the highway, he managed to think happy thoughts and avoid regurgitating his earlier meal over Maggie's lap. This was an important milestone for him. His relationships with the opposite sex often ended badly, sometimes in a humiliating fashion, but he had somehow held it together.

In fact, he had held it together much better than he could have imagined. There were plenty of instances when he found himself short tempered. Severe internet latency could provoke rage. Pop quizzes could elicit vociferous protests. But point a gun at his head, and he was clear-eyed and levelheaded.

The circumstances were disconcerting. The gunmen had not only taken Israel and Judah hostage but had also rounded up Maggie, Sahara, João and Samson. There had been some sort of shootout as they were leaving the factory. Israel couldn't tell exactly what was going on because they were whisked away so quickly. All he knew was that one moment, he was preparing to check out a customer at the Sant'Anna factory, and the next moment, he was being thrust into the back of a white van by three men in mustachioed pirate masks with assorted weaponry.

He was seated in the second row of the van, behind the armed driver in a pirate mask, and next to Maggie, whose hand he gripped. João was seated to the right of Maggie, with Samson in his purse on his lap. In the seat in front of João was another gunman in a pirate mask, presumably the ringleader, and behind him was another gunman in a pirate mask, presumably a muscle man. The muscle man who was seated behind João in the third row was next to Sahara, who was leaning on Judah for emotional support. Or perhaps it was the other way around. It was difficult to tell. It was a chaotic and tense situation, with lots of yelling in English and Portuguese, which got even more tense, once they were chased by two maniacal police officers on a motorcycle.

"That female cop is riding like a lunatic!" cried the driver.

"Get us to the port," shouted the man in the passenger seat. "If they corner us, they'll have blood on their hands."

Israel watched in morbid fascination as the driver reached into the cup holder for a pistol, rolled down his window and fired multiple shots at the pursuing police officers. A minute later, there was the sound of an explosion, followed by another, that sent the van swerving erratically until the driver finally got it under control and into the marina beside the 25 de Abril bridge.

When the van eventually came to a stop, after a gut-wrenching doughnut in the parking lot near a dock, the ringleader turned to the driver. "Hold them off until backup arrives. I'll be back in a minute. We need free passage out of Portugal," he said, opening the door of the van and snatching João's purse. "If negotiations go south, kill them all."

Then he was gone.

With the van's engine shut off, everyone sat in silence for what seemed like an hour. The ringleader's rapid vanishing act seemed to shock the remaining gunmen as much as it shocked the hostages.

At last, Israel spoke. "He's a hard bargainer, I gather," he said.

"Shut the hell up," growled the driver.

"I should shoot you now," said the strong man.

"He took my Samson!" cried João.

"Be quiet!" shouted the strong man.

"You guys are screwed," said Sahara.

"He took my sweet, baby boy!" cried João.

"The pigs are here!" exclaimed the driver, rolling down his window before reaching for an Uzi under the passenger seat and firing at an approaching police car.

A couple of minutes later, the parking lot was filled with squad cars, their strobe lights flashing, their sirens blaring. Israel thought he could hear at least one helicopter overhead.

"I know you all have a plan, but you might turn yourself in," he said. "The prison establishment in Lisbon has nice bedding and attentive customer service."

"He'll be back," said the driver.

"That's what they all say," said Sahara. "If he truly cared, he would have taken you with him."

"We're in a committed relationship," said the strong man. "We've worked together for years."

"Except that he abandoned you when it mattered most," said Maggie.

"Someone needs to stall the police, or we'll all get arrested," said the driver. "I'm sure that's what he had in mind."

"You don't have to rationalize his behavior," said Maggie.

"You don't think … I mean, he wouldn't be using us to save his skin?" asked the strong man.

"It does seem like a real possibility," said Judah.

"Without a doubt," added Sahara.

"Shut the hell up, João!" cried the driver. "Don't listen to them!"

"What did I say?" asked João.

"The other João," exclaimed the driver.

"Oh, I see," said João.

"He's exhibiting classic displacement behavior," said Maggie. "Don't let him take his anger out on you. He's unmoored. He's furious at your boss."

"I am not!" yelled the driver.

"Yes, you are!" yelled strong man João.

"I'm being perfectly reasonable!" shouted the driver, leaning out the window and firing his Uzi in the air.

"See? He's taking out his aggression against everyone but your boss," said Maggie.

"What was our relationship with Sérgio really about?" asked strong man João. "What about those late-night conversations? The discussions about our future. His empathetic listening. Were they all a sham?"

"You're a sham," shouted the driver.

"Now you're being defensive, João," said strong man João.

"I am not!"

"Yes, you are!"

"Am not!"

"You are!"

"Hold on a second," shouted Judah, interrupting their argument. "How many Joãos are there in this car?"

"João is a common name," said strong man João.

"Yeah, it's traditional," said driver João. "You got a problem with it?"

"No, just wondering," said Judah. "João's a good ..."

He was interrupted by a loudspeaker. "This is the police! Step out of the van with your hands in the air!"

"Screw it!" yelled driver João, turning and pointing his Uzi at Maggie. "Psychologist lady! Get out of the van … slowly, with your hands in the air."

Strongman João kicked the seat in front of him, causing João to jump in his seat. "Open the door, fake boy João!" yelled strong man João, before turning to Sahara. "And you … yeah, you … come with me."

"You," driver João shouted to Maggie, "get out and come around to my side of the van … and don't get any ideas or I'll kill your sister, there."

Maggie opened the sliding door, ducked her head, stepped around Israel and out of the van. Driver João followed her outside, ducking below the driver's-side window to avoid being shot by a sniper. Then, he pulled Maggie roughly toward him so his mouth was against her neck. He pressed the muzzle of the Uzi into the side of her abdomen.

"Okay, pretty lady, you're my ticket out of here," he said, breathing heavily.

A moment later, strong man João was holding Sahara similarly on the other side of the van, with a pistol pressed against her chest.

"We want free passage out of Portugal, and then we'll release the hostages!" shouted driver João at the gathered police.

"Let us go, or else!" bellowed strong man João.

Israel glared at driver João. His face was turning red and he got angrier and angrier.

"Drop your weapons! You are under arrest!" blared the police from a loudspeaker.

"Hell, no!" shouted driver João. "You let us walk free, and we'll let the hostages go. We are not going to prison."

"Bring out a negotiator if you want to see your hostages alive," shouted strong man João.

There was a moment of silence. Israel thought he could see the police huddling, apparently discussing options. *Get your stinking lips off my Maggie*, he said to himself.

"I don't think you'd like to see this pretty little thing in a bloodied body bag, now, would you?" driver João shouted, his lips brushing Maggie's neck.

Israel felt his muscles twitching in ways he never had experienced before.

"It would be such a shame for her to be shot by the Portuguese police while being filmed by the international press corps, wouldn't it?" driver João yelled.

"Yeah, not a good look," shouted strong man João.

Driver João moved his hand down Maggie's neck and toward her chest. He laughed as he stared at the police, challenging them to overreact.

Israel growled. It was a deep, guttural, primordial sound, fomented from a part of his being that he didn't realize existed. It emerged from a cave in Spain's Atapuerca Mountains, a club in hand, as it faced a saber-toothed tiger. It hiked through open grasslands with flocks of sheep, threatening wolves with skinned hides. It rumbled on horseback past scattered villages, chasing marauders with a spear. It crossed the Ionian Sea by trireme, mooring along the coast of Laconia, transforming into the warrior Alexios from Assassin's Creed, so intimidating that the Cult of Kosmos feared his wrath.

And there it took hold, causing Israel to place one foot outside the van, then the other, as he rose up, arms at his sides, fists balled, eyes ablaze with fury, and stomped toward driver João. He was on a mission. He was a member of the Peloponnesian League. He was fighting for a sacred honor. He was fiction turned into reality. He was pixels turned into skin and bones.

Driver João turned his head, then did a double take as he saw the madman approaching. *Don't you see I have a sub-*

machine gun? said João, without saying anything. *Don't you see that I'm a gangster?*

Israel and driver João locked eyes. *Don't you see that you've messed with the wrong guy?* said Israel without saying anything. *Don't you see that you're touching my woman?*

Israel placed his left foot in front of his right foot, then, in one swift movement, launched his right foot into the driver's kidney, causing him to buckle, drop the Uzi at Maggie's feet and crumple to the ground. Before he could raise his head to see what had hit him, and not to be outdone by Israel, Maggie did a spinning crescent kick that knocked João's pirate mask off and threw him onto his back and into a battered state of unconsciousness.

"J. J.?" Israel asked.

Strong man João, startled at this latest development and unsure about his next move—he wasn't the brains of the operation--loosened his grip on Sahara just enough to receive a sharp elbow to the stomach. He staggered backward, shaking his head, while Sahara raised her fists in a defensive stance.

"We Cruzes are many wonderful things, but forgiving is not one of them," said Judah, grabbing a crowbar from the van and launching it like a trident at strong man João's head. João dropped like a concrete Jersey barrier from a crane.

Sahara lowered her hands and stared at the prone figure on the ground. "Aquaman?" she asked at last.

"Good guess," said Judah cheerily.

"We have to cosplay that," said Sahara, running up to Judah and wrapping her arms around him.

A Reuters cameraman stepped forward to get a better angle of the scene with his handheld broadcast camcorder.

"All clear?" someone shouted.

A police officer raised her head above the yellow Renault parked in front of them and raised her hand in the air. "All clear!" she shouted.

Israel squinted at the officer in the distance. "Is that Detective Metrass?" he asked.

"Was she the woman riding like a lunatic?" asked Maggie, grasping both his hands.

"I believe she was trying to save us," said Israel.

One of the members of the maritime police stepped out of his pickup truck, stared at Israel and Maggie for ten seconds, then brought his hands together. Another police officer rose from behind the Renault and began clapping.

"Is that Officer Sequeira?" asked Judah as he began to walk hand-in-hand with Sahara over to Israel and Maggie.

"I think it is," said Israel.

"He's clapping for you," said Maggie.

"He's clapping for all of us," said Israel.

Police officers were filing out of squad cars, clapping their hands and forming a crowd as they approached the scene of the crime. A helicopter swooped over the marina.

"Unbelievable!"

"Did we just witness Bruce Lee?"

"That crescent kick was *devastating*."

A gaggle of reporters ran up to Maggie and Sahara, microphones in hand.

"Make way! BBC here!"

"Reuters! Where did you learn those moves?"

"RTP! Excuse us. Tell us about the chase."

Israel looked down and realized he was holding Maggie's hands. "I'm not letting you go," he said under his breath.

"What was that?" asked the reporter from the BBC.

"I was just saying …" Israel glanced at Maggie.

"Israel and Judah Cruz!" blared someone through a bullhorn.

"Detective Metrass?" Israel shouted back.

A police siren rang out intermittently, parting the crowd like the Red Sea. Whoop, whoop, whoop.

A blue police van with white stripes and Detective Metrass in the passenger seat pulled up to Israel and Maggie. She had her head out the window and a bullhorn in her hand. "Get in," she said.

"Not again," Israel lamented.

"We need to bring you into the station," Detective Metrass said.

"We just got out of prison," Judah cried.

"It's been a long day," Israel added.

"Detective Metrass, on what grounds are you arresting these individuals?" asked the reporter from the BBC.

"We were the ones taken hostage," Sahara cried.

"You can't be serious," Maggie exclaimed.

"I'm very serious," said Detective Metrass, tossing the bullhorn into the back of the van. "We need to get those ankle bracelets off you."

PART IV

CHAPTER THIRTY-TWO

Detective Metrass Closes the Case

Detective Metrass was seated on a chair behind a panel desk, stage left, facing an audience in a small theater. There was a bottle of water in between a name card and a gooseneck microphone anchored to the desk. The event would likely last the full two hours, and there were at least a dozen reporters in attendance, sitting in the front row.

To her right sat Officer Sequeira. To his right sat Luís Noronha, the national director of the Judiciary Police. A technician finished adjusting Luís's microphone, scurried offstage, then motioned to the crew in the back of the theater that the event was to begin now.

"It was nice for them to give us front row seats," said Israel.

Israel was seated in between Maggie and Judah. Sahara and João were seated to the left of Judah. Samson was curled in a ball on the floor beside João.

"You played a central role in this case," said Sahara.

"Especially Israel," said Judah. "I do wonder if we would have been kidnapped had Israel not aided and abetted J. J.'s, or should I say João Joaquim's, release from prison."

"A traditional name," added João.

"I never would have guesscd it," said Israel.

"Well, he kidnapped us," said Judah. "They wanted us out of the picture."

A hush fell over the audience as Luís reached for the microphone and cleared his throat.

"Ladies and gentlemen," he said at last. "I am pleased to be here with you today to discuss a critical milestone in our effort to fight organized crime."

He took a small sip of water from his bottle.

"We captured the criminal ringleader, Sérgio Ricardo de Carvalho, last evening as he was attempting to flee the country. His arrest and the arrests of his accomplices, João Abreu, João Barbosa, João Ferreira and João Joaquim Cruz, all of whom are Portuguese nationals, has dealt a devastating blow to their criminal operations. These arrests have led to further arrests in the United States, through our close partnership with the FBI and the DEA. Domenico Di Stefano, a senior member of the Chicago mafia, and his lieutenant, Angelo "Sweet Tooth" Vena, were arrested and face multiple felony charges for international narcotics trafficking, money laundering and extortion, among other crimes. Their arrests led to the arrest of a Brazilian national, Antônio Mattos, based out of Miami, who was cxtradited to São Paulo and faces similar charges.

"None of this could have been possible without the vigilance of our investigative units. Detective Oceanna Metrass, who heads our national drug trafficking unit, has brought honor to the Judiciary Police through her dedicated leadership and commitment to pursuing justice, even when the odds were stacked against her. I will turn the microphone over to Detective Metrass momentarily, but I want to make one last statement. A country cannot function if people are not held accountable to laws. To any criminal, foreign or domestic, who thinks they can get away with illegality inside our borders, thereby taking away our justice, think again. We are a nation of laws, and if you choose to break them, we will find you. The case we closed on Friday shows our commitment to the ceaseless pursuit of justice. I am proud and humbled to serve as the national director of the Judiciary Police, the greatest law enforcement agency in the world. With that, I yield to Detective Metrass."

"Thank you, Director," began Detective Metrass. "It is indeed an honor to serve as a member of the Judiciary Police under your leadership. This case was a complex one, involving multiple transnational syndicates specializing in cocaine distribution through a manipulative system of extortive methods, in which susceptible, you might even say gullible individuals, were targeted for smuggling purposes ...."

Israel's mind wandered. *This is SO boring.* Israel shut his eyes.

"It's also worth stressing," Detective Metrass went on, "how important it is to have a diverse workforce. As a woman, and one of the very few female detectives in the Judiciary Police, my point of view on cases typically differs from that of my male counterparts. Not drastically, I'll add, but enough to offer insights into the psychology of persons of interest. This diversity of perspective can be found in all kinds of people, and since the Judiciary Police is concerned with the well-being of all Portuguese society, it's of paramount importance that we continue to hire officers who represent us in the truest and broadest sense."

Detective Metrass was interrupted by a question from the audience.

"Is it true that Sérgio was found half drowned on the banks of the River Tagus? Can you explain why his clothes were torn, and how he received lacerations and puncture wounds?" asked a reporter from RTP.

"It's an interesting story," said Detective Metrass. "It's clear he encountered an overwhelming force of nature."

"Some have said he was thrown off balance by a swooping helicopter and swept away by an undercurrent," said the reporter.

"That's a plausible theory," said Detective Metrass.

"I heard he was attacked by a police dog," said another reporter.

"My sources suggested an altercation with the PSP gang," said another.

"All reasonable hypotheses," said Detective Metrass. "The evidence suggests otherwise. Officer Sequeira, would you like to answer this question, given your direct communication with the search party?"

Officer Sequeira lowered his microphone and leaned in.

"It was the chihuahua."

CHAPTER THIRTY-THREE

Israel and Maggie Head to the Airport

Unshackled from police monitoring devices and free to move about Portugal at will, as a minor celebrity, Israel decided to leave the country. Two weeks after their kidnapping, Israel sat in the second row of a Mercedes Metris passenger van beside Maggie as the taxi driver took them to the airport. Judah and Sahara sat in the third row, and João sat up front in the passenger seat with Samson on his lap.

They had spent the past two weeks lazing about in a beach house in the Algarve overlooking the ocean, near the popular Benagil Cave. The weather had been pleasant, still cool but warm enough to lounge outside in hammocks or on beach towels by the water. It was during this time that Israel, unencumbered with any responsibilities, had clarifying thoughts.

He had given Maggie the azulejo shortly after Detective Metrass had removed their ankle bracelets, and they were freed of charges. He had felt emboldened after his well-placed front kick against driver João and felt that he needed to communicate his feelings to Maggie. Timing was everything. It certainly was in the case of Israel and Maggie's kung fu imitations. Israel knew he had to make the move when their passions were most inflamed.

"There's something I need to show you," Israel said.

"That's right. We were interrupted at the factory," Maggie said as they walked out of the police station.

Israel pulled the painted tile of the galleon from his pocket and handed it to Maggie, who stopped in the middle of the sidewalk to look at it. Judah, Sahara and João continued walking ahead of them.

"You've turned my world around ..." Maggie read the inscription, her voice trailing off.

Israel held his breath. He had spent days working on this poem. It had a nice musical quality to it. The word "pithy" came to mind. Then again, he wasn't sure if poetry was his calling. He had tried to paint the words in a calligraphic style.

Maggie held the tile in her hands, tracing the words with her index finger. Israel shuffled his feet, uncomfortably. "I can explain ..." he began.

"Shh," Maggie shushed him as she continued examining the tile.

Israel looked at his feet. *Well, I tried at least. It's not like I had anything to lose.*

He felt her fingers on his chin. He looked up, and before he knew what hit him, she planted her lips on his.

It was at this moment that he could see the appeal of drugs. The sensation of ecstasy was so overpowering, he was certain his body had taken flight. He was Icarus flying toward the sun, but here he faced no threat of melted wax. Maggie was the center of the solar system, and he was a big blue marble pulled into her orbit, her gravity overpowering and full of life-giving energy. This was no artificial stimulant. It was truth. Raw, unvarnished truth.

"Aww! You two are *so* adorable!" cried João.

The decision to leave Portugal was as much Maggie's as it was Israel's. Although she had traveled to the US once before, on a high school trip to New York City, she wanted to see more. She wanted to see the famous national parks. The Grand Canyon. Yosemite. The rugged wildlands England could not offer.

They had discussed options during their stay at the Algarve. They talked about taking Amtrak's California Zephyr to Yellowstone. Israel mentioned his fondness for zydeco music, and its fusion of cultures.

"You never know who you might encounter on a train," he said.

They ended up deciding on a two-month itinerary, hiking the Pacific Northwest Trail, booking an excursion through a tour guide. Once complete, they would spend a month or two traveling from Seattle to San Diego before flying back to the UK. Israel had decided to complete his studies in London. There were plenty of options. He was confident that with Maggie's help, he'd get into a university somewhere in the city so he could be with her as she began her term at the University of the Arts London.

Judah, Sahara and João, meanwhile, were planning to continue their travels across Europe. Next up was Spain. Judah had developed a keen interest in the culinary arts, which had only increased since meeting Sahara, and was planning to visit the Culinary Institute of Barcelona.

"There's a bunch of prestigious culinary schools in the UK too," said Sahara. "You can study there once our travels are over."

Maggie had ordered a DNA ancestry kit for Israel, which arrived by mail the day after the kidnapping. He had immediately collected his saliva sample and mailed it to the company and had discovered his test results on the taxi ride to the airport, to his great fascination.

"So, you're Portuguese after all," said Sahara, from the back of the van. "Isn't that a bit of irony?"

"I always thought you looked Portuguese," added João.

"I thought you were skeptical of these types of tests?" asked Judah.

"I suppose I had a change of heart," said Israel, glancing at Maggie, who was sitting beside him.

"So, what else are we?" asked Judah, impatiently.

"Based on our ancestry," said Israel, "we are forty-nine-point-nine percent Ashkenazi Jewish, from Belarus; twenty-five-point-five percent Spanish and Portuguese, with the strongest associations to the Canary Islands, Andalusia, Galicia and the Azores and Madeira archipelagos; fourteen-point-nine percent from sub-Saharan Africa, mainly Nigeria; and nine percent Indigenous American, which I assume is Taíno, given they were the original inhabitants of Puerto Rico. The rest is undefined."

"We're mutts," said Judah. "We don't fit into a neat category."

"We all are," said Maggie. "We're multiracial and proud of it."

"That's right. We're citizens of the world," said Israel, staring out the window as they approached Lisbon Airport. "We're like seawater. We're full of dissolved compounds from all corners of the globe. And if blue is the color of Earth from space, then we're most definitely not black or white or brown. We're blue, and I can't think of a more beautiful color than that."